Don't Cry For Me
Aberystwyth

THE LOUIE KNIGHT SERIES:

Don't Cry For Me Aberystwyth

Malcolm Pryce

BLOOMSBURY

First published 2007

This paperback edition published 2007

Copyright © 2007 by Malcolm Pryce

The moral right of the author
has been asserted

Bloomsbury Publishing Plc,
36 Soho Square,
London W1D 3QY

www.bloomsbury.com

A CIP catalogue record
for this book is available from
the British Library

ISBN 978 0 7475 9317 1
10 9 8 7 6 5 4 3 2 1

Typeset by Palimpsest Book Production Ltd, Grangemouth, Stirlingshire

Printed by Clays Ltd, St Ives plc

All papers used by Bloomsbury Publishing are natural, recyclable products
made from wood grown in well-managed forests. The manufacturing
processes conform to the environmental regulations of the country of origin.

www.louieknight.com

To Wilhelm Warth

I would like to thank my editor Mike and agent Rachel for all their help and friendship.

Mrs Powell's first cousin had left Patagonia and gone back
home to Wales.
'He *has* done well,' she said. 'He's now the Archdruid.'

In Patagonia, Bruce Chatwin

Aberystwyth at Christmas. The smell of pine drifts along the Prom mingling with the reek of bladderwrack, toffee apple, vanilla and wet donkey fur . . . From somewhere beyond the spires of the old college children sing 'O Little Town of Bethlehem', and the siren from the distant prowl car wails in harmony. The ice man shivers behind his empty counter and in a filthy alley in Chinatown a man in a red-and-white coat with a long white beard lies dead in a pool of his own gore. In happier times the red robes of his office – like the red cross of Switzerland – conferred a species of neutrality in the never-ceasing disputes that wash over the Prom; but these are not happy times. The cruel melancholy of his death is heightened by an extra finesse: his manhood has been hacked off and placed in his mouth. And with the last of his strength the man has dipped a finger in his own blood and written a word on the pavement: 'Hoffmann'. With the blood beginning to freeze and glitter like raspberry ripple, the school art teacher, Mrs Dinorwic-Jones, kneels beside the dead Santa and prepares to draw a chalk outline around the corpse. Just like so many times before; but this is not like the times before. Her hand shakes uncontrollably and tonight the white chalk line zig-zags in and out like the outline of an electrocuted polecat. Aberystwyth at Christmas. Compliments of the Season.

Editorial, *Cambrian News*, Christmas 1989

Chapter 1

WHEN I ARRIVED next morning flakes of snow were swirling like moths in the penumbra of the street-lamp outside the office. There was a car parked on the kerb and two moths sat inside. The Moth Brothers. Two men in their late fifties who took care of debt collection for the druids. The difficult cases, the type that are often fulfilled by a transition to the state that proverbially pays all debts: the state of not being alive very much. They were identical twins; so alike, it was said, that the only way their mother could tell them apart was from the pattern their tiny moth teeth left on her nipple when she suckled them. In later years it was their victims who had to be identified by their teeth. They had heads that were bigger than they should be, and big eyes that were placed too far to the side of the head. Their skin had the pallor of candle wax and the texture of ear wax. No one knew whether they had always looked like moths or had grown to look like them the way some people grow to resemble their pets. Maybe they acquired the name because they usually came out at night; or maybe it was something do with the habit they had of leaving their clients' clothes full of holes. When they saw me they stepped out of their car and followed me up the stairs into the office. I didn't offer them a drink.

'We've come to claim our reward,' said Meic. I knew it was Meic because he had a big M on the front of the sweater he wore under his jacket. Othniel wore an O.

'Reward for what?'

'The Father Christmas murder. We know who did it. That means we get some books, right?'

'On philosophy,' added Othniel.

'By some Danish bloke. Exis . . . exis . . .'

'Stentialism, that's our favourite.' Othniel pulled out a copy of the *Cambrian News* folded to the classified ad. 'See?'

I took the paper and made a great play of reading it, even though I knew what it said. They fidgeted while I read, so I took some more time.

'We haven't got all day,' said Meic.

I put the paper down and regarded them. 'It certainly seems to be in order, all here in black and white. Anyone who gives me useful information that helps track down the culprits gets a signed first edition of the works of Søren Kierkegaard. First editions are difficult to come by so I can understand your excitement.'

'We're all a-tizz,' said Meic.

'OK, then, who killed him?'

Meic pointed at Othniel and said, 'He did!'

Othniel pointed at Meic and said, 'He did!'

'There's only one set of books.'

'We don't mind sharing.' They laughed.

'And I bet you've both got alibis, too.'

'That's right.'

'Let me guess. You were with him and he was with you the whole night.'

'That's right,' they said in unison. 'The whole night.'

'So there'd be no point me trying to run you in.'

'You don't think so?'

'Not with alibis provided by two upstanding members of the community.'

'We hadn't thought about that.'

'Couple of nice guys like you, loved by everyone, what sort of jury would convict you?'

'Oh dear, it looks like our attempt to turn ourselves in has been thwarted,' said Othniel.'

'No books for us,' added Meic with mock gloom.

'And given the way you both look so alike, you couldn't absolutely swear in a court of law that it was Meic you saw on the night in question and not your own reflection in a puddle or something; and you, Meic, couldn't absolutely swear it was Othniel you saw and not a reflection in a puddle or something, isn't that right?'

'That's a good point,' said Meic. 'He and I look so much alike the only way I know who I am is to look at his jumper. But what if someone swapped them during the night? How would I know?'

'In fact, we recently beat up a chap from the philosophy department who made precisely the same point. He said it had to do with discontinuity of the narrative self.'

'Apparently there's no way anyone can be sure that the memories they wake up with belong to the same person who went to bed.'

'You could wake up as a different person and there'd be no way to tell.'

'He still doesn't know which one of us hit him.'

'And to be honest, in light of the doubt spawned by his scepticism, neither do we.'

They laughed.

I laughed, too, although it was no more genuine than theirs. 'There you go: if you couldn't tell, how could we believe the word of any witnesses the court produces? Are there any witnesses?'

'We're not sure.'

'I guess for their sake we have to hope there aren't.'

'That's right, Christmas is a time when families should be together, not attending funerals.'

'OK. Just out of curiosity, why did you kill him?'

'Why not?' said Meic.

'Maybe we just didn't feel very Christmassy,' said Othniel.

'Bah, humbug!' said Meic and laughed. 'And besides, don't you hate they way they turn up earlier every year?'

'The decorations in the shops went up in October.'

'It's certainly very irritating but I wouldn't kill a man for it.'

'Maybe we have a lower irritation threshold.'

'Maybe. But I'm still not persuaded by your motive. I need more than that to give you those books.'

'It's all to do with a taxonomic problem we have,' said Meic. 'That means something to do with how you classify things, y'see. And as purists we're a bit tired of Father Christmas being wrongly classified as a Christian icon.'

'Wrongly expropriated, in fact,' added Othniel.

'You saying he's not a Christian?'

'No, we're not saying that exactly. The name Santa Claus is derived from St Niklaus of Myra, in Asia Minor, a fourth-century Christian bishop. Now we got nothing against this chap—'

'He once resuscitated three girls who'd been murdered and pickled in brine,' said Meic.

'Of course,' added Othniel, 'if he'd resuscitated some girls we'd pickled in brine we wouldn't be very accommodating about that.'

'When we pickle someone we expect them to stay pickled.'

'Some people would call us old-fashioned.'

'Although not to our faces.'

'No, not to our faces.'

'Tell me about the taxonomic problem.'

'Santa Claus is an upstart. The real Father Christmas is the pagan god Odin who brought presents at the time of the festival of Yule, which celebrated the winter solstice, the death of the old year. The early Christians put their festival on the same date so that everyone could swap over without giving up their favourite rites.'

'Which we don't think is very fair on Odin.'

'I can see why that would annoy you. Apart from wanting the books for your library, why are you telling me?'

'So we don't have to kill you, too.'

'Do you have to kill me?'

'If you stuck your big hooter in places where it had no business being inserted, and found some evidence that might be embarrassing to us in this connection, we would have to kill you, wouldn't we?'

'Not necessarily.'

'Oh, believe us, we would.'

'Would that be such a problem for you?'

'It would be an unnecessary inconvenience.'

They stood up and left, adding, 'And this is the season of goodwill.'

I think it was the second Thursday before Christmas when the woman claiming to be the Queen of Denmark called about the ad. It was one of those melancholy winter afternoons; the sky had that flat translucent greyness which filters through the window of the office like the glow you get from an old TV tube after it has been switched off. The sort of translucence that used to puzzle me when I was a kid and still had the capacity to stare in wonder at the sky. The sort of sky that communicates in some arcane way that snow is on the way. There is only one way to describe a winter sky like that. Plangent.

There was the usual distant hum of traffic and a silence in the room that called for the slow tick of a grandfather clock to give it shape; but we'd sold the clock to pay to keep Myfanwy at the nursing home. So I tapped my pen on the desk and sighed every now and again. Calamity Jane, my partner, was sitting in the client's chair practising the art of the hunch. She was holding a book in front of her face in the awkward attitude of one who has spent her seventeen and four-fifths years on the planet viewing the act of reading with disdain and has never acquired the correct posture for it. Then one day she discovers a book on a subject which fascinates her and sits there spellbound like a kid at a magic show. The book was an old training manual for operatives of the Pinkerton Detective Agency in Los Angeles. Don't ask me where she got it; it was stolen. The chapter she was reading described the scientific approach to the hunch and prescribed a number of methods for cultivating it. I wasn't so sure such a thing was possible but the technique she was trying entailed sitting still and allowing the mind to focus on the infinitesimal feelings and intimations that might or might not constitute the approach of a hunch. If you didn't know, you'd think she was cultivating the art of aplomb. Calamity and I had been partners for a number of years and in that time I'd seen her brash and hotheaded, defiant, effervescent, full of joy, optimistic, noisy, brave and always suffused with the unsullied wonder of youth; but I'd never seen her sit still. I was grateful to the Pinkertons, even if the scientific art of the hunch did strike me as moonshine.

The phone rang and Calamity picked it up, and said without taking her eyes off the page, 'Louie Knight Investigations.' She listened, nodded and said, 'I'll see if he's free.' That's what I mean about aplomb – this was the Queen of Denmark on the line, remember. She reached the phone over to me.

The voice on the other end of the line spoke the sort of English that was almost too perfect to be from a native of these shores and lent credence to her claim.

'It's about the dead Father Christmas,' she began. 'We read about it in the *International Herald Tribune*.'

'It also made the *Shropshire Star*.'

'The article said there was no identification on the body . . .'

'That's what they say; no one knows who he is or where he's from.'

'On the contrary, Mr Knight, everyone knows where he's from. Father Christmas comes from Greenland.'

The sharpness in her tone made me pause for a second. Then I said in the sort of voice that gives nothing away, 'That's a good point.'

'Somebody should tell them.'

'Who? The police? I expect they already know. They were children too once, difficult though it is to believe.'

'Then why don't they publish the fact?'

'Sometimes in cases like this they don't publish everything they know. Cops like to keep a few things up their sleeve. It makes them feel smarter than the criminals. It's all to do with psychology.'

'God preserve us from cops who try to be clever.'

'I have a lot of sympathy with that view. How exactly can I help you?'

'Greenland is a self-governing overseas administrative division of Denmark, which makes the dead man an honorary citizen of my country. We take attacks on our citizens very seriously. You see where I'm heading?'

I said a picture was beginning to emerge.

'I would like you to investigate the murder. I've put a small advertisement in the classified section of yesterday's *Cambrian News* giving details of a reward for significant information which helps you crack the case. It's a signed first edition of the complete works of Søren Kierkegaard. As you know, Kierkegaard first editions are hard to come by.'

'I've never heard of him – the 'K' section in my school library got burned down.'

'A great man, he wrote about despair.'

'I've heard of that.'

'I leave it to your discretion how to disburse the reward. It's spelled S, Ø, R, E, N with a little dash on the O like a lopsided Saturn. Good luck!'

She hung up and I looked at Calamity. She said, 'It was a pay phone.'

In books the PI would probably treat a call from the Queen of Denmark, especially when made from a pay phone, with a degree of scepticism; but in books they don't have to eat whereas in Aberystwyth it is a daily necessity. And I'd been in the game long enough not to care too greatly about my clients' bona fides since they seldom had any. An hour later a messenger arrived with a postal order for five hundred pounds.

We banked it and wandered down to Sospan's ice-cream kiosk for a small celebration. Hard currency upfront without even needing to beg was a rare occurrence for us. Sospan was sitting in his box, huddled in front of a brazier of coals, his normal expression of wan insouciance getting ever bleaker as the flesh of his cheeks melted away. They never cover it in *National Geographic* but the life cycle of the ice-cream man is a fascinating spectacle. Towards the end of summer Sospan overeats like a bear laying in a store of fat for winter. From dawn to dusk he grazes, dipping into the rich takings of summer, and for a few brief weeks his white coat balloons out until the buttons pop. Then business drops off, he starts to live off his fat, and around the end of November he swaps his summer coat for a thick white quilted winter one. It does little to disguise the fact that he is shrinking like a wraith. Just after Christmas, with the last of his ebbing strength, he closes the box and goes to sleep for three months, generally emerging again around the same time as the snowdrops.

'Sospan, have you heard of a man called Søren Kierkegaard?'

'The one who writes his name with an O that looks like a wobbly Saturn? 'Course I have. Teleological suppression of the ethical. *Fear and Trembling*, *Despair* and *The Sickness unto Death*. And don't bother offering me the signed first edition, I've already got one. My grandfather left me it in his will.'

'You've seen the ad, then?'

He pulled out a copy of the *Cambrian News* from under the counter and began rummaging around inside for the classified ad. I stopped him, closed the paper to the front page and read the report on the Father Christmas slaying. He'd been found in a Chinatown alley a few nights back, lying in a pool of blood.

He'd been shot twice, and while he lay dying the assailant had chopped off his manhood and put it in his mouth. Mrs Dinorwic-Jones, the art teacher who regularly drew the chalk outline round the freshly slain, was said to be in a state of shock. The final detail was the most intriguing. With his dying strength Father Christmas had dipped his finger in his own blood and written on the pavement the word 'Hoffmann'.

Chapter 2

CALAMITY ARRIVED at the office next morning carrying a bundle of butcher's paper and a copy of the *Cambrian News*. She spread the butcher's paper on the floor and handed me a marker pen.

'What's going on?'

'JDLR,' said Calamity.

'I'm still no wiser.'

'JDLR. It's what the Pinkertons say. It means Just Doesn't Look Right.'

'What doesn't?'

She pointed to the front page of the paper. It carried a photo of the celebrated chalk outline.

'What am I looking at?'

'Doesn't his posture strike you as unusual?'

'He's been brutally murdered.'

'Even so, it doesn't look natural.'

'He fell awkwardly.'

'That's my point: you can't fall like that. Look.'

She did a slow, dignified collapse onto the floor, roughly in the same attitude as the corpse.

'Draw round me.'

I took the cap off the pen and drew her outline.

She got up and looked down. 'See? His foot's facing the wrong way. He's lying on his left side, his right knee is touching the ground on top of his left leg. There's no way you can get the right foot to face backwards like that unless you break the leg.'

'So maybe he broke it.'

'The report doesn't say anything about a broken leg.'

'Maybe it's just a mistake in the drawing.'

'Mrs Dinorwic-Jones has been teaching life study classes all her life. She wouldn't get something like that wrong. There's only one explanation.'

'Which is?'

'He did it deliberately. He took his leg out of the trousers and stuffed his hat in the trouser leg and boot, then twisted it round to face the wrong way.'

'Where's his real leg, then?'

'It's pulled back and up, inside the thigh, like actors who play Long John Silver.'

'Why would he do a thing like that?'

'It's a signal. He was dying. He had just a few minutes left to live. So what does he do? He writes "Hoffmann" in his own blood. Who's Hoffmann? Good question. My hunch is, either he recognised his assailant, who happened to be called Hoffmann, or it's a message written to an accomplice called Hoffmann or about a subject of mutual interest to them both which is connected with someone called Hoffmann. So the accomplice reads about the murder and the word "Hoffmann" and realises that Santa has hidden something in the alley for him and has used the phoney leg routine to point to it.' She started to gather up the sheets on the floor.

'You mean, he's hidden something in the alley?'

'Yes.'

'And pointed to it with his leg?'

'Phoney leg.'

I laughed. 'OK, we check the alley. Do we have anything else to go on? I'm not saying the phoney-leg routine isn't promising or anything, but it would be nice if we – you know – had something else.'

Calamity took out a notebook and flicked it open. 'The DOA is called Absalom. Arrived in town two or three weeks ago; no one is exactly sure when. Kept himself to himself. Took a job as Father Christmas even though he was Jewish. There's mention of a woman.' She opened the *Cambrian News* to the scandal pages. There was a picture of a mousey-looking Welsh woman in a stovepipe hat, in her early twenties probably, beneath a lurid headline: 'SANTA SLASH MOLL IN STOVEPIPE HAT MOOLAH MYS-TERY'.

I skimmed the first paragraph. It was a feeble attempt to insinuate a sinister explanation of where the girl got the money for her hats.

'She's the harp player out at Kousin Kevin's Krazy Komedy Kamp,' explained Calamity with a slight air of hesitation.

We swapped knowing glances. The holiday camp at Borth was not one of our favourite haunts, in contrast to most holiday camps they had a strictly enforced 'No Dicks and Sleuths' policy. They were good at spotting disguises, too.

'We'll take a ride out there,' I said.

'We also need to get some knitting needles.'

'What for?'

'Ballistics.'

'Oh, of course.'

'Been reading about it in the Pinkerton book. What you do is you stick the needle in the bullet holes in the wall and shine a flashlight along the line of the needle. That way you find out the trajectory, and you can work out where the firing came from.'

'Is that so?'

Calamity assumed a nonchalant air. 'Fairly standard scene-of-crime m.o.'

'I've never come across it before.'

'If Jack Ruby's lawyer had tried it he probably wouldn't have fried.'

'Jack Ruby didn't go to the chair. He died in hospital while awaiting a retrial. Embolism, I think.'

'Same difference.'

'And he shot Lee Harvey Oswald from three feet away. You wouldn't need to stick a knitting needle into Lee Harvey Oswald to find out where the firing came from.'

'It was just a . . . a . . .' She consulted the Pinkerton book. 'An illustrative example.'

'That's all right, then.'

'I thought we could check the alley, see if the scene-of-crime boys missed anything.'

'Is that likely?'

'Of course it is. They only see what they're expecting to see, because they arrive loaded with preconceptions. You have to empty your mind of the obvious and just see what turns up.'

'And I bet that's in the book, too.'

'It's all in the book, Louie.'

Outside the Chungking Express a police car with out-of-town plates was parked. We pushed through the door into the main parlour. It was the usual cuckoo's nest of oriental bric-a-brac: lanterns, vases, model junks, silk dragons, a lacquered cabinet, Buddha and Confucius . . . objects side by side that would have occupied separate wings in a museum.

It was still early and the dining room empty except for a man eating an early lunch. A white napkin was stuffed a touch flamboyantly into his shirt collar. He wore a crumpled and stained suit that might once have been well cut and had an air that suggested the tailors of Swansea or Llanelli. Even without seeing the car outside I could smell cop. He looked up as we walked in, cast a glance and returned to the task of spooning the last drops of sauce from his plate into his mouth. We sat at an adjacent table. After deciding that no more could be scraped off the dish he threw it down with a rough clatter and dabbed his chin with the napkin. He shouted in the direction of the kitchen. 'Hey, chop chop!'

I grimaced and he noted it from the corner of his eye. And I noted that he noted.

A waitress appeared in the doorway leading to the kitchen and at the same time the door to the Gents opened and a police constable walked out drying his hands on the thighs of his trousers. He looked at me and made a strangled scoffing sound that implied he knew who I was. I didn't recognise him. He walked over and joined the cop, who turned to the girl and said, 'Hey, stop staring and clear away this shit.'

She was in her early twenties, slender in a scarlet cheongsam embroidered with golden flowers; her face was as smooth and expressionless as alabaster. She began to clear. The slit in her cheongsam opened over the thigh and the two cops stared with no attempt to conceal their lust.

'No thanks, we haven't got time for dessert,' said the big cop. The deputy guffawed dutifully. Or maybe he genuinely thought it was funny.

The girl flinched and moved her leg to let the parted fabric fall back. I winced again.

This time the cop looked over. 'Something wrong with your eye?'

I said nothing.

'Every time I look round, I find you looking at me like you got soap in your eye.'

'It's conjunctivitis.'

'My auntie had that, too – purgatory it was. She never looked like she had soap in her eye, though. I reckon it's something else. Maybe you can see something on our table we got that you haven't?'

'You mean apart from that inimitable Swansea sophistication?'

'Ah!' The cop nodded as if all had become clear. 'Now I get it. I get it. It appears that quite by chance this fine Aberystwyth morning I have stumbled on someone purveying an item I greatly disdain. Namely the wisecrack.'

'The wisecrack?'

'I disdain it. Always have, always will.'

'I'll bear that in mind.'

'I would recommend that you do. Because to crack wise in my presence is not wise at all. It's stupid. I call it cracking stupid.'

He picked up the corners of the napkin and wiped his mouth again, unnecessarily.

The deputy chuckled with a sycophantic air. 'Oh, he just loves to crack wise, this one does, he's famous for it.'

'You know this man?'

'He's a peeper. He's working the Santa case,' said the deputy. 'He's got an ad in the paper.'

The cop put on that smile you get to recognise after a while, the one they wear just before they hit you. 'Must be getting slow in my old age. Normally I can spot a shamus two blocks away.' He furrowed his brow as he contemplated the seemingly paradoxical nature of what he was witnessing. 'A shamus working a murder case. That's kind of hard to believe.' He leaned towards me. 'Didn't they tell you peepers are not allowed to poke their snouts into murder investigations? I'm sure they must have told you that.'

'I thought maybe we could work together as a team.'

The deputy chuckled again. The cop's smile deepened. It was clear I was asking for trouble and that was his favourite request. But also it was clear he was a connoisseur of situations like this, and preferred to savour them rather than rush things.

'Oh yes, a purveyor of the dumbcrack.'

He stood up, threw the napkin down, and walked to the door. The deputy followed.

The sour cop continued to talk to himself, shaking his head in mock incredulity. 'A peeper who likes to crack stupid, and he's working a murder case. It must be Christmas.'

The girl began clearing the table.

I said, 'I guess he must be the new community policeman.'

The girl looked at me, but said nothing. Carried on clearing.

'Know his name?'

She paused. 'Erw Watcyns. He's from Swansea. He likes the food and hates the people. Our favourite type of customer.'

'Were you working the night the guy got killed in your alley?'

It was as if she hadn't heard.

'Yes, I know. No one saw or heard anything. Could have happened in your kitchen and no one would have seen anything.'

'Why should we care? The affairs of the round-eye are no concern of ours. You'll be wasting your time asking round here. Even with your Kierkegaard.'

'I know. I can understand why you don't want to talk to the cops. I wouldn't, either.'

She said nothing.

I took out a business card and put it on the table. 'An old man killed in an alley at Christmas, that's a terrible thing. All we're doing is trying to find out why. It's not a lot to ask. You can find us at this address if you hear anything that might help.'

'We won't say anything to the police,' added Calamity.

'In fact, if you want to get up the nose of the cop who was sitting at that table, talking to us might be a grand idea.'

The girl stopped clearing and stared at us. Calamity smiled at her.

'We've nothing to say.'

'Mind if we look in your alley?'

'It leads to the street, it's not ours.'

'We're polite people, we always ask first.'

She shrugged. 'It's not our alley.'

The alley led nowhere unless you considered a yard full of bins a place worth going to. It smelled of stagnant drains, hot laundry water, soy sauce and barbecued pork. There didn't seem much reason to go down there and you wondered why the Father Christmas had. Maybe he was dragged there. It wasn't a great place to die; or to spend much time while alive. I waited patiently in the entrance while Calamity held the newspaper in front of her and tried to match the image with the layout of the alley.

Finally she found it, nodded, put the newspaper down and followed the direction of the wrong-ways-round leg. She turned to face a wall. There were drainpipes, and a bricked-up window. She started scrabbling around the window ledge and I walked over.

'Are you going to do the ballistics thing with the knitting needles as well?'

'I thought I'd wait until after dark.'

'Doesn't seem to be much here, just litter.'

Maybe the litter is what we're looking for.'

She ran her finger along the ledge, pushing through a wedge of dirty, rain-sodden paper. Sweet wrappers, a scrap of something, coloured chits ... it didn't seem like much. The sort of detritus that gathered on ledges in alleys everywhere.

'You have to look for the *Gestalt*,' said Calamity.

'What does that mean?'

'I'm not sure, I think it's something about looking at something but not seeing it. Like not seeing the wood for the trees.' She picked up a red chit of paper with a number on it.

'You think that's it?'

She looked at me with a glint of excitement in her eyes. 'It's a receipt from the Pier cloakroom.'

I was about to say that didn't prove anything. It could have just blown there. No reason to suppose the dead man hid it here and did the phoney leg routine to point it out. I was about to say that but then I noticed a man standing at the end of the alley watching us. He wore a black hat with a wide brim, and a long black coat. His beard was long and grey and wispy like candyfloss spun from cobwebs. Calamity put the chit in her pocket and we walked back along the alley towards the man, feeling strangely guilty. When we reached the street we avoided his gaze and walked to Pier Street and then right towards the sea front. The man in the black coat followed. We walked some more and I glanced over my shoulder.

'Is he still following us?' asked Calamity.

'Yes.'

'Maybe we should go to the hat-check office a bit later.'

I agreed. At the Prom we stopped and stood by the sea railings, watching the nothing that was going on out at sea. The man took a few hurried steps and put a hand gently on my shoulder. I turned to face him.

Seen close up, he was strangely indistinct, wrapped in layers of smeared greyness like a wet sky, or watercolour washes on wet paper. Only the thin darker line of the brim of his hat against the knobbled cloudscape had a discernible edge. There were holes in his coat.

'My name is Elijah,' he said. 'I represent the government and people of Israel. I can arrange to provide bona fides if you require it.'

'How can we help you?'

'Your little girl has an item belonging to the people of Israel. I must insist you surrender it to my safekeeping.'

I looked at Calamity, who feigned surprise.

'Do you have an item belonging to the people of Israel?' I asked.

'Not me, boss.'

'She says she doesn't have it. She's an honest kid.'

A weary look passed across his face, which seemed already deeply lined with the imprint of a life spent upon a thankless quest.

'Of course she says that.' He removed his hat and then replaced it. He seemed to be perspiring in the cold morning. 'She says that, even though she knows I stood in the alley and watched her take it.'

'Supposing she did find something in this alley you mention, what was it doing there if it belonged to you?'

'Did I say it belonged to me? I recall saying it belonged to the nation of Israel. I have the honour to represent them, I do not aggrandise to myself the notion that I embody them.'

'That's a fair point, but it's still hard to understand how a nation can lose something in an alley.'

'To you, perhaps, but my people have lost many things in their sad history . . .'

'Not in alleys.'

'Did I say it was lost? I do not recall saying it was lost.'

'You implied it.'

'We didn't find it,' said Calamity.

'No, how could you find that which was not lost? You stole it. That much is clear.'

'Tell us what you are looking for and maybe we can help you look for it.'

'I have been working in the shadows of this world and with the spectres who inhabit it for over forty years. Do you not think I might by now have tired of people feigning ignorance?'

'Maybe I'm not feigning.'

'Feigning ignorance is a difficult stratagem to employ, perhaps the most difficult of all. There are very few people who can do it convincingly. You are not one of them. Time is running out. Mr Knight, please surrender the item and go in peace.'

'What item?'

He sighed. It was a phoney sigh. Feigning a sigh is a difficult stratagem.

'Tell us how an item belonging to the people of Israel happened to be in an alley belonging to the Corporation of Aberystwyth.'

'As if you didn't already know.'

'Humour me.'

'A man was recently cruelly slain in the alley and mutilated in a fashion which shocks even a people whose name has become a byword for suffering.'

'A man called Absalom.'

'Perhaps. He has had many names, as indeed I suspect have you.'

'My name has always been Louie.'

'It is inevitable that you say that. But have you always been a private detective? My information is that you have not. Your current occupation is a tactic, a brilliant one, to cover your investigation into this man you call Absalom.'

'How come you know him?'

'He was my brother. The item he hid in the alley was meant for me. He placed it on the window ledge and with the last of his dying strength wrote "Hoffmann", confident that the shocking manner of his death would be reported in the world press and that the word "Hoffmann" would agitate an elaborate and sophisticated series of tripwires which would cause a bell to ring in the offices of the organisation for which I work. He knew as surely as if he had sent it by registered mail that his message scrawled in blood would reach the awareness of me, his brother. And to help his brother in his search he inserted a rudimentary signal of incoherence in the arrangement of his scene of death such that a policeman would overlook it but one with trained eyes, one who knew there was something there to look for, would not.'

He made a summing-up gesture with his hands. 'And thus we arrive at the scene in the alley, where your little girl – your very smart little girl – decoded the signal and found the hidden item.'

'I'm not his little girl, I'm his partner.'

'What's the item?'

'That I do not know; there you have the advantage of me.'

'Who is Hoffmann?'

He looked annoyed at what he perceived to be my amateurish play-acting. 'It is time to stop fooling, Mr Knight. Or there will be more unnecessary deaths.'

'We're not fooling, we really don't know who Hoffmann is.'

'So you say, but how can that be?' He tilted his head and regarded us quizzically. 'You know, I am still trying to guess who you work for.'

'I can tell you that. It's the person who put the ad in the *Cambrian News*.'

'Ah, yes. The Queen of Denmark. I forgot.' He stepped away from the railing and paused in the motion of turning away. A look of gnomic purpose crept across his features.

'Mr Knight, if you are indeed who you say you are, if you are really a nobody, a . . . a . . . a nothing, just a scrap of newspaper blown along in the wind of the Hoffmann case, I must ask you to reconsider your position.'

'Who is Hoffmann?'

'Indeed! Who is he? How many men over the years have uttered that deceptively simple phrase? How many times have those syllables quivered on the lips of a dying man? Who is Hoffmann? I myself have sought the answer to this riddle. In Moscow, in Warsaw, in Buenos Aires, in Jerusalem, in Zurich and London and Washington; in Peking and Kamchatka, in Berlin and Ljubljana. . . Who is he? An enigma for sure. A myth perhaps. A riddle, yes. Perhaps the greatest spy of the late twentieth century. Maybe the greatest who ever lived.'

He paused and stared up the Prom towards the Pier, as if the answer to this the deepest of mysteries, the riddle of Hoffmann's identity, could be found up there somewhere amid the rusting ironwork that was a home to a thousand seagulls and pigeons.

'I see that we will make no more progress today. Perhaps after another innocent person has been killed you will begin to appreciate the gravity of this situation. And it is indeed most grave. You see, Mr Knight, you and I and your little girl are standing before a unique fissure in the topography of the epoch. Hoffmann has decided to come in from the cold.'

Chapter 3

THE OLD JEW wandered off in the direction of the kids' paddling pool and sat down on a bench. He stared out to sea but it was clear he was still observing us. Two workmen in overalls were pasting posters to boards attached to the sea railings. Two posters that represented in many ways the twin poles of love and terror to be found in the collective Aberystwyth heart.

One advertised a new movie, *Bark of the Covenant*, featuring Clip the Sheepdog. Clip had been the canine hero of the war in Patagonia at the end of the '50s; a beloved star of the *What the Butler Saw* newsreels, the Welsh Lassie. After the end of that insane conflict the dog had been stuffed and now sat obediently in a glass case in the museum on Terrace Road, his muzzle permanently fixed in the bright smile that they said was a high-water mark of the taxidermist's art. The movie was a re-release, the director's cut. The other poster bore a different sort of smile, the grin of a man less beloved than Clip: it was the face of my old games teacher, Herod Jenkins. The bogey man who haunted all our nightmares. Years ago in school I had watched him send my consumptive schoolmate Marty off on a cross-country run into a blizzard from which he never returned. In later years Herod had tried to blow up the dam and drown our town. His face, too, was famous for its smile, or rather the horizontal crease across his face that he called a smile.

Calamity and I watched the two men dip their brooms in watery wallpaper paste and sweep them rhythmically across the paper. The long, slow arcs, like windscreen wipers, smoothing out the horizontal crease in the paper, but doing nothing for the one in Herod Jenkins's face. According to the poster Herod Jenkins had found work at the circus: 'Samson Agonistes, half man, half bear!' It was a role created bespoke by the tailors of fate. Circus strongman, the last refuge for a renegade games teacher who has run out of options. The circus was parked about twenty miles outside town, at Ponterwyd. They didn't dare cross the county line and come any closer to town because Herod was a wanted man in Aberystwyth. Although wanted only in the technical legal sense. I shivered.

'What do you reckon?' said Calamity.

I put a fatherly arm across her shoulders. 'If he was telling the truth, and he really doesn't know what the item you found is, he doesn't know it's a hat-check receipt, right?'

'Right.'

'So there's no reason why we should tell him. We'll come back and pick it up another time.'

'I'm aching to know what it is.'

'Me too, but sometimes you just have to be patient about these things.'

'So what do we do now?'

'We'll go to the Kamp and then talk to Father Christmas's girlfriend.'

We drove out to Borth with heavy hearts. We hated going to Kousin Kevin's Kamp; we always got thrown out. It was only a matter of how far we got inside the perimeter gate before it happened.

After the turning at Rhydypennau we bade farewell to the sun. The world was grey. It was just one of those accidents of geography. All the rocks found along this coast are grey, buff, beige or dirty mauve. In other parts of the world the hills are quarried for bright, shining Carrara marble. Just a little accident of geography, that's all, but it is surprising how much it can affect the contents of the human heart. Try as you may, you can't imagine people lolling about in togas and sandals, drinking wine, in buildings made of slate. Just as it's hard to imagine them beneath the bright hills of Liguria, in their halls of white marble, sitting in crow-black rags, stirring cauldrons and tending spinning wheels like they do in Talybont.

We drove in through the perimeter fence and past the guard house, under a bleak wrought-iron sign, and on to the car park. The snow that had fallen a few days ago still remained here on the north-facing slope. Against the whiteness the buildings looked darker and more sombre, a world of two tones which reminded of those arty photography exhibitions they sometimes held up at the Arts Centre on campus. The sort of blurred, out-of-focus snaps that normal people threw away but that won prizes if you exhibited them.

'You can get rickets if you stay at this place too long,' said Calamity.

'How do you know?'

'I read about it in the paper. They recommend you to eat mackerel while you're here because it's high in vitamin D.'

I reversed into a parking space and butted the rear of the Wolseley Hornet up against a wire-netting fence on which was stapled a metal sign showing an Alsatian dog in silhouette attached to a leash held by a clown.

'Judging by past experience we won't be here more than ten minutes so you should be OK. If you start feeling dizzy, let me know.'

I was wrong. We were there less than six minutes.

Any time after mid-October was low season at the Kamp and it would get lower and lower until about late March. The only blip was around New Year when a few people turned up who had won weekends away in the works' raffle. But it was too early for that, and as we wandered through the lines of dark brooding barracks we saw almost no one except the odd Klown slouched in a doorway, and up by the perimeter a party with buckets and spades digging in the kitchen garden. We headed straight down the rows and followed the smell of frying to the refectory.

It was warm and stuffy inside and reeked of fried bacon and tea that had been stewing in a big silver urn since the days of Noah. A few families sat eating from meal trays at long trestle tables. Nearer the door a man sat alone, scooping soup from a wooden bowl. We sat at his table.

'Mind if we join you?'

He paused and looked and said nothing.

'Great place isn't it?'

His eyes narrowed but he kept on eating as if there was a time limit and he was up against it. It was probably true.

'You been here long?' I beamed at him.

He put the spoon down and said, 'Why you asking? I've done nothing wrong.'

'Just being friendly.'

'We were looking for the harp player,' said Calamity.

'The one in the stovepipe hat,' I added. As if there were any other type.

The man narrowed his eyes and regarded us for a second; then, having decided it was safe to divulge this piece of information, said: 'She doesn't come on till the evening.'

We feigned disappointment.

'Did you know she was seeing the Father Christmas who got whacked?' said Calamity.

The man choked on his gruel. He picked up his bowl and spoon and scurried over to one of the Klowns. He spoke to him, turning and pointing to us as he did. The Klown took out a notebook, wrote something down, and then left the room. We decided to leave, too.

'What are we going to say to the stovepipe hat girl when we find her,' said Calamity.

'Well, we could always try the subtle approach you just used there; that seemed to work quite well.'

'Yes, I goofed. We need to be more oblique.'

'You can say that again.'

'The Pinkertons wouldn't have done it like that.'

'What would they have done?'

'Psychology. That's what they'd have used.'

'I'm all for that.'

'If we go straight in and ask the party about her relationship with the DOA, she'll clam up, right? We have to find a way to make her drop her guard. We achieve that objective by enlisting her sympathy.'

'How do we do that? Say our dog's got a thorn in its paw?'

'No, but you could pretend to be sick and we could knock on the door.'

'I've got a better idea. You pretend to be sick and we knock on the door.'

'Why me?'

'Because they will feel more sorry for you, especially as you will look so sweet with those ribbons in your hair.'

'What ribbons?'

'The ones we will buy on the way.'

'I'm not wearing ribbons.'

'Think of it as going undercover.'

We were interrupted by the sound of an explosion somewhere towards the car park. Calamity and I exchanged glances and without needing to discuss it turned our steps in that direction.

A man wearing chef's whites rushed out of the kitchen and came up to us. 'Can I help you, sir?'

'No, we're just going over to the car.'

'Your car?'

'Yes, we heard something over there, sounded like a crash.'

'Wouldn't you prefer to go to the bus stop? There's one due any minute.'

'Bus stop?'

'It's a wonderful service, sir, truly wonderful. You really shouldn't listen to those idiots who disparage it. Really you shouldn't.' He looked at me with a beseeching expression and watery eyes filled with imploring anguish. His voice was thin and had the whine that a regularly beaten dog gets. 'Please, sir, it really is a wonderful bus.' He grabbed my sleeve. 'I wish I had time to take it myself.'

'But we've got a car, we want to go to our car.'

His face fell and a look of utter hopelessness swept across it. 'Your car, yes, of course you do. And why not? If I had a car, I'd want to go to it too. It would be crazy to expect anything else.' He let go of my sleeve with the air of a man whose last hope of salvation has disappeared. 'It was foolish of me. Absurdly foolish.'

'I'm sorry but we really must be going.'

'You can come, too, if you like,' said Calamity.

The man struggled with himself in the grip of his anguish. He grabbed his wrist and twisted it. 'But what are you going to do when you get to your car?'

'Drive home, I suppose.'

'But that's a crazy plan . . .'

A man in a tuxedo and black bow tie appeared from around a corner and joined us. 'Is there a problem?'

'He wants to drive home,' said the chef.

The man in the tuxedo grinned with joy. 'My word, sir, my word! A sportsman, a true sportsman.'

'We were going to drive to Talybont.'

'I see, sir, you are an optimist. A man who, if I may be permitted the observation, sees always the doughnut and never the hole.' He turned to the chef. 'Don't you agree, Johnny?'

'Absolutely Mr Fortnightly. You have to admire it, you really do.'

The man who was Mr Fortnightly allowed a look of wan sadness to transform his face. It was acting, but it was good acting. 'Ah, but alas, sir, I suspect even you would be rather less sanguine if you were to see the condition of your car now.'

'Why? What's happened?'

'I fear a rock may have hit the fuel tank.'

'Is someone throwing rocks?'

'Rocks are a common feature of the sea shore.'

'But our car isn't on the sea shore . . . is it?'

'Yes.'

'But how did it get there?'

'Plummeted.'

How?'

'I'm afraid there you have me, sir. You will have to take the matter up with Mr Newton.'

'Where can I find him?'

'He's in Westminster Abbey. Unless you are a modernist, in which case you would probably have more sympathy for the view of Mr Einstein . . .'

'You're referring to Sir Isaac Newton, aren't you?'

'Indeed, sir. Your car has been gripped by the mysterious force of gravity and fallen off the cliff. In doing so, it has sustained what both the aforementioned physicists would describe as a massive increase in entropy, to a degree that would severely prejudice your plan of driving it home.'

We reached the car park and found, to our relief, that our car was still there. But the one next to it was being winched up from the beach. The two men exchanged gleeful glances and then burst out laughing. The man in the tuxedo handed me a card on which was written, 'Kongratulations! You've just had your leg pulled by Johnny Sarkastik and his assistant, Mr Fortnightly.' He grabbed my hand and shook it, saying: 'Well done, sir, what a sport!' Then he lowered his voice and added, 'You had a lucky fucking escape this time, didn't you, snooper.'

We interpreted this as an invitation to leave and drove to

Talybont. On the way we stopped a district nurse who pointed out the cottage where the harpist lived. It was set away from the road at the end of a small lane, built from slabs of grey stone under a mauve roof of slate gleaming in the watery air. Dank weeds and grasses grew up against the walls and gave off a strong vapour of rottenness; a horse stamped in a stable nearby.

We stood in the doorway and knocked, Calamity doing her best to look sick and woebegone.

The door was opened by a girl wearing a red flannel shawl over a white blouse and a black-and-white checked skirt; on her feet were shoes with shiny Tudor buckles. She looked younger than the photo in the newspaper – about nineteen, perhaps – and prettier. She smiled.

'I'm so sorry,' I said. 'My daughter has had a nasty turn. Could we trouble you for an aspirin?'

'Oh, you poor little mite,' said the girl, automatically lowering herself a few inches as if Calamity were a five-year-old. She pressed the back of her hand against Calamity's brow.

'All I need is an aspirin,' said Calamity with thinly disguised hostility.

'She really isn't very well,' I said.

We were invited into the kitchen and seated at a table of unvarnished wood. The old man of the house sat in a rocking chair next to an open fire. He had thin white hair and white whiskers, and bright pink cheeks. A book rested on his knees, old and worn like a Bible or some ancient religious tract. Reading glasses lay on the book. Another man, much younger, stood with his back to us, staring out of the window. He stood stiffly erect, without the softness of the old man. Three stovepipe hats hung on a stand by the door. The girl picked up a sooty black kettle from the hearth, brought down cups and saucers from a Welsh dresser set against one wall, and made us tea.

'You have a nice cup of tea, now,' she said, 'and I'll have a little word with the spirits to see what we can do for you.'

'Please don't go to the trouble,' I said hastily. 'She'll be fine. All she needs is to sit down for a few minutes and a little aspirin.'

'Nonsense, it's no trouble. It's a pleasure to be able to help you.'

'That's if you are who you say you are,' said the man standing at the window.

The girl screwed up her face in consternation. 'Peredur, please!'

He about-turned like a soldier on a parade ground. 'I mean no disrespect, but who are you? We don't know. You could be anyone. We don't take kindly to strangers bringing the troubles of Aberystwyth here like mud on their shoes.' He wore a tight black jacket, cut like a frock coat, and had a dog collar. His face was young and glowed with the conviction of the zealot.

The girl walked over and put her hands either side of his face. 'Please, Perry.'

He jerked away.

'Look,' I said, 'we didn't mean to cause you folk any problems. Maybe it's better if we leave.'

'No,' said the old man. 'Please do not be offended by Peredur's sharp tongue. He forgets his manners sometimes.'

'We're not offended,' I said. 'We understand your caution. These are dangerous times. Why, a department store Santa was murdered in town last week.'

There was a palpable increase in tension in the room.

'I expect you heard about it,' I added.

'Yes,' said the old man. 'We read about it – Arwel does work in the village and he brings us the papers sometimes.'

'And we have a wireless,' said the girl with a nervous look at Peredur. 'We sometimes listen to the BBC.'

The back door opened and a man came in carrying a shotgun and with a leather bag slung across his shoulder. His hair was thick and curly, jet black. He pulled a dead hare out of the bag and slung it down on the table. Dark blood where the jaws of a trap had closed was congealed in a ring around the hare's hind leg.

'This is my brother, Arwel,' said the girl. She poured him a tea. He nodded but didn't offer to shake my hand.

'These people are from the city,' the girl said.

He nodded again but said nothing.

'Fancy that!' said the old man. 'Tell me, I hear they have cappuccino in Aberystwyth now. Is it true?'

'Yes,' I said. 'It's true.'

The man smiled and gave a slight shake of his head. 'My, my. And an escalator? I hear there is an escalator there now?'

'No, I don't think so. I think the nearest one is still in Shrewsbury.'

He looked slightly crestfallen, as if a trip on an escalator was the one dream still left burning in the embers of his life.

'Oh, yes, of course. Shrewsbury, not Aberystwyth.'

'Have you been on one?' asked the girl.

'Yes, many times.'

'We were wondering,' said the old man. 'Do you need special shoes to stand on them?'

'No, not at all.'

'And is it true that when the step reaches the top it re-appears moments later as if by magic back at the bottom?'

'Yes, I suppose you could say that.'

He shook his head at the wonder of it. 'Fancy that!'

'We met a man in the village once,' said the girl, 'who came from Aberystwyth. He gave father a coconut. How about that!'

'It was from the funfair,' the old man added quickly, for fear I be misled into a misunderstanding about the climate of Aberystwyth. 'He won it in a contest. Have you ever seen one?'

'Yes, I've seen one or two.'

'They say the coconut tree provides more materials for man than any other tree on earth. They eat the fruit, and cook with the milk. From the trunk they make ships, and the husk gives them matting; the leaves can be woven to provide shelter, and this is only the beginning of what that marvellous tree does. Burning the husk wards off insects—'

'Oh, father, don't start on your silly old tree stories.' She turned to us and smiled. 'Father used to be a rocking-chair maker. All he ever thinks about is wood.'

Ignoring his daughter, the man continued, 'And do you know why a Stradivarius violin sounds better than all the others? It's because of a mini ice age they had in the fourteenth century. The long cold winters made the spruce trees grow slower so the rings were more tightly packed and this extra density gives a Strad its unique sound.'

'That's very interesting,' I said politely.

Peredur cut in impatiently. 'I'm sorry if you have had a wasted journey but we have no aspirins here. There is a pharmacist in the village.'

It was time for the wild card.

'Hey you're not the girl in the papers, are you? The one who was going out with the dead Father Christmas?'

She flinched and looked down at her shoes.

'My daughter gives her free time to play harp to the poor holiday-makers at the Kamp,' said the old man. 'And for this the papers print lies about her.'

'I may have met him once or twice,' said the girl with a slight stammer. 'But that's all. Nothing more. Peredur doesn't ... doesn't like me talking to men.'

'Why, is he jealous?' I laughed.

Peredur flushed. 'I regard that as impertinent!'

'Oh, I'm sorry,' I said, 'I didn't mean to cause offence.' Even though that was exactly what I meant.

'Perry, please!' said the girl.

'The imputation is abhorrent to me,' said Peredur.

'Oh, now! The man didn't mean anything by it.'

Peredur spoke through gritted teeth. 'Banon, I flattered you with the hope that your heart was not like the hearts of other women in this town – a toy, a sailing boat sent hither and thither by the storms of trivial passion and adolescent sentimentality. Perhaps I did you too great a compliment.'

'Come on, folks!' I chirruped. 'It *is* Christmas!'

They all looked astonished by this remark; silence fell with the suddenness of a guillotine. The girl began to polish her silver buckles. The old man found something interesting to look at outside the window. Peredur fixed me with a cold stare. He spoke slowly and enunciated each syllable lest I miss one. 'It is precisely this loathsome trivialisation of the sacred truth of the Christ Mass represented by the ... the institution of the department-store Santa Claus that I abominate.'

'Christ Mass is a time of grieving in this household, you see,' said the girl. 'We're Church of the Sacred Insubordination.'

'I don't think I've heard of that one.'

'We are an austere Church,' said Peredur. 'Our beliefs are considered too severe for many of the people round here. We believe that the truth about God is contained in the Old Testament and that the New Testament is a perversion of his message by His Son.'

'Jesus lied you see,' said the girl.

'Like a lot of children he disobeyed his father,' added the girl's father, giving her a meaningful stare.

'But ... but ...' I struggled for a response. 'What about the bit, you know, "A new commandment I give unto thee, that ye love one another"?'

'He made it up,' said Peredur.

'He was very naughty,' added the girl.

'And for two thousand years mankind has been deceived.'

'Are you sure about this?' I asked.

'The evidence is there in the gospels but people just don't have the eyes to see it. Has it never struck you? The startling difference in the personality of God between the Old and New Testaments? How do you account for such a thing? Do you suppose God, the divine and immutable, underwent a personality change? Or that He is somehow schizophrenic? That He perhaps drank a potion like Dr Jekyll to transform His character? It is absurd. The true God, as revealed by His prophets, is stern and vengeful, quick to anger, jealous and terrible to behold. And yet He is fair and loves us after His fashion, but demands obedience. He is, in fact, like most fathers. He wants only what is best for His children but He is wise enough to know that the route to their felicity does not lie through the fields of softness and indulgence. "Spare the rod and spoil the child" was never more truly written than about God's children. What He categorically is not is sentimental. And yet the New Testament, the outpourings of Jesus, is a febrile, toffee-coated chocolate box of vile and corrupt sentimentality. Love thy neighbour? How can a man in Aberystwyth follow such a precept? Oh, yes, I know they will say it is not literally true but we are not shilly-shallyers here, sir. For us a gospel is precisely that: gospel. The true and undiluted, literal word of God. If it says we must turn the other cheek, we suppose it to mean that. And yet who could take such a precept seriously? Is it not obvious, when you consider it, that Jesus was taking the piss when He said that? Love, forgiveness, charity . . . it is all the grossest sentimentality, foisted on a credulous world by a disobedient son. He was a terrible disappointment to His father.'

Calamity sneezed. ''Scuse me.'

'Oh dear!' cried the girl, seemingly grateful for the opportunity to divert the conversation from Peredur's gloomy liturgy.

'You poor little thing, all the time we've been prattling away and you there still suffering. Wait a moment.' She put her face into her hands and started to groan. She groaned for a whole minute and then looked up.

'I've spoken to the spirits and they recommend a little salve of wormwood, betony, lupin, vervain, henbane, dittander, viper's bugloss, bilberry, cropleek and madder. That should do the trick.'

'All I want is a goddam aspirin,' said Calamity.

'Don't use bad words, Mary-Lou!' I said with the sternest voice I could muster.

'One of my salves is much better than a silly aspirin,' said the girl. 'You just boil it up in sheep's grease, place under an altar, sing five masses, strain through a cloth and use it to anoint your face after meals.'

'It works best at five-night-old moon,' said the old man.

'Oh, Dad!' laughed the girl. 'You are so old-fashioned!' She smiled at us conspiratorially, adding, 'If you replace the viper's bugloss with blackthorn bark and boil it in ewe's milk it's good against goblins, too.'

'And if you say, "Wizen and waste shrew till thy tongue is smaller than a handworm's hipbone,"' said the old man, 'it's effective against a chattering woman.'

The girl flushed. 'Oh, Dad, really! You always go too far. You know I don't like to hear such talk.'

The old man winked at us and said, 'See what happens? I send my daughter to the school in Talybont and they send me back a feminist.'

We stood up and I said, 'Maybe we'll try a chemist.'

The girl showed us out to the car. I slid into the driver's seat and she bent forward and whispered with a nervous backward glance at the cottage in case Peredur was in the window, 'I'm sorry about Peredur. He's frightened, you see. They say the man was killed by gangsters and it is better not to get involved.'

'Is it true what the papers say, about you and . . . the dead man?'

'You mean Absalom? Most of it is lies, of course.'

'You knew him?'

'You mustn't tell Perry.'

'Oh we won't.'

'You see . . . I went to Aberystwyth. To see *Bark of the Covenant*. Perry would go mad if he found out. He thinks Clip is a graven image. He hates idolatry.'

'Of course we won't breathe a word.'

'I met him in the queue for the movie. He was a Jew, you see, and I was wearing my stovepipe hat because they told me I would get a concession on the ticket if I did. And Absalom saw my hat and thought I must be a Jew and started talking to me. He asked me what tribe I was from.' She giggled.

We forced polite smiles.

The girl looked over her shoulder again and leaned further into the car window. 'I had dinner with him afterwards. But you mustn't tell Peredur.'

'We won't.'

'We talked, you know, about things. Mostly about hats and stuff and the best way to re-black the brim. He had some good tips.'

'Did he say anything unusual?'

'Well, the funny thing is, he did say something rather odd. He said, "After seeing this movie tonight my life is fulfilled." And I said, "Yes, it was a jolly good film, wasn't it?" And he said, "No, I don't mean that. I mean tonight at the cinema I saw a man, a man whom I have sought all my life. My quest is ended."' She smiled. 'He was ever so posh!'

I pressed a card into her hand.

'If you think of anything that might help us, feel free to drop in to our office.'

She stuck the card up the sleeve of her blouse along with her handkerchief.

'It's in Aberystwyth,' added Calamity.

The mention of the town lit a small fire in her eyes. 'Ooh!'

'And merry Chr . . . er . . . Christ Mass.'

'No, you mustn't say that – it's like saying merry funeral or something.'

'Happy New Year, then.'

'No, you mustn't say that, either; God doesn't like it because it implies there was something wrong with the old one.'

'What about "Oh, the baby's knuckle or the baby's knee, Where will the baby's dimple be?"' said Calamity. 'Can we say that?'

'I've never heard that one.'

'It's traditional.'

'Well, then, I think it would be suitable.'

I dropped Calamity at her bus stop and drove back to the office. The sky was overcast and, though it was still only mid-afternoon, the cloud had snuffed the last dregs of light from the day. Occasional flakes of snow fell. There was a small crowd gathered in the street outside the office. But, for once, they hadn't come to complain. They were watching a crane winch a fat man into a garret across the road.

The woman from the all-night sweetshop said, 'You've just missed the reinforced bed. You'd think he'd find somewhere on the ground floor, wouldn't you?'

'Who is he?'

A man leaning against a lamppost spoke from under the brim of a fedora hat pulled down low. 'Nobody knows.' He had a slight American accent and was impeccably dressed: two-tone black and white brogues, sharply creased, generously cut trousers. A silk handkerchief peeped out of the breast pocket of a coat of midnight blue. The discretion of the handkerchief was good: just enough to see it. Most people get that bit wrong. The man walked off.

I stared up, along with the other good burghers of Aberystwyth. Flakes of snow, invisible in the gathering dusk, smarted coldly for the briefest of moments on my eyeballs. The man was a round shadow slung beneath the crane, with short arms and legs sticking out and giving the outline of an inflated rubber glove. He turned slowly, swivelling on the end of the chain as, down below, workmen in hard hats shouted instructions to the crane operator. As he turned he came to face us for the briefest of seconds and then the momentum swept him on to more orbits. Round and round. And then, a kid turned up dressed in a red tunic and red pillbox hat like a bellboy from one of the fancier hotels. He was holding an insulated food box, and said, 'Who ordered the pies?' There was no answer but fifteen bystanders turned to look at him and then with synchronised movements pointed at the fat man hanging from the crane. The kid walked over and handed the pies to the foreman. I stared up at the man for whom the pies were intended, and as he swivelled and turned again to face us my gaze was caught and locked for a second by two sharp bright points of light that were his eyes, set deep in the dark, shadowy pumpkin of his face.

Chapter 4

T HE PROM gleamed in watery golden sunlight like a newly washed doorstep. A thin dusting of crystalline snow speckled the pavement, glittered in the sun, and turned at the edges to water. Breath was fog and cheeks smarted.

Sospan stirred a steaming pan of mulled-wine-flavoured ripple. The vapour of cinnamon, cloves and rum made my eyes water and mingled with the sharp, sweet scent from the Christmas tree in the corner of his kiosk; on the roof the fibreglass cone had been squirted with snow from a can, smelling of pine. He lifted the wooden spoon and tested the mixture with the air of a chef, nodded approval and turned down the gas.

'I love Christmas,' he said. 'Although it won't be the same this year. Not with ... without ... you know.' He looked away, avoiding eye contact, with a sheepish air. For once his unerring instinct had led him astray and he had brought up a subject which might be a breach of decorum. He had meant to say, 'without Myfanwy singing at the Pier carol concert'.

Myfanwy was my girlfriend, a former nightclub singer from the Moulin. It was a cherished tradition in Aberystwyth that she sang every year at the carol concert, but this year it did not look like it would be honoured. In the summer she had been kidnapped by gangsters and I rescued her. When I found her she was very sick, but she could have been a lot worse – she could have been dead. For a while after, she had hovered on the edge of consciousness, in a way that suggested rejoining Aberystwyth life was a plunge into a deep pool for which you needed to summon up the courage. The light inside her flickered on and off like a faulty fluorescent light. And then one day she woke up and smiled and started eating and everything seemed fine except for one thing. She couldn't sing. It was as if the town hall clock had lost its tick.

'I was talking to the chap at the home,' said Sospan, 'and he says there's nothing physically wrong — nothing wrong with her voice. It's a mental thing. Blocked, she is.'

I nodded politely but said nothing and wished he would choose another subject. Mercifully he moved to the ice dispenser and started to polish it. Calamity stamped her feet to keep out the fresh cold. A man appeared from the direction of the Pier, ambling slowly, and leading a train of mules like a gold prospector arriving at the foot of the mountain. It was Eeyore, my father. I watched his gait for signs of the slowing that must inevitably come for a man now over seventy but he seemed unchanged, no more soporific than the donkeys who were sixty-five years his junior. There were only five this morning: Antigone, Erlkönig, Firkin, Sugarpie and Gretchen. A slimmed-down troupe to reflect the fact that no one ever bought a ride between late October and March. It was partly a bid to conserve feed and not unnecessarily wear out hoof metal, but also a statement by my father that maintenance of the ritual had a value beyond the money that accrued from the rides. A value which he might have found difficult to put into words but which he felt in his bones just as he would have felt something amiss, a sense of letting the side down, if he had let bad weather serve as an excuse for staying at home. Or perhaps it was a more deeply personal fear: the recognition that the day he first stayed at home would be the beginning of a pattern in which those days would gradually outnumber the days he worked. Until one day the time came when he didn't go out at all, and we stood at his bedside and discussed in whispers what we would do with the donkeys once he was gone.

Calamity kissed him on the whiskery cheek and Sospan poured out another ice.

I put a hand on Antigone's head and nodded a greeting. 'Everything OK?'

'I'm doing fine,' said Eeyore. 'The donkeys are a bit sad – it always happens.'

'They don't like Christmas?'

'It's the pain of exile. They feel it keenly, especially when the cold gets into their hooves.'

'What are they exiled from?'

'Originally donkeys are from Palestine, aren't they? And Lebanon. Lands of heat and dust and shady cypresses and cedars. Olive groves and orange trees. Life, a long, pleasant travail along a series of oases like green and blue beads on a chain of sand; tinkling fountains, the glitter of the pure clean water drawn from the well in the hot sun, and laughing virgin girls bearing sherbet and feeding them figs from the palm of their unsullied hands.'

Sospan looked up at the mention of laughing virgins and said gloomily, 'And now here they are in Aberystwyth.'

'Not all donkeys come from Palestine,' said Calamity. 'Some come from Mongolia.'

'Sure,' said Eeyore. 'But the ones that give the rides to the kids on the beach are from the Holy Land. The ones from the steppes are too bad-tempered – they bite and kick. You wouldn't have caught Jesus riding one of those on Palm Sunday.'

I ran my hand down the mane. 'Do they really miss Lebanon?'

'Not in an obvious sense. Not like they'd miss their stable if we moved to a different part of town; but deep down in their souls they know, they remember a sunny land to which they'll never return. It's the darkness at this time of year, you see, the deadening of the spirit that accompanies the dying of the year.'

'That's what Christmas is all about,' said Sospan. 'It's a winter festival to mourn the dying of the light, the sun slipping into the sea and leaving us in everlasting grey mournful twilight.'

'That's it,' said Eeyore. 'We have this awareness born into us, we don't like it but we understand it, but they don't. They come from a land of perennial sunshine.'

'They look OK to me,' said Calamity. 'Did you get the thing?'

Eeyore looked puzzled for a second and then said, 'Oh!' as he remembered. He delved into his pocket and pulled out a brown envelope. In a bid to throw the old Jew off the scent we had given Eeyore the Pier hat-check voucher to redeem. He handed it to Calamity. It was unopened and she looked at me.

'It was your hunch, kid.'

She tore off the end of the envelope and took out a photograph. It was old and torn and faded, in sepiatone. It showed three people, two men and a woman, posing in what looked like Victorian Sunday best, or Edwardian – I was never too clear about those things. It could have been fancy dress but something about the attitude of those posing suggested it was real, that this was one of those special occasions which don't come along often in a lifetime. It was inscribed in the elegant, flowing script that even the milkmaid used in the days before Biro. It said, 'Mr & Mrs Harry Place and their dear companion Mr Robert LeRoy Parker. DeYoung's Studio, Lower Broadway, New York City. 1901.'

Calamity stared at it for a while and when it refused to surrender its meaning handed it to me. I turned it over. It was stamped '*Ex Libris* Mossad'

I gave it to Eeyore.

He chuckled and ran his thumb across the surface of the picture. 'Didn't think you were into this sort of thing,' he said.

We looked at him.

'Wild West. Didn't think it was your cup of tea. Least, I don't remember you ever being interested. Even as a kid it was always cops and robbers rather than cowboys and stuff.'

'What are you saying?'

'The photo.'

'It's from the Wild West?'

'Oh yes. Last of the great outlaws.'

Calamity said, 'Who?'

He tapped the picture with his index finger. This is Butch Cassidy, and this is the Sundance Kid. The woman is Sundance's girlfriend, Etta Place. She and Sundance were travelling under the names Mr and Mrs Harry Place. Robert LeRoy Parker is Butch Cassidy – that's his real name, although he often used the alias Santiago Ryan. DeYoung's Studio, Lower Broadway, New York City. 1901. This is a famous picture, the one they took before catching the ship to Patagonia.'

Calamity tried to speak but her jaw was too far agape. I curled my index finger and held it gently under her chin, as if coaxing a bird to step on it, and slowly I closed her mouth.

'Butch Cassidy!' she gasped. 'And Sundance!'

'I thought they went to Bolivia. It was in the movie.'

'That's right,' said Eeyore. 'In the Hollywood version they go straight to Bolivia and within six months are dead in a blaze of gunfire. In real life they sailed to Buenos Aires on the SS *Herminius*. With the loot stolen from the Union Pacific *Overland Flyer* they bought a ranch out in Patagonia near the Welsh settlement of Chubut. Stayed there two years.'

'It's the Pinkertons' greatest unsolved case,' said Calamity.

'What's unsolved? They died in the marketplace in Bolivia.'

'The Pinkertons have never accepted that,' said Eeyore. 'They think the outlaws faked their own deaths so they could return unmolested to the States. For the Pinkertons the case is still open. But the real mystery is what happened to the girl, Etta Place. She disappears from the historical record not long after this was taken. No one knows what happened to her. Although they say she was carrying Sundance's child.'

Calamity gulped the remains of her ice cream down in one. 'I've got to go.'

'Where to?'

The post office. I've got to fax them.'

'Who?'

'The Pinkertons.'

She strode off, fired with the conviction of youth. I made to follow her but Sospan called me back. He grabbed my forearm and leaned forward out of the box, looking up and down the Prom as if enemies were all around and the secret he was about to divulge was too precious to risk. 'I know it's probably not a good time, what with you worrying about Myfanwy and all that, but if you're interested, I might be able to get a few tickets for *Bark of the Covenant*.'

Chapter 5

TINKER, TAILOR, whalebone-corset maker, rich man, poor man, beggar man, rock maker, druid. They all used to turn up at the Moulin, the nightclub where Myfanwy used to sing; formerly in a basement, now at the end of the Pier; a dark, neon-blue dingle filled with cigarette smoke, whisky fumes, louche trollops in stovepipe hats, and libido on draft. It didn't really matter what state in life you occupied, as long as you didn't sit in the druids' seats. They all came, and Myfanwy sang to them. And because the songs she sang weren't rude ones, but nice popular anthems detailing the eternally recurring cycle of hearts won and hearts lost, even the ladies from the Sweet Jesus League against Turpitude could come. Just as soon as they had finished protesting outside and excoriating Myfanwy as a harlot straight from Babylon.

Tinker, tailor, seaside-rock maker, crazy golf pro, hobo, clock winder, beggar man, mayor. He came, too, and was humble enough to leave his chain at home. Flickering neon signs fizzed in the rain-drizzled streets: Eats, Whelks 24 hours, liquor and sadness.

Tinker, tailor, mason, Rotarian, hotelier, donkey man and hotdog seller, shepherd, nightwatchmen, and people who are just nobodies. They stand in Peacock's with their bitter spouses discussing socks. Nobodies who sit on the Prom watching nothing. Did they ever expect it to be like this?

Tinker, gaoler, Soldier for Jesus, librarian, whelk catcher, beggar man, ex-con, bent cop. They all came. And while they danced, while the music played, they could forget for a while;

take a trip to the washroom and wash their faces in a tributary of the Lethe. Tinker, tailor, mudlark, warlock, fisherman, stovepipe-hat stockist, effigy maker, gravedigger.

And the people on my client's chair.

It was a private nursing home paid for by an anonymous bene-factor. I didn't know who; perhaps some high-ranking druid, an admirer from the days when she sang in the Moulin Club; or a member of the town council. For the first two months I had footed the bill but it wasn't easy. No one ever got rich fighting crime, just ask Eeyore – a cop for thirty years before he became the donkey man; more collars than a Chinese laundry, and he ended up just as poor. Aberystwyth, queen among towns for irony; perhaps nothing was more so than this: that there was so little money to be made in law enforcement when there were so many villains, so many laws to be enforced.

It had been built as a seminary some time earlier in the century. One large grey three-storey block to which a reluctant architect had seemingly had his arm twisted into adding some decoration. He'd probably read all the latest architectural jour-nals and wanted the purity and elegance of Bauhaus, dreamed of winning a major prize somewhere far away and prestigious. But the Church fathers – perhaps fearful of the warlike reputation of the townspeople – insisted on turrets and battlements. So he'd scribbled on a pointless turret, some arched windows and an oaken door studded with iron. Then he quit and caught the train to Shrewsbury. Now it sits serenely in a nice park at the top of a hill overlooking the town. Slate quarries and gorse towards the back, and a paddock of horses. Gorse is not a great thing to have in your garden; it seldom lifts the jaded heart. But every spring it burns with buds of yellow flame, and when you see the same fire reflected in the eyes of a mare aglow with pride for her foal you always wish you'd brought some sugar lumps along.

It was a good place to recuperate. The wind could be bad in

winter. It could knock you off your feet sometimes, and rattle the windows so violently it made you stop your darning and turn round to stare anxiously at the panes. Sometimes it howled in a way that was unsettlingly human, as if the wind collected all the voices of wanderers who had been lost in its storms, and replayed them. But it wasn't always like that, and in all seasons the view was wonderful. It gave you perspective. Instead of being witness to a myriad trivial heartaches and sorrows, betrayals and acts of meanness, you looked down and surveyed the broader sweep: the heroic little town thrust out into the bay, the sea slowly gnawing away at the edges like a mouse with a piece of cheese. From up here you could see the long, straight line of the Prom and the characteristic zig-zag at Castle Point like a cartoon lightning bolt; or, depending on your mood, the valedictory blip on the heart monitor of a man who has just died.

Myfanwy lay in bed, propped up on pillows, asleep. The watery winter sunlight made her cheeks glow like amber. She looked well. Someone had disfigured her chestnut tresses with two childish yellow ribbons. The sort they tie to oak trees when someone comes out of prison. They sat knotted on either side of her head in some strange insult. I knew she would have hated them. They were redundant: it was not possible for her hair to be a mess any more than a lion's mane can be dishevelled. It was the same colour as the chestnuts in Elm Tree avenue.

Gently, I undid the ribbons and put them on the side table. She had been like this almost four months now. The doctors said there was nothing physically wrong as far as they could see. She just seemed happier asleep. In the moments when she woke up, she was often sullen, and withdrawn, cold almost, like a kid who ate a piece of pie baked by the Snow Queen. I wondered if she blamed me for what had happened in the summer; or resented me for bringing her back from the dream world. Or maybe it was the loss of her voice, her very essence, that had hit her hard. But she looked well today.

I listened to her breathe, watched the gentle rise and fall of the sheets. I smoothed them out and then ruffled them again. Listened to her breathe: like the sea on a windless day, slow and soft and pitched precisely on the threshold of audibility. I pressed the back of my hand to her cheek, like a mother checking the temperature of a pale child, like a boy stealing an apple. And then I leaned forward to kiss her cheek. Strange, the mild sensation of guilt that the motion evoked. As if standing over the sleeping form of one's girlfriend was a forbidden pleasure. Myfanwy would not have begrudged a kiss, I knew. But all the same . . . Maybe it is the vulnerability that is revealed in a sleeping form. It makes you feel like a peeping Tom, his eye to the keyhole, watching two lovers at play in a walled garden. And you know the slightest noise, such as the crack of a twig underfoot, will reveal your presence and destroy their joy; sully it with the pall of having been observed.

I leaned forward to kiss her cheek below the ear.

'Hello, Louie.' A voice crashed through the serenity like a felled tree. 'She looks lovely, don't you think?'

I jerked round to face the intruder. It was a nurse, with a fat boyish face, standing stiffly and shapelessly in a white pinafore dress. The dress was too tight; the buttons strained and divided her torso into segments like a giant millipede. Damp patches of sweat darkened the fabric of her blouse under her arms. Her hair was straw-coloured and cropped in a way that suggested a pair of kitchen scissors and a head bent over a bowl on a kitchen table, a bowl which on other occasions would be used to soak feet.

'I made her look nice. I knew you would come today.'

I smiled uncertainly.

'You don't remember me, do you?'

'Er . . .'

'It's OK, you don't have to pretend. My name's Glenys. We were in the same class in school.'

'Oh . . . I . . .'

'You don't remember, I can see it in your face. Please don't pretend.'

'It was so long ago.'

'Yes. It doesn't matter. You needn't worry about me. Why should you? You've come to see Myfanwy. She's much better. Would you like me to wake her?'

'No, please. Don't wake her.'

She needlessly plumped up the pillow. 'The ribbons are mine, I wore them for my second baptism. I knew you would like them. Are you sure you don't want me to wake her?'

'Yes. I'm quite happy sitting here.'

'It's ever so easy. You just put your hand over her mouth and hold her nose. She wakes up in a jiffy. I do it with all the patients. You're looking well.'

'Thanks. You too.'

'I've put on weight, specially round the knees.' She looked down and my gaze followed of its own accord. She was wearing tan woollen tights on legs without shape, the tights wrinkled at the fat ankles. Below them were black sensible shoes with scuff marks on the toes. 'It's all this running around after the invalids, you see. They treat me like a bloody servant. My legs were my best feature in school.' She began to smooth down the bed and apply herself to tidying chores. I wished she would leave.

'Five years I sat behind you and you never turned round once.'

'As I say—'

'I sent you a Valentine card and you thought it was from the girl from the estate. You asked her out and she said no.'

'I remember that.'

'She's dead now, so they tell me. Brain haemorrhage.' She picked up a litter bin and walked out.

Myfanwy sighed and shifted position. There was something deeply calming about that sigh. A sign that wherever it was she was wandering, whichever somnambulant world closed to us, it was nice there and bathed in warm sunshine. Perhaps she was walking through the marram grass at Ynyslas in summer. The day we had our first picnic. A hot blue sizzling day when you had to squint to look at the sea; a day of champagne and strawberries and whispered words; a day I keep locked away in a vault and seldom take out, for fear that exposure to the sun will fade it, and the joy it brings will seep away, like a perfume slowly loses its scent with time.

I walked to the window and looked out at the town. A woman wandered in and sat on the chair I had vacated. She was in a dressing gown, and wore her grey hair in pigtails like a Red Indian squaw. Her features were finely drawn and hinted at lost beauty. There were bandages on both her hands. She took Myfanwy's hand and spoke.

'I do envy you being able to sleep like this. I haven't slept a wink for thirty years—' She made a tiny startled movement, like a gazelle which picks up the scent of a predator on the breeze. 'Who's that?' she whispered. 'There's someone here. Someone by the window . . . I can smell liquor.' She sniffed the air. 'Captain Morgan rum, if I'm not mistaken.'

'I'm sorry, I was . . .'

'A man! Oh, you must be Louie.'

'Yes.'

'I'm blind, you see. Myfanwy always talks about you.'

'That's kind of you to say.'

'How old do you think I am?'

'Oh, I . . .'

'Don't say it, you'll upset me. I'm only forty-six. That shocked you, didn't it?'

'No.' She looked twice that.

'I can tell from your voice that it did. I've had a hard life. I'm the oldest resident. Did you know that? That's what fooled you, you see. I haven't got my stick. That wretched nurse keeps hiding it.'

'Is Myfanwy your friend?'

'Yes. My name's Evangeline ... Miss not Mrs. I was never married. Who would want me? Oh, but there was a time, oh yes, a time when I was desired.' She stood up. 'Well, I must be going. I know better than to play gooseberry to two young sweethearts.'

'You're very welcome to stay.'

'This place used to be a seminary, did you know that? "Seminarium" means nursery garden, from the Latin for seed, like semen. A place where they grow priests; you need to spread a lot of dung to do that. I knew a priest once, many years ago; he used me as a seed bed but they didn't believe me. He was a beastly priest, or was it the other way round? Heigh-ho, there is a willy grows aslant a brook ...' She paused as if trying to recover a lost train of thought. 'I was desired once, too. But that was long ago.'

She stepped slowly to the door and I said, 'Does Myfanwy really talk about me?'

'All the time.'

She reached the door and added, 'Myfanwy says you drink too much rum. I think she was right.'

'It's my aftershave.'

'Well, then, you drink too much aftershave.'

Before leaving, I dropped in on the doctor. He was sitting at his desk showing a series of cards to a small mongrel dog who sat on a chair. The cards showed pictures of various objects that might interest a dog.

'The vet says he needs worming,' the doctor explained without looking up. 'Please take a seat.'

I pulled up another chair to the desk.

'That's their answer to everything: worm tablets. But what's the point of removing the parasites if you don't address the fundamental psychosomatic causes?'

He held out a card with a picture of a cat and the dog growled. The next card had a bone on it and the dog licked his nose.

'You see!' said the doctor as if this proved something.

'Dogs have psychological problems, too?'

'Of course. They have two eyes like us, a heart like us, two lungs like us, a brain like us. Why do people suppose they don't also have the same neuroses?'

'I've just been to see Myfanwy.'

'Yes, she's looking better.'

'She seems to sleep a lot.'

The doctor paused and put on his concerned face. 'She seems a bit – how should I say it – a bit reluctant to join the party. It's as if she's happier in dreamland or wherever it is she goes.'

'I can understand that.'

'We need to coax her back. We need to help her see that life is worth living and she will be happy again.'

'How do we do that?'

The doctor put the cards down and made a steeple of his fingers as he warmed to his theme. 'One thing you could do is bring in an item with sentimental value for Myfanwy, something that has associations of happier times. It doesn't have to be anything dramatic – a photo or an ornament or something. Just leave it in her room. It could help.'

'I've got some of her records, she gave them to me after our first date. I think she would like those.'

'Excellent. That would do splendidly. We could play them to her; music has the most remarkable curative properties in this respect.' He returned his attention to the dog. The next card showed two dogs copulating and the patient wagged his tail.

Downstairs in the hallway I ran into the nurse again.

'Hello, Glenys,' I said with forced cheeriness.

'The name doesn't mean a thing to you, does it? No one ever called me that. You all used to call me Tadpole.' Her eyes watered at the memory and she stuck a pudgy fist into the socket and screwed it round. 'Tadpole,' she repeated and her mouth became distorted into the shape of a figure-of-eight lying on its side.

I still couldn't remember her but the sight of her pain, still vivid after so many years, made me squirm. 'Oh, now I remember. I'm so sorry, kids can be very cruel, it shocks me when I think about it.'

'You never cared about me at all.'

'Oh, that's not true. I really liked you.'

She looked at me. 'Really?'

'Of course. We all did.'

The hand shot back up to the eye and she began to cry. 'Now I know you're lying. You never cared about me. Maybe if I'd been called Hoffmann, that would have been different.'

I blinked in surprise.

'That got you, didn't it? Yeah, that got you.'

'Did you say "Hoffmann"?'

'Might have done,' she snivelled.

'Do you know something about Hoffmann?'

'Maybe I do and maybe I don't.'

'Oh, come on.'

'I saw the ad in the paper. I don't want your lousy books, if that's what you're thinking.'

'Tell me what you know.'

'I used to nurse a man who had been a soldier in the war in Patagonia. They tortured him with an electric telephone generator. He used to cry out in the night, cry out the name "Hoffmann". Bet you didn't know that.'

'No, I didn't. Who was this soldier?'

Her face lit up in triumph. It was a small victory but I suppose people like Tadpole take what they can get. She minced off, seething with glee. 'That's for me to know and you to find out.'

I ran after her. 'Look, Nurse Glenys, I'm sorry the kids in school called you Tadpole—'

'That's it butter me up, now I've got something you want.'

'You saw the ad in the paper. You know I'm looking into the murder of Father Christmas. It was a shocking crime.'

'Yeah, I know. They cut off his doodah and stuck it in his mouth. I know how that feels. But I don't care about him.'

I sighed. 'OK, Tadpole, if you don't want to tell me, I can't make you.'

She paused and considered for a second, then said with a sly edge to her voice,

'I could take you to see him if you want.'

'To see who?'

'The soldier who used to cry out "Hoffmann" in his dreams. That's if you give me what I want.'

'How much do you want?'

'I don't want your lousy money.'

'What do you want, then?'

'A date.'

I looked at her in surprise, which she mistook for disdain. Her face crumpled up and the fist shot straight to the eye. Her voice rose to a whine. 'See, I knew it. Just a lousy date and look at you . . .'

'You mean, like dinner at the Indian or something?'

'What's the point? You can't bear the thought of it, can you? It's written all over your goddam face. I'm a leper, I know. Eugh! Look at him! He's going out with stinky Tadpole!'

I touched her arm softly. 'I'd love to. It would be great to catch up after all these years. We could have dinner and maybe go to the Pier afterwards for a dance. Would you like that?'

She smeared the tears away with the back of her fist. 'That . . . that would be nice, but . . . but . . . there's something else, something else I really want.'

'Yes, what?' I said with a cold feeling of dread. 'Tell me what you really want.'

'I want to go and see the new movie about Clip.'

Chapter 6

'YES,' I SAID. 'I will accept a reverse-charge call.'

'Hold on, please. Go ahead, caller.'

Pause. Click. Rustle. Flustered breathing.

'Oh, my goodness! What have I done? What have I done?' said the Queen of Denmark. 'I couldn't find a coin. Can you believe it? My head's on ten million of the damn things but there isn't a single one in the palace.'

'That's OK, just keep it brief; international phone calls don't come cheap.'

'Yes, of course. I'm sorry. I was just wondering if you'd had any responses to the advertisement.'

'Not many, I'm afraid.'

'How many?'

'Well, not any, actually.'

'Oh dear ... Do you think the newspaper will give us the money back?'

'I would be highly surprised.'

'Oh, dash it all. It cost forty pounds.'

'I'm sorry but the problem is the reward. This philosopher—'

'Kierkegaard.'

'It's not a great motivator.'

'I suppose I'm a bit out of touch. What if I were to offer them a duchy or something? Or a bit of Africa – we've still got some somewhere.'

'That might be interpreted as taking the mickey.'

'You must think I'm a dreadfully silly old woman—'

'Not at all. I think it's great that you're showing an interest.'

'I really called because I was bored.'

'Don't you have anything to do?'

'Opening a shopping mall this afternoon. How dull is that? My mum used to launch ships.'

'You build ships in Denmark?'

'Begging your pardon, Mr Knight, we are a race of seafarers. Have you never heard of the Hanseatic League? Where do you think the Vikings came from?'

'Never really thought about it.'

'Our boys used to come over in their longboats and whup your sorry asses. Oh, God! What have I said? I'm so sorry—'

'There's no need to be. I underestimated your nation – I thought you just made bacon.'

'Despite our small size our influence on the world stage has been quite considerable. We invented Lego.'

There was a pause and then she burst out laughing. 'Oh Lord! What have I said? I'd better get off the line and stop wasting your money. I'll call you next week when you might have something for me.'

'See if you can find some coins next time.'

'I'll get some specially minted.'

'Did the Danes really invent Lego?'

'Stop teasing.'

'I'm not, I was just thinking about the reward in your ad. Forgive me for saying this, but Lego's a lot more popular in Aberystwyth than the works of Kierkegaard.'

'You think it would make a better reward?'

'I think so.'

'My God, what a brilliant idea. We could offer the centenary set.' She hung up.

I left the receiver cradled against my cheek and watched Calamity. She was writing out index cards with a marker pen, a frown of deep concentration on her face; acrid inky fumes surrounding her in a cloud. She wrote 'Dead Santa, name:

Absalom' on one and pinned it to the incident board. She wrote 'Butch Cassidy' and pinned it to the board. She followed that with the 'Queen of Denmark', 'Rocking-chair Man' and 'Emily'.

She felt my gaze on her and looked across. 'Every scrap of information has to go up because you never know which ones are the significant ones. If you just concentrate on what you think is important you often overlook the crucial stuff.'

'Is that so?'

She slapped the Pinkerton manual. 'It's all in here. Incident-board tectonics. It's a new science.'

I nodded. 'Makes me wonder how I survived all these years without that book. Where did you get it, anyway?'

'Eeyore gave it to me. He got it from the police library.'

'I didn't know he was still a member.'

'He isn't. It's a rarity, this book. The man at the antiquarian bookshop offered me fifty quid for it.'

'How did he know you had it?'

'He asked me to get it.'

'From the police library? What's Eeyore going to say?'

'He gets fifty per cent. He needs a new manger.'

'Is there a chapter in there on fencing stolen goods?'

Silence.

'So what went wrong?'

Silence.

'What happened?'

'Huh?'

'Why didn't you get the fifty quid?'

'I started reading it.'

I watched her work, aware of a strange feeling fizzing inside my chest. It wasn't one of those feelings we easily find names for; none seems quite right. An emotion which, paradoxically, has a physical representation: pins and needles of pride. When I first met Calamity she was an amusement-arcade hustler, with the bad complexion and glassy look that come from a troglodytic life spent in dimly lit caverns staring all day at fruit machines. She would have regarded a trip to the town library with about the same relish as dogs view their monthly bath. She was the sort of kid who was going nowhere and had it all mapped out. The sort you tend to look warily at when they congregate in groups, the sort you damn at first sight and regard as evidence that the world is going to pot. And yet.

'You don't believe in it, do you?'

'I didn't say that. If it helps you work, that's fine. I keep my incident board in my head.'

'It's supposed to help you see the links and interconnections between the pieces of the puzzle. Things which aren't obvious.'

'I've got a guy in my head who does the links for me – he works the night shift.'

She pinned up another card.

And yet. And yet here she was: focused and determined. And with less cynicism than a newborn puppy. After removal from the amusement arcade her eyes had acquired a natural brightness; it would dim with the coming years, I knew, but it was still good to behold. Having her around was a tonic and I didn't want to do anything to curb that bright heart. But sometimes I had to.

'You do understand about what I said? Faxing the Pinkertons and that?'

'Sure.'

'I know you're pretty excited about it, but really you can't just dance off with a fresh piece of evidence and spill the beans – even to the Pinkertons.'

'It's all right. I understand.'

'I mean, it's not like they're going to be interested or anything.'

'It's all right, Louie.'

'I don't like to stop you, but . . .'

'Can we drop it?'

'As long as you're OK about it.'

'You're the boss, right or wrong.'

'Honestly, Calamity, this time I'm not wrong. Who's Emily, anyway?'

'She rang earlier when you were visiting Myfanwy. She's a student at the theology college in Lampeter. Apparently, everyone out there is pretty excited about the Kierkegaard books. She says she's got information on the Father Christmas case.'

'Really?'

'He went to see her last week.'

'Did you tell her the last student we had from Lampeter ended up with a "Come to Sunny Aberystwyth" knife between the ribs?'

'I thought it better to gloss over that bit. Anyway, she's not from the Faculty of Undertaking. She's from Jezebel College.'

'I don't know that one.'

She consulted her notebook and said without understanding, 'Comparative ethnography of the icon of the fallen woman in Cardiganshire.'

'They study that?'

'Seems so.'

'Kids of today, eh? We never had the opportunities when I was young. What's that roll of celluloid in the corner?'

'Acetate film. Anti-glare coating for the incident board. A guy dropped it off here earlier.'

'What sort of guy?'

'Just a guy. He was a salesman. Left it as a free sample. He said it would work well on our incident board.'

'In case you get snow blindness from staring at it.'

'It was free, what are you worried about?'

I called Meirion at the *Cambrian News* and we arranged to meet at the museum in half an hour. I arrived early and stood for a while pondering in the gloom and enjoying the calm that fills the soul in a world of musty linen, penny-farthings, and whalebone corsetry. Clip the Sheepdog stood mutely in his glass tomb, ear permanently cocked for the Great Farmer's whistle. The dead Santa had been to see him and afterwards said his life was fulfilled. That had to mean something. Was it something about the dog or the war? The casual visitor could visit the town and leave without ever knowing about the war that had been fought in 1961 for the colony of Patagonia. It was one of those things kept hidden from view, a war no one wanted to talk about – the Welsh Vietnam.

The settlers left Wales in the middle of the nineteenth century to start a new life. They sent letters home complaining how hard and unforgiving the land was; wresting potatoes from the soil was like wrenching coins from a miser's hand. And yet, paradoxically, when the war of independence erupted they spent three years irrigating the land with their blood, rather than surrender the colony. Some people saw it all as a monument to an essential truth about the human condition: to contrariness, or man's deep-seated need to moan. But not me. For all the names of obscure battles we memorised in school, the campaigns and mountain ranges, the lamas and lamentation, the one image that has remained with me across the years is the strange story of their arrival on those far off shores. The story of the first day. The good ship *Mimosa* was anchored out in the bay, men were wading ashore; and one man – the perennial early bird – ran ahead and climbed a nearby hill to view the promised land. What happened next must surely have crushed their spirits and made them want to turn back. But emigrating in those days was a life sentence against which there was no appeal. Everything you had was sold to buy the dream, the one-way ticket; there was no surplus and no returning. You had to admire their guts; or their desperation . . .

What did the man see, that first Welshman on the top of that hill? The Welsh Cortez? He saw the cruel wisdom which had been available to him at his grandmother's knee, but which he had scorned because of her simple ways; and because knowledge only becomes wisdom once you have paid a high price, and traversed oceans for it. He saw a simple truth: that a man who arrives in the marketplace to sell dreams from atop a hastily upturned crate, and who casts anxious looks around every now and again as if in fear of arrest, is not to be trusted. He saw that a man who claims to have the cure for all known ills in his small bottle of cordial and wears clothes covered in patches is not to be believed. He saw that a man who has found what all men since the beginning of time have sought, a promised land, might reasonably be expected to go and live there himself; not sell tickets with an air of furtive desperation in the marketplace.

But hope, like love, is a powerful drug that subverts all calls to reason. Patagonia! Where the soil was so rich you could cook and baste with it; rivers so full of gold it took two people to carry a bucket of water; lambs which made the ground tremble as they walked, and arrived ready-seasoned from grazing in the vales of mint. A blessed grove where troubles were unknown; but which, strangely, only Magellan had heard of. A far-off land named after a race of Indians who had vanished from this world and whose only imprint in the sands of time seemed to have been – and oh, the cruel irony of it – the fact that they had big feet. What did he see from the top of that hill? The Welsh Cortez? No one knows. He disappeared into thin air. The very first settler: climbed to the top of the hill and was never seen again. Don't tell me that isn't an omen.

Meirion had said he'd bring the paper's film critic along, but when he arrived there was only him. Then I saw he was wearing a different hat and I understood. He greeted me with a warm smile and took a stick of rock out of his pocket and went through the slow ritual of removing the cellophane. He pointed at Clip. 'They say it's the second most enigmatic smile in the history of art.'

'After the *Mona Lisa*?'

'That's right, but without the guile.'

'I didn't know they used dogs in war.'

'They used loads, they just don't like to talk about it too much. They're ashamed, you see.'

'What of?'

'Of what you have to do to get a dog to disobey his natural instinct and run headlong into machine-gun fire.'

'What do you have to do? Throw a stick?'

Meirion smiled. 'No. You have to use the dog's deep love and devotion, his loyalty to and trust in his master. There's nothing else on earth quite like a dog's love for his master. And it's freely given. A bit of food, a bit of kindness, a few soothing words and a pat on the head, some slippers to fetch, that's all it takes. Then, once you've got it, once the dog loves you so much he will trust you absolutely and do anything you say, you can send him into the minefield.'

I grimaced at the picture Meirion had painted. 'So what's the story about the new movie, *Bark of the Covenant*?'

'Technically it's not new. It's just been re-cut. The director's cut, I suppose you'd call it – he's dead now, but he left detailed instructions on how he wanted it. Clip was a kind of Lassie, you see. He used to star in the newsreels shot in the *What the Butler Saw* format. At first it was all factual stuff, but because the news was rarely good they started to embellish it a bit. Before long Clip became so popular back home no one wanted to hear about the war unless Clip was in the story. So they blurred the boundaries between fact and fiction. In fact, they didn't so much blur them as blow them away. They started producing full-length features masquerading as newsreels. *Bark of the Covenant* and *Through a Dog Darkly* are the most famous. Last spring some workmen rebuilding the Pier found a walled-up room with a runic inscription above the door. Inside they found an archive of lost Clip footage. Some enthusiasts restored the movie and transferred the print to 70mm.'

'What did the inscription say?'

'I don't know but I can guess: "A curse upon all who enter" or something like that.' He laughed. 'I mean, when you get a druid inscription above a sealed chamber it doesn't usually say, "Come in and make yourself at home".'

Before he left, Meirion gave me a newspaper clipping which he thought I might find interesting. It was from a few weeks ago and told the strange story of a man who had hung himself after seeing the premiere of *Bark of the Covenant*. He had been a taxidermist. Meirion gave me the address and said the man's daughter was living there now. The house was nearby, on Bryn Road, and I decided to pay her a visit. The girl, her eyes still red with crying, peeped round the door at me and invited me in. I was shown to a chair in a small sitting room in front of a gas fire that hissed softly in the gloom. The mantelpiece was arrayed with the usual knick-knacks, stuff which I could tell had belonged to her dead father and mother: cheap silver-plated candlesticks, a Coronation mug, miniature brass elephants set beside a brass shell case from the Great War; framed photos of various dead people, and a south-coast seaside resort where a young couple grinned awkwardly into a camera forty years ago. A brass letter holder stuffed with letters and cards, none of them from abroad. The accumulated detritus of a life, all that was left of the good times two people had shared. Put them all together in a box and sell them through *Exchange and Mart*, you might get the cost of a second-class stamp.

'I'm so sorry,' said the girl, dabbing her eyes. 'I . . . I . . .'

'Take your time,' I said gently. She was somewhere in her mid-twenties, wrapped up in a bilberry-coloured mackintosh which looked like it might be quite an expensive model, belted tightly at a narrow waist. Her hair was cropped in a pageboy bob, ivory colour, the way they did it in Flemish paintings back in the time when the Flems went in for painting. She was very pretty, with clear blue eyes and tear-stained cheeks which some would describe as pellucid. It was the sort of complexion they use to advertise cosmetics even though you never get a complexion that good using powder. Two weeks ago her father had gone to see the new Clip movie and after that he had walked down to Trefechan Bridge by the harbour, attached a length of cord to the central light fitting, and hanged himself from it. He swayed like a pendulum in the breeze all night and was found in the early light by a fisherman going to work. If he'd been my dad, I would have cried, too.

She picked up a tissue and with a determined effort to move things along blew her nose with a sharp and unseemly 'parp' sound.

'You say he hanged himself after seeing the movie, but does that imply simply a temporal relation like saying it was after the six o'clock news, or are you implying there is a causative connection?'

'I'm sorry, I . . .'

'I mean, when you say "after" do you just mean after the movie, or do you mean he killed himself because of something he saw in it?'

'Because of what he saw, yes, there is no doubt about it. No doubt whatsoever.'

'There's usually doubt about these things . . .'

'You didn't know my father. His life was ruined by that dog.' She gave me a look which challenged me to make light of such a claim. I left the gauntlet where it lay. 'You've seen the stuffed Clip at the museum?' she said.

'Plenty of times.'

'What do you think of it?'

'I don't generally think about it. To me it's just a dog in a glass cage.'

'What about the smile? Do you agree it's like the *Mona Lisa*? Mysterious, enigmatic, but with perhaps a little less guile?'

'Not really. All collies look like that.'

'My father hated that expression. It destroyed him.'

'That's quite a strong opinion to have about a stuffed dog's smile.'

'For you perhaps. But my father was a taxidermist. He had a wonderful career ahead of him. He could have been one of the greats . . . perhaps the greatest of all. With work on show in Moscow town hall or the Sorbonne. But life is full of what-might-have-beens isn't it?' Her head was lowered but she raised her tear-filled eyes as if to seek my complicity in this bitter truth. 'Oh yes, he never stopped finding fault with Clip. There was never a day when he did not criticise the piece for various technical failings: ears too sharply angled, tongue too pink, the line of the spine not straight enough . . . but he knew they were irrelevant, like criticising Michelangelo for getting David's head out of proportion. Secretly he knew the truth: it was an act of divine creation. Angels must have reached down and anointed the stuffer while he worked. The day my father saw the unveiling of Clip at the museum he felt like Salieri when he first heard the music of Mozart. His heart was shattered. He spent the rest of his life on his allotment; never stuffed another piece. With time, of course, the pain subsided. But then they re-released the movie and it all started again. We tried to stop him going, but it was no use. He came home after the movie with a face the colour of ash. Fetched something from his room and walked out into the night. That was the last time we saw him alive.'

Christmas is a time of rituals, some that have lost their meaning and some that acquire new meaning as the years pass and folks' memories assume new forms. After I left the girl's house I went back to the office to prepare for a modern Christmas ritual, one which had only recently come into being and which had a deeply personal significance for me. It was the annual swinging of the cricket bat. That sacred wand of willow with which, five years ago, I had knocked my old games teacher, Herod Jenkins, out of a plane door. For the rest of the year it stands in the corner of my office, in the place at the foot of the hatstand reserved for umbrellas and walking sticks. And once a year Gwynfor from the Rotary Club comes and takes it away. People pay 50p for a swing and with the proceeds some needy children acquire a new climbing frame or a day trip to Chester Zoo. Such are the quixotic strategies that Dame Fortune uses, planting the seeds of future joy in the loam of past tragedy.

Herod Jenkins survived the fall from the plane; Planet Earth just wasn't hard enough. It's only made of rock. Since then he had been on the run from the law with my former cleaner, Mrs Llantrisant. They made an improbable Bonnie and Clyde, robbing the same sub post offices from which they drew their pensions. Now, it appeared, they had taken employment at the circus, Herod using that famous upper body strength to earn his keep, to provide for his moll, as a strongman.

If only his victims had been possessed of such strength. The photo of my schoolmate Marty stands on the desk in the office. Propped next to it is a Christmas card from his mum which arrived two days ago. She never forgets. Just as none of us, not me nor Gwynfor nor anyone else who was there, will forget the time in the third year when Marty was sent off on that cross-country run into the blizzard and never returned. The weather had been vile that day; snow falling so thick the sheep on the hills suffocated as they stood. Herod was not hostile to the concept of postponing games in bad weather, but it never got bad enough on Earth. Only beneath the liquid methane clouds of Saturn, they said, where storms raged unabated for centuries at temperatures of minus 190°C, and winds howled at more than 2000 kilometres an hour did it start to look doubtful. A lightning bolt hits the ground-keeper's hut and discharges in one flash more power than is generated on Planet Earth in ten years. OK, no games today.

I poured a rum and began to rub linseed oil into the talismanic bat. Before long I heard footsteps on the stairs outside and Gwynfor walked in, red-faced, chubby, cheery. We shook hands, and said how good it was to see each other again. Even before the sentence was finished his eyes were trained on the bottle. We drank to our health and we toasted dead Marty. We used to laugh at his lack of athletic prowess, the silly way he ran. Marty the seer, the saint, the one the gods loved, but not much. The day he came back with the X-ray showing the shadow on his lung he was almost exultant, as if it proved what he had long been trying to tell people: he was not meant for this world. He was a poet and had the poet's disease to prove it: consumption. The white death. That dark spot on the lung worn as a badge of honour by Shelley, Kafka, and that bloke played by Dustin Hoffman in *Midnight Cowboy*. He named his budgie Hans Castorp in honour of the diagnosis. 'Who is that?' I said. 'Oh, he's a bloke from a book called *The Magic Mountain*.' Sometimes he liked to mystify. But if it hadn't been for him, what would I be doing today? I didn't know, but I knew I wouldn't be a private eye.

Gwynfor took the bat and walked across to the door. I crumpled up a piece of paper and bowled. 'Howzat!' he cried, the ball of paper thudded against the window pane and, as if the gods were anxious for our party not to lose sight of its serious purpose, a van drove past outside with a loud-hailer on the roof inviting us to the circus at Ponterwyd. The shadow fell. Gwynfor looked glum. He nodded, finished his drink in one go, wished me a Merry Christmas one more time, and left with the bat.

Chapter 7

PEOPLE WHO ARE afraid of the dark are not being unreasonable. Our deepest fears arise from instincts developed at the dawn of time when the world was much emptier. There were not many folks about. Human beings were the hairy guys in fur swimming costumes, stooping a bit because they were still getting used to standing on their hind legs. They were harmless to everybody except themselves. All the early indications were, they didn't like themselves much. In those days, if you happened to be walking through the vast untamed wilderness and encountered that greatest of rarities, a stranger, someone from another tribe, the safest course of action was to kill him. That's why they invented the police. But that experiment quickly turned sour, one of those cases where the cure was worse than the disease.

So humanity tried something more sophisticated. They invented something called the greeting. Just a little form of words, a comment on the weather, made as an opening gambit, trivial in content but far-reaching in its implications. It allowed men and women to come together and live in things called towns. Because they discovered a strange thing about the greeting. Nutters were incapable of exchanging pleasantries of this sort. It's the same today. There has never been a more effective way of singling out the benign from the malign.

But it doesn't work so well at night. If you encounter a stranger at night in a place where there are no street lamps, it is always an unnerving experience. Tadpole lived in a copse beyond the top of Penglais Hill where there were no lights, where the sun seldom reached, where families were often closely knit in ways proscribed by the Bible. A world with a high likelihood that anyone you encountered in the dark would be a nutter.

I had to leave the car at a five-bar gate held closed by a wire and counterweight strung over a pulley. The path was overgrown, a dark tunnel through wet black trees. I traced the route by gingerly testing the texture of dead leaves under my feet. Up ahead was a dark shape which might have been a clearing or quarry, or maybe the back door to Pluto's realm. There was no light, except for a brief glimpse every now and then through gaps in foliage of the rectangular green direction sign at the side of the main road. It got smaller and smaller. The sounds of cars getting more and more muffled. I've always found those signposts strangely comforting, with the myth of order in the chaos that they suggest. You may be leaving town, they seem to say, but you will always be connected by the ribbon of tarmac, and you can't go anywhere that those most prosaic of people, the council road menders, have not been before. But it was clear from the path beneath my feet that they hadn't been here. An owl hooted. A lone star glimmered through a black cobweb of twigs and branches that groaned in the invisible breeze as if shaken by a giant's hand. In my pocket my hand clutched the jar of Eye of Newt pesto that Tadpole had phoned and asked me to bring.

I came to a clearing in which stood a cottage. The windows were dark apart from one downstairs: black curtains edged with a glimmer of light. A man stood in the yard sharpening an axe at a grindstone, sending a flurry of blue sparks into the night. To the side of the house, there was a washing line hung with items that instinct warned one not to scrutinise; beyond that was a lonely grave. An invisible dog growled; the man stopped grinding and looked up.

'Evening!' I said.

There was no answer.

He was a fully grown man, maybe fifty or so, doing a man's

chore. But there was something about him that suggested a boy. It was difficult to say what it was, his demeanour perhaps, or his wardrobe – something about the cut or style of his clothes told you, in a way you couldn't define, that here was a man in his fifties who was still dressed every morning by his mother. A man who lives his life in the feverish embrace, in too close and suffocating a communion with a mother's love. A man who says little except for occasional grunts, and whom people refer to as 'one of God's children'. Until the time, that is, when the sheriff arrives late at night at the back door with a posse of men with frightened faces. The family sit in scared silence round the supper table, listening as Mother talks long and low under the porch. Then she comes back, her face having aged ten years in the space of that conversation, and says, 'Billy will be going away for a while.' And the men come in and take him away, their eyes narrowed and glittering with hate; and Mummy has no one else to dress and must face the terrors of this world alone.

I knocked on the door and Tadpole opened with the air of someone who has been peering impatiently through the curtains for the past hour. Yet when you finally arrive she makes you wait before answering to make it appear that she has forgotten that you were coming. The smell of Tadpole's house was a sour mixture of infrequently washed flesh, soot, onions and dripping smells from the pantry; and the stultifying thickness of air breathed in rooms where the windows had years ago been sealed shut by paint, and the only fresh air that arrives enters via the chimney.

I'm not sure exactly what I had expected. A gauche attempt at dolling up, perhaps; a moth-eaten dress stored in the back of a wardrobe in a room no longer used; a dress last seen in a sepia vignette of Gran and Granddad on a day trip to Llandudno. But I was wrong. She was wearing military uniform. She had black trousers, sharply creased, with red piping down the inseam; a black military tunic with gold braid on the sleeves and epaulettes and medals on the chest. The whole ensemble mirrored in the brightly polished convex toes of her shoes. She looked like a bandsman who plays the French horn in a gazebo on Sunday afternoons. Her hair, the colour of wet straw, was parted man-style and plastered down with something that might have been Brylcreem but could just as easily have been beef dripping. In the porch light I saw with grisly fascination that little flakes of dandruff were scattered in the furrow of her parting, like corn-flakes from Lilliput.

She noted my surprise and mistook it for delight. 'Not bad, huh?' she said doing a pirouette. 'I felt really stupid trying on a frock so I thought I would wear my Soldiers for Jesus uniform. It's the one we wear for ceremonial occasions.'

She led me into the small sitting room. Her mum was sitting in an armchair at the fireside, knitting. She gave me a look of appraisal but registered no verdict on her face, neither approval or disapproval.

'Mum, this is Louie, remember? The boy from my class in school.'

Again there was no hint as to how she received the news. The man from outside came in and Tadpole's mum said something to him in Welsh and he went to the kitchen and started to brew tea. In the light of the sitting room I saw his face had a strange brightness which suggested that, although he watched the same events through the windows of his eyes as the rest of us, the narrative he invented to explain them was utterly alien.

I stood by the fireplace and, because no one spoke, said: 'Was that a grave I saw outside under the washing line?'

'Yes,' said Tadpole. 'It was the lodger.'

'What did he die of?'

'Happiness.'

There was another silence and I examined a photo above the fireplace. It was a school photo from long ago. 'Upper School 1927', said the caption. I ran my gaze across the sea of lost faces, faded into fuzzy black-and-white and no doubt many of them faded into the grave by now. In the back row there was a face that stopped me. It seemed vaguely familiar and there was a vicious pin right through it, between the eyes. I stopped and peered closer.

'It's Mrs Llantrisant,' said Tadpole brightly.

I touched the pin. 'Is this witchcraft?'

'Yeah. Mum's trying to whack her.'

'Mrs Llantrisant used to swab my step,' I said stupidly.

'We know. Now she's run away to the circus with Herod Jenkins.'

'Mrs Llantrisant is a nasty old busybody,' said Tadpole's mum.

Tadpole took me upstairs and showed me her room. It was a shrine to Clip. The walls were festooned with memorabilia: film posters, publicity shots, Clip scarves and Clip toys. In pride of place over a bed with a Clip coverlet was a framed paw print. 'It's real,' said Tadpole. 'The man at the museum did it for me with the stuffed Clip. What do you reckon?'

'It's fantastic,' I said.

'Yeah, I think so too. Mum says I love Clip almost as much as I love Jesus.'

'High praise coming from a Soldier for Jesus.'

'Ha ha, Louie you're so funny.'

All tickets for the movie had long ago been sold, but Meirion in his role as *Cambrian News* film critic had managed to pull a few strings for me, a fact which seemed to impress Tadpole to an unusually high degree. The queue wound down Portland Street and onto Queen's Road. Tadpole talked the whole time about Clip and her other obsession, Jesus. I tried to ask about the tortured soldier but she wouldn't be rushed. In the manner of obtaining the solicitude of men, life had obviously taught Tadpole to bargain hard and to use what little resources she had frugally.

'Never give a man what he wants until you've had all you want,' she said wisely. 'If I tell you now you might run off, mightn't you?'

'Of course I wouldn't,' I said and prayed no one I knew would pass by and see me with Tadpole. I cursed the slow progress of the queue.

At the entrance to the cinema Tadpole pointed to the posters and said, 'Oh, look at that.'

It was a poster for the circus. The guy with the paste and broom still having had no luck with the horizontal crease in the strongman's face.

'Your old games teacher. I bet you never guessed he would end his days blowing up rubber gloves and wrestling tigers.'

'No, strangely, the thought never crossed my mind.'

We sat in the darkened auditorium, near the back, and waited. The excitement built up like static in the air before a thunderstorm. Tadpole held my hand. I leaned over and said, 'So what was the name of that soldier you told me about?'

'Oh, Louie, not so fast! Didn't anyone ever tell you not to rush a girl?' She giggled in a way that gave her words an alarming double meaning. Eventually the lights dimmed, music started up, and thunderous applause broke out as the title *Bark of the Covenant* appeared, rippling over the red velvet curtains, which slowly began to wind back.

The movie began with an introductory spiel, superfluous to us but perhaps done with an eye to the jury at Cannes. Europe in the early years of the nineteenth century. Everywhere people are on the move, a great restlessness, a great yearning to be free from tyranny. Loud boos from the audience as we watch the appalling injustice of an absentee landlord turfing a peasant from his land, sending the family off to starve. Is it Wales or pre-revolutionary France or the vast steppes of Russia? It's hard to tell because it is all three. The brave families set out in boats for the New World. A map appears with probing arrowheads pushing sailing ships west. Some head north: the huddled masses on Ellis Island, the lice inspections, and inoculations, grim-faced nurses examine scrofulous urchins from the European slums. Some go south to Uruguay and Argentina. From Wales they go Patagonia. Life is hard, but they struggle grimly and carve a toe-hold on the unforgiving land. They water it with their blood and their sweat and when the war of independence starts no one wants to leave; there are too many crosses on the hillside, and that counts for something. Cut to footage of the queues snaking down the street outside the recruitment office. The Legion embarking at Milford Haven, sweethearts in tears, tickertape, the feeling of a great adventure, they'll be home by Whit. But things don't turn out that way. Patagonia is a harsh country where people do not fight by the rules laid down by Clausewitz. Like all guerrilla fighters the enemy determines when and where to join battle; at other times he simply dissolves and evaporates into the countryside.

A nation looks for a hero, the stentorian voiceover informs us. And who answers the call? Clip does. Cut to close-up of Clip the Sheepdog on a Welsh hillside. His ears prick up at some unheard summons, his head swivels. Comprehension lights up his bright intelligent eyes. He understands. He turns and runs home across the hillside; he reaches his master and barks a few words, and carries on running. We see him trotting down the road past the postman, 'Hello, Clip, old boy, where are you off to in such a hurry?' Soon he arrives at the recruitment office. 'Hello, Clip, old boy,' the men in the queue say. They pat and stroke him. He runs on into the office and by the magic of cinema runs out pulling a trolley bearing his army kit. To the people back home, says the voiceover, he was just good old Clip. Cut to Patagonia, where Clip is running between the lines: carrying messages, impervious to the shells exploding all around. But to the peasants of Patagonia, the voice continues, he was something else: a vision, an inspiration, a hero, the dog that saved the hour, he was – the voice pauses for dramatic effect – he was *Pata Brillante*, or . . . and before he can say it everybody in the cinema shouts, 'Bright Paw!' Everyone in the audience except me raises his or her hand, crooked at the wrist, in emulation of a dog offering his paw to shake. They sing the famous Bright Paw song to the tune that was later stolen by Champion the Wonderhorse. Tadpole nudges me and grabs my wrist and pulls it up into the correct shape. I, too, make the gesture of the Bright Paw salute. This is an unusual case.

'Pata Brillante! Pata Brillante! El Perro Maravilla!'

I turn my head to look at Tadpole. She is singing her heart out. Her eyes are on fire, cheeks glistening with tears. The singing carries on for a while and then peters out. We watch enthralled as Bright Paw scampers across ridges, doggy-paddles through the foam of torrential rivers, runs headlong but miraculously unscathed into machine-gun fire. He dodges mines that explode a fraction of a second after he passes. He was a hell of a dog, that was for sure.

The movie tells the famous story of the Mission House siege. The men of the 32nd Airborne are bivouacked at the Mission House, marooned in bandit country. Clip heroically passes messages between the Mission House and HQ a hundred miles away, by using the legendary secret passage of the Incas that only he knows about. The situation is desperate, and General Llanbadarn, returning from Buenos Aires, decides to stake all on a bold, audacious, and some would say suicidal reconnaissance patrol. The men are afraid. Very afraid. On the eve of battle there are whisperings of mutiny among the ranks. And then lo! in the light of the silvery moon an angel appears among the men, plucking the terror from their hearts, filling them with courage. An angel on a white horse holding a flaming sword aloft. Next day at dawn the men ride out and fight like lions. Losses are heavy, the battle desperate, but the day is won and the honour of the Legion saved. Clip, though he manages to limp back to camp, dies from his wounds and pays the ultimate price. Tadpole was inconsolable.

Normally when the first bar of signature tune starts up there is a stampede for the door, but tonight the people of Aberystwyth,

*or pasture, in their gaunt and haunted eyes the look of a dog
that has lost his youth by the age of four, the people rallied.
There was a revulsion against the pitiless and mindless
slaughter, an unstoppable groundswell of public anger. Within
six months the decision had been taken to bring the dogs home.*

The men, of course, stayed on for another three winters.

After the movie we went to the Indian restaurant in Eastgate
Street and sat at a table in the window. Tadpole, cheeks still glistening with tears, examined the menu carefully, while I glanced
nervously at my watch. We needed to be quick, because the pubs
would be chucking out soon and the Indian restaurant would
become a scene which made the battlefields of Patagonia seem
a picnic.

'Oh, Louie, I don't know what to have. It all sounds so good.'

'Don't agonise. It's not really good, it's just well written.'

'Oh, Louie, you're such a cynic.'

I tapped my fingers and stared out at the darkened street. Across
the road a man in a fedora stood in an alley. He met my gaze
and hurried off. I'd seen that hat before but I couldn't remember
where.

'How about telling me the name of this guy.'

'Which guy?'

'Yes, you bloody well did. It was a deal.'

'I didn't say I'd tell you his name. I said I'd take you to see him.'

I paused, slightly taken aback. 'So when are we going to see him?'

'We just did.' She giggled.

I looked at her in cold fury as the implication became clear.

'He was there on the screen.'

'It was a cast of five thousand!'

'That's not my fault.'

I stood up and threw a tenner down on the table. 'Here, enjoy your meal.'

'But, Louie, you said you'd buy me dinner.'

'That's right, but I don't have to sit and watch you eat it. No wonder no one liked you at school.' I stormed out and as I passed by the window I saw in the corner of my eye Tadpole sitting grief-stricken, her fist pressed into her eye, her mouth disfigured into a figure-of-eight. It was a pose I was starting to get quite familiar with.

I hurried down Eastgate Street towards the office and saw up ahead the man in fedora and black and white shoes. He turned into Stryd-y-Popty. I quickened my pace. He was waiting in the shadow of the door to my office and I grabbed his arm and dragged him into the light; but it was the wrong man. It was someone wearing a Jew's broad-brimmed hat and sporting a long grey beard; a man in a coat full of holes. Elijah.

'There's been another death,' he said and tut-tutted in a manner that suggested it wasn't anyone close.

'Is that a fact?' I said.

The man in the fedora slipped out of the doorway across the street and hurried towards Great Darkgate Street. We both watched him slink away.

'You have a friend,' said Elijah.

'I thought maybe he belonged to you.'

'He's not my friend.'

'Who is he?'

'I really don't know.'

'Maybe if I bang your head against the wall it might help you recall.'

'There is nothing to recall. It is you he is following. Such visitations are commonplace in cases involving Hoffmann.'

'So who has died?'

'A girl, an innocent girl. You'll read about it in tomorrow's paper.'

'Why should I care?'

'There will be more.'

'More papers?'

'More deaths.

Chapter 8

NEXT MORNING Calamity bought a copy of the newspaper and read it as we walked up the Prom.

'It's Emily Bishop,' she said. 'The girl who rang about the ad. The fan of Kierkegaard.' She handed me the paper. 'Do you think there's a jinx on us?'

'What makes you say that?'

'She was from the college in Lampeter. The last student we had from there didn't last long, either.'

'At least we got to shake hands with that one. I'm not even sure if this one counts. All she did was ring.'

'Still a bit spooky, though.'

'Maybe they're accident prone in Lampeter.'

'Or maybe we are.'

I crossed the road at the junction with Pier Street and Calamity followed.

'Aren't you going to tell me where we're going?'

'Can't you guess?'

'The Cabin isn't open yet.'

'We're not going there, we're going to the hobby shop.'

'What for?'

'If you want to find out about a man's secret weaknesses, those shameful vices he would rather conceal from the light of day, where do you go?'

'Lots of places. Depends on the vices.'

'Yes, but as a guiding principle you talk to the madam, the procuress, whoever it is who supplies his shameful lusts.'

'OK. That's good, that's psychology. I approve of that.'

'You see, there's something puzzling me about *Bark of the Covenant*. It tells the story of the Mission House siege. Now, on the odd occasion when you actually turned up in school, you must have done the history of the Patagonian War, right?'

'Yes, although my memory of it is a bit cloudy.'

'What did they teach you about the Mission House siege?'

'I don't think we did it.'

'That's right, nor did we. No one did, because everyone knows it was a military disaster. None of the veterans from that war will talk about. it And yet in the movie it's a famous victory. The murdered Father Christmas goes to see it and says his life has been fulfilled. You don't normally say that after to seeing a film, do you?'

'Not normally.'

'As he lies dying he writes "Hoffmann" in his own blood. According to Tadpole, she used to nurse a soldier who fought in the Mission House siege and who cried out "Hoffmann" in his nightmares. Are you following me?'

'I think so.'

'So maybe we should try and find out what really happened at the Mission House siege. The version that didn't make it to the big screen.'

'OK.'

'We'll talk to the man in the hobby shop.'

'Is he the madam?'

'Yes, sort of. He supplies people who come in for stuff to make models of battles and stuff. He's bound to know.'

'Uh-huh. Maybe we should try one of the techniques from my Pinkerton book to get him to talk.'

'Yes. We could buy some rubber hose off him for our submarine model, and then hit him with it.'

'They don't do that. They use psychology. It's called Interrogative Misdirection.'

'How does that work?'

'Tell me how you were going to handle the interview.'

'I was going to walk in and ask him if he's seen the Clip movie.'

'That's your first mistake. You shouldn't let him know what you're after. You've got to use subtlety, like the Pinkertons. You start by asking him about something you're not interested in. It's like a conjuror, you see, you have to use misdirection. You divert his attention to this something else and then casually slip in the real thing. We'll share it. You ask about something you're not interested in, and I'll use one of the techniques to steer the conversation round to Patagonia. Agreed?'

I considered for a second and then laughed. 'OK, we'll let the Pinkertons handle this interview.'

We walked up Pier Street and Calamity, having chalked up a small victory for the Pinkertons, became expansive. 'Yes, there's definitely room in this game for a more systematic and scientific approach in line with the precepts and methodology established by the Pinkertons.'

'Did you read that in the preface?'

'It's empirical.'

'I bet you read that, too.'

'What if I did? It's true, isn't it? We rely too much on outdated methods.'

'Is that so?'

'Take the Butch Cassidy case, for instance.'

'There is no Butch Cassidy case.'

'How do you know? There might be. If we just contacted the Pinkertons—'

'Calamity!' I said sharply as we reached the doorway to the shop. 'There is no Butch Cassidy case. It may be the most celebrated case of the Pinkerton organisation but it's not our case. Ours is the celebrated Hoffmann case.'

'But they're linked.'

'No, they're not.

I opened the door and we walked in, entering a world in which the real one had been miniaturised and rendered claustrophobic and obsessive. There were flocks of miniature sheep on papier-mâché hillsides arrayed alongside armies of footsoldiers from Lilliput; kits to build Aberystwyth Castle scaled down to fit on the dining-room table; kits to make fishing boats and the brigs that took the settlers to the New World in the last century; replica spinning wheels ... Pride of place went to a scale model of Aberystwyth Pier as it was in the days before the sea chopped off the end and left a vestibule leading to nowhere – although that was a popular destination in the town. The detail was impressive: it even had a miniature fibreglass boy with a calliper on his leg, standing at the entrance, for ever soliciting charity from the stony hearts of the townspeople.

'Can I help you?' The voice belonged to a man behind the counter; a small greasy man with an obsequious air, a shiny bald pate, a pair of tortoiseshell-framed glasses that had been repaired with sticky tape, and that cloying look of deep understanding which is shared by the ice man and the brothel keeper. He smiled, an invitation to me to unburden myself and a reassurance that, whatever it was I was after, he would probably have it and in such quantities that I need not worry that I was alone in my obsession.

'I'm looking for a gift ... for a friend.'

The man nodded and smiled but made little attempt to conceal the fact that he didn't believe me. No one ever came into this shop and admitted he was shopping for himself.

'He's a trainspotter.'

The man nodded again and said, 'And you'd like to buy him a little something?'

'He's not a close friend.'

'No?'

'Really an acquaintance.'

'Mmmmm.'

'I met him at the railway station.'

'Where else?'

'We just talked a bit, you know.'

'It's not a crime in this shop, sir, as you see. Are you sure it was a friend?'

I ignored the insinuation and carried on, feeling strangely ill at ease. I wished Calamity would hurry up and subtly misdirect him.

'Nothing extravagant, maybe an 0–0 gauge sheep for his layout or something.'

'The mockery is never far away, is it?'

'I'm sorry?'

'My friend, I would say the best gift you or any man could give to this –' he paused in a way that cast doubt on the trustworthiness of the next word – '*friend*, as you call him, would be to stop classifying him by that disgusting epithet.'

'Which one?'

'Spotter.'

'They don't use that word?'

'Only those who revile them call them that. Call him a cranker, or a basher, and he will thank you far more sincerely than if you were to buy him a model signal box, which I suspect is what you with your limited understanding had in mind when you came in.'

'Cranker?'

'It's their chosen term.'

'Do you use it?'

'I am just the dealer. I supply what my customers desire. I take no sides. I'm not proud of what I do, but neither am I ashamed. A man must make a living in this world and there are worse ways of doing it.'

I began to sweat around the collar.

'Oh look, Louie!' Calamity cried in a voice suffused with insincerity – the voice a wife in a farce uses to deny the presence of her lover in the wardrobe. 'Look at this!'

I allowed my attention to be diverted to a model layout of the Fairbourne railway.

Fairbourne is a small town just below Barmouth on the Mawddach estuary, about thirty or forty miles north of Aberystwyth. The estuary is even more beautiful than the one we have at Aberdovey, if such a thing is possible. But Fairbourne itself is not so interesting, apart from a lovely beach and the little train that runs the entire length of it.

I bent forward to take a better look. 'This looks very accurate.'

'It is,' said the shopkeeper. 'Only the magnificent pointlessness of the journey is missing.'

'No, not that,' said Calamity. 'I meant this.'

It was a scale model of Clip the Sheepdog. I moved across and the shopkeeper dutifully stalked me from behind the counter. If any of this was fooling him he was doing an excellent job of concealing it.

'We sell a lot of those,' he said.

'He must have been an amazing dog.'

'Yes.'

'I saw the movie. Quite a famous victory.'

'Yes, famous,' he said in a voice that suggested he didn't think so.

'Wasn't it?'

'Who am I to say? I just sell the little toy soldiers, I don't comment on the broader historical sweep.'

He gave me the obsequious smile that the private detective in Aberystwyth comes to recognise like the yelp of a faithful dog. The smile that says: my lips are sealed and can only be unlocked by a special pass key, available from all good off licences. I took out a flask of rum and waved it in front of his obsequious face.

'Why don't you break the rule of a lifetime and comment on the ... what was it?'

'Broad historical sweep.' He pulled over a teacup. 'What are rules for if not to be broken?'

I poured a generous measure into his cup and took a gulp from the flask because I hated to see a man drink alone.

'It's difficult to know where to begin,' he said.

I poured another shot into his cup. 'Does this make it any easier?'

'A bit of lubrication never hurt.' He gave a wan smile, full of understanding of human frailty, especially his own.

'Just so long as we don't flood the engine. Tell me about the Mission House siege. What happened there?'

'Wooh!' He pretended to be startled and rolled his eyes as if the task was beyond the compass of mortals.

'Look, buddy,' I said, snatching his cup away from him, 'I'm not sure if you understand the mechanism at work here. I'm pouring libations into your cup not because you're a darling of the gods but because I want you to tell me something. Information that in any decent town I would get for nothing.' He reached for the cup and I held it up by my ear, out of his way. He watched it like a dog watches the butcher.

'Does that make sense to you?'

He nodded, still staring at the cup.

'What was the mission about? What was the objective? Surely you can tell me that?'

'Great mystery surrounded the precise nature of the objective. It seemed to involve a lot of getting shelled; a lot of stealing enemy barbed wire; a lot of walking across open ground towards machine-gun outposts.'

'How do you steal barbed wire?'

'Not easily, that is for sure. And not without a terrible loss of life. But General Llanbadarn wanted them to bring some back. No one knows why. He had just come back from Buenos Aires. He kept a woman there, so it was said. Not that that explains it, but there were some who suggested the objective stemmed from a boast he made to his mistress.'

'Stealing barbed wired seems like a pretty crummy objective,' said Calamity.

'It was certainly no Monte Cassino. But it was always the same when he came back from Buenos Aires – he invariably had a new plan, one which was distinguished only by being more completely stupid than the previous one.'

'Are you saying the men weren't allowed to run?'

'They were told to proceed at walking pace so as not to destroy the symmetry of the lines. The cameras were there, you see. Although they did not last long.'

'I don't understand why anyone would order his troops to walk into machine-gun fire.'

'That's because you aren't a military man. General Llanbadarn was old school. He learned his tactics by studying the great battles of World War I, particularly the Somme.'

'Was the Somme great?'

'In magnitude, yes. The magnitude of the carnage. In terms of troop dispositions there are arguably far better models in the annals of military history: Salamis, Agincourt, Custer's last stand . . . but the Somme had one factor which made it especially attractive for a strategic thinker of General Llanbadarn's rare mettle, namely, he had heard of it.'

'He sounds like an idiot.'

'Military historians are a disputatious lot but on that point there is unanimity.' He stopped and pointed at my ear. I put the cup back down in front of him and refilled it.

'The men were, of course, terrified. They had heard the rumour that the general wanted the barbed wire to give to his mistress as a trophy. There was talk of a rebellion. That's when they saw the angel. She filled their hearts with the fire of courage and off they went. And this is where the true story parts company with the version portrayed on screen.'

'They were all slaughtered?'

'Yes, of course. But there was something else. Something truly terrible happened that day, even worse than the slaughter. But no one knows what. They refuse to speak about it. A handful of men limped back to camp; Clip died in mysterious circumstances; and the chaplain went mad.'

'How mad?'

'Oh, utterly, utterly bonkers. The neurobiological equivalent of a man's hair turning white overnight.'

'But you don't know what happened?'

'It's a military secret. You could ask the chaplain; he preaches at the community shelter by the war memorial; but, as I say, he lost his marbles and has never recovered them.'

I held the flask in front of his face and waggled it. 'You sure you don't know?'

'Sincerely I don't. As I say, no one will talk about it. Is there anything else I can help you with? If you're thinking of modelling the battle you'll need some of these.' He placed a curatorial hand on some toy soldiers. The label said, '32nd Airbourne'.

'Is that how you spell airborne?'

'Alas, no, they were not really the airborne – they had no planes. They were from Fairbourne. Dropped the "F" in a hopelessly misguided attempt to big themselves up.'

I walked to the door and he held it open with a cloying smile.

'What makes you think I want to model it, anyway?'

'All that stuff about the trainspotters was a smokescreen. I knew as soon as you walked in what you were after. Goodbye. Oh, and if you do want to make a model of the Mission House siege, don't forget this.'

He handed me a small plastic figurine of an angel.

Outside the door Calamity looked peeved and said, 'It's not supposed to work like that.'

'I guess he must have read the Pinkerton manual before you. You can't win them all.'

She gave me a sour look. I sent her off to check up on the dead student, Emily Bishop, to see if she had a roommate who might talk. I had an appointment with Myfanwy.

* * *

Something about the way the date with Tadpole ended last night had made me uneasy about leaving Myfanwy in her care. I went back to the office, picked up her LPs and made the climb up to the top of the hill. Everything seemed fine when I arrived. Myfanwy was asleep again and Tadpole was combing her hair and spreading it out over the pillow. It seemed to me to be an unwarranted invasion of the patient's privacy, and not really within her remit, but I wasn't sure whether I should say so. She looked up at my entrance and we locked glances. It was one of those moments, the first meeting after a quarrel or something like it.

She beamed at me. 'Louie, I'm so glad you're here, I was so worried. About what happened, you know, last night. I was horrible, I don't know how you will ever forgive me.'

'It's OK, don't worry about it.'

'But how can I not? I cheated you. I said I'd give you the man's name and then I didn't. No wonder you hate me.'

'I don't.'

'Look, here it is, I've written it down for you.' She handed me a slip of paper on which was written, 'Caleb Penpegws. Corporal or something. In the army. The one that went to Patagonia'.

'I'm sorry, I don't know all the details.'

'This is fine.'

'What have you got under your arm? Looks like records.'

'The doctor told me to bring them in. They might cheer Myfanwy up.'

'Oh, how lovely! Let me help you.' She took the records and put them down on a table. 'I'll see if we can find a record player.' She walked up to me and looked into my face. 'Do you forgive me, then?'

'There's nothing to forgive.'

'But I was horrible last night.'

I waved the slip of paper and put it in my pocket. 'This more than makes up for it.'

'You forgive me, then?'

'Of course.'

'Oh, Louie! You are so wonderful!' She threw her arms round me and pulled me in and kissed me on the lips. I tried to struggle free but they obviously do a lot of press-ups at the Soldiers for Jesus boot camp and I found her grip hard to break. She continued pressing her lips on mine, making a long drawn out "Mmmm" sound. I found myself staring over her shoulder at the sleeping face of Myfanwy. And Myfanwy was staring, eyes wide open, at me.

Chapter 9

OUR GAZES LOCKED for the briefest fraction of a second before she closed her eyes again; not simply closed, but pressed tightly shut like a defiant child's. I drew up a chair and picked up a magazine, to give the impression of one settling in for a long wait, but really hoping for Tadpole to leave. Eventually she did after wasting time doing needless and irritating tidying-up chores.

I put the magazine down. 'Stop pretending, I know you're awake.'

No reaction. She carried on feigning sleep.

'Oh, come on, Myfanwy.'

Still no reaction.

'Oh, please, Myfanwy. I know what you saw but it was nothing. She was just thanking me.'

Silence.

'I know you can hear me.'

Silence.

'This is ridiculous. You don't seriously think there's something between me and . . . and that thing, do you? They call her Tadpole. It's an insult to frogs.'

Silence.

'This is silly.'

Silence. Or was that a slight, stifled 'Hmmmph'?

'You're not supposed to sound exasperated if you're asleep. You want to pretend to be asleep when you're not, that's fine. But you can't go "Hmmmph" as well.'

There was a pause and she said, 'Are you still here?'

'If you're going to speak you might as well open your eyes.'

'I didn't like what I saw last time I did that.'

'That wasn't what it seemed.'

'How many times have I heard that?'

'You think I want to kiss a girl who looks like that? It was like being a kid again, getting grabbed by my auntie.'

'Is that how you talk about me when I'm not around?'

'Are you nuts? How could you think such a thing?'

'Oh, I wonder how. Maybe because I saw you snogging my nurse. What sort of guy does that? Has a fling with the nurse right by the bedside of his dying girlfriend—'

'You're not dying.'

She opened her eyes. 'How do you know? I might be.'

'Myfanwy.'

'Nobody would care if I did.'

'Everybody would care.'

She closed her eyes again.

'Open them up, for God's sake.'

'Don't have to if I don't want.'

'That's childish.'

Another stifled 'Hmmmph'.

'I risked my life for you. Do you hear that? Risked my bloody life.'

She opened her eyes. 'I didn't ask you to.'

'You didn't have to. I would have done it whether you wanted me to or not.'

'So stop boasting, then.'

'Huh?'

She was smiling. And then she said in words suffused with a warmth I hadn't heard for months, as if the splinter of ice in her heart had finally melted, 'Oh, Louie, I've missed you.'

She lurched forward into my arms. I grabbed her as one catches a child about to run into the road, and hugged her.

'Oh, I've missed you so much,' she said. 'Even when I was

sick and far away I knew I was missing you, even then. I just felt it. I can't explain how . . .' She broke free of my embrace and brought her face up close, inches from mine, as she tried to explain with a strange urgency. 'I don't know how, but it's like being in a deep dream and yet still knowing . . .'

'It's OK, it doesn't matter.'

She considered for a second and smiled. 'No, I s'pose not. You're here now. Just stop chasing the nurses, OK?'

'I'll do my best but it's not easy when they look like Tadpole.'

She giggled. 'Where's my present?'

'It's on order.'

'What is it?'

'You know I can't tell you that. It would ruin the surprise.'

'But you don't know what I want.'

'All right, what do you want?'

'A white Christmas.'

'That's what I ordered.' She grinned and let her head sink back onto my chest.

In the corridor on my way out I ran into Miss Evangeline, the blind woman who had visited Myfanwy's room the last time I was here. She had been waiting for me.

'Come with me,' she said. 'I want to show you something.'

She ambled along the corridor, feeling the wall gently with her hand. She took me to a small bedroom and bade me sit on the bed. The room was bare, almost monastic. I suppose if you are blind you don't need to put much up in the way of decoration. She opened the drawer of a bedside cabinet, took out some photos and held them out to me. They were pictures of her thirty years ago as Borth Carnival Queen. She sat regally aboard a float, surrounded by lesser members of the royal household: carnival princesses, I guessed; along with courtiers and ladies in waiting. She wore a one-piece swimming costume with a satin sash across her chest. On her head sat a tiara and in her hand was a sceptre.

Her face was gentle and heart-shaped, almost overwhelmed by the beehive hair-do and severe kohl-rimmed eyes that mimicked Dusty Springfield. On her face that bright look of expectancy, the one we wear in our teens on the threshold of life, the look full of latency, the one that pierces us when we see it years later in a snap at the back of a drawer. She had been a good-looking kid and I presumed that was what she wanted to hear.

'Yes,' she said. 'I was desired once. Ooh! Did you hear that?' She grabbed my arm and became still. We listened, Miss Evangeline's hand resting on mine. The bandages on her hands were fresh. Two safety pins glistened.

'How did you hurt your hands?'

'My hands? Oh yes. I can't remember. It's so long ago.'

'Aren't they getting better?'

'The doctors say so, but what do they know? Listen!'

'I can't hear anything.'

'It was the horse. In the paddock, do you hear? I often hear her whinny. She's got a foal. Listen. There it is again.'

'You've got sharper ears than me.'

'I'm not making it up, if that's what you think.'

'Of course not.'

'People say I make things up.'

'Oh! I heard it that time.'

'One day that little foal will be a mare with a foal of her own. I had a child once but they took it away. I wonder if she ever thinks of me? Do you think she does?'

'I'm sure she does.'

'Now you're making things up. She probably doesn't even know about me. She was too young to remember. It was different in those days ... What if they never told her about me? She would never know. Oh, there she goes again. She loves her foal, doesn't she?'

'I never met a mare that didn't.'

'One day they'll both be boiled up for glue. The glue will stick the boards of my coffin. And they'll plant me in the garden so the worms can eat me, and shit me out to fertilise the soil, and make the grass grow. And the foal will eat the grass and all that will be left of Miss Evangeline is a whinny. Do you ever think of things like that, Mr Knight?

'Yes, very often.'

'You should. None of us have very long.' The distant, dreamy expression on her face clouded with a vagrant urgency. 'Promise me something, Mr Knight. Will you do that?'

'Only if you stop calling me Mr Knight.'

'Louie?'

'Yes.'

'Don't let Myfanwy go. Whatever she says, don't take any notice. She's a silly goose sometimes. Do you promise?'

'I promise.'

She fumbled for my hand, and squeezed it. 'I think it's time. Do you know the bench outside the gate that overlooks the town?'

'Yes.'

'Will you walk me to it?'

'Of course.'

'I go every day. I've got a friend. But she's not allowed in here.'

We walked down the path to the bench. Miss Evangeline's friend was already there, waiting, sitting with her back to us, looking out at the prospect of Cardigan Bay. It was Lorelei, the one-eyed streetwalker. She allowed the thick powder on her face to crack in a thin smile of recognition when she saw me; a look of understanding passed between us, the look shared by two people who have spent too many hours of their lives walking the Prom late at night. She had take-away tea in Styrofoam cups and placed them on the bench between us.

'I'm sorry there's not one for you,' she said. And Miss

Evangeline said, 'He can have some of mine. Don't forget the ...'

Lorelei took a quarter-bottle of spirits from her bag and fortified the tea. We drank a toast to the new year.

'Me and Lorelei went to school together,' said Miss Evangeline. 'Sometimes we just sit here and don't say a word.'

I left them to their tea and silent communion, went down the steps that led to North Road, and headed for my own personal confessor. Sospan. He was still there, leaning over an empty counter, staring out to sea.

'Not closing early for Christmas?' I said.

'You should know me better than to ask that.'

'No one would hold it against you if you did.'

'Does the wolf take Christmas off?'

'Not as far as I am aware.'

'So how, then, can the shepherd?'

'Is that what you are?'

'Not precisely, but I have my role.'

'And what is that?'

'I provide spiritual sustenance.'

'With ice cream?'

'That is the vehicle.'

'But it's just frozen milk, isn't it?'

A hint of annoyance darkened his countenance. 'You think milk isn't important? Milk is the staff of life.'

'I thought that was bread.'

'The spiritual staff.'

'I see.'

'It's the first food you ever taste, the essence of the bond between mother and infant. The bond before the great betrayal.'

'What was the great betrayal?'

'It's what your mother did to you, and you never forgave her.'

'I never even met mine. What did she do?'

Sospan paused and blinked, as if it was difficult even now to talk about it.

'What did she do?'

'Weaned you, didn't she. Took away her breast.'

'Oh, I see.'

'You never really get over the shock of that. Did you know in some cultures the mother puts wormwood on her nipple to make it taste nasty? It's in *Romeo and Juliet*: "When it did taste the wormwood on the nipple / Of my dug, and felt it bitter, pretty fool"'

'So how do you differ from the milkman?'

Sospan winced and a look of resignation stole across his face, as if the realisation was dawning that he had chosen the wrong person to try and express the ineffable to.

'Mr Knight, I'm surprised at you. I can only assume you are trying to provoke me. That's like asking how the wine the priest gives with the sacrament differs from the stuff you get in the pub. In one sense it may not differ at all, in the purely technical sense of its provenance. But it is invested with symbolic freight of the most far-reaching consequences for those who believe. For them it represents the blood of Christ.'

'What does your ice represent?'

'Balm.'

'Balm?'

'A mother's love.'

'So you are like the big mother figure?'

'I prefer to regard my role as that of a shaman.'

'What about the flake?'

'What about it?'

'What does that symbolise?'

'Nothing, you big twit. Not everything has to mean something. You should read your Freud. You know what he said? Sometimes a cigar is just a cigar. It's the same with the flake.'

I took my ice cream and wandered down the Prom towards

the harbour. At Castle Point I found Eyeore standing across from the Old College, looking flustered. Three donkeys, led by Ariadne, waited patiently.

'What's wrong, Dad?' I said.

'Barbarians in the citadel,' he said. 'That's what we are.'

'Are we? How so?'

He held out the book he was carrying. A guidebook to Wales published in the 1920s. 'Read this and it breaks your heart, to see how things used to be, and what we are now. It's like those pictures of a peasant farmer in Egypt, ploughing his field with oxen, irrigating his field with water from the Nile. A timeless ritual unchanged for centuries, like African farmers everywhere, except for one thing: He's got the Great Pyramid of Cheops at the bottom of his field. He doesn't know how it got there, nor what it is. No one knows. It's been there for hundreds of years, left by a vanished race of superior beings. He's a barbarian in the citadel. Just like us.'

He pushed the book toward me, opened to a page. 'You see? The Royal Pier Pavilion; in those days it was seven hundred feet long and had its own orchestra. What is it now? Thirty feet, the rest blown away by a storm and never replaced. And then there's the bandstand, home to "first-rate municipal bands" and "excellent London companies". It was an age in which they were not ashamed to do things properly.'

Eeyore looked at me, brows furrowed in a pain almost palpable as he struggled to articulate the urgent truth hidden among the seeming pleasantries about bathing machines, 6d a time.

'At what point did we change from being the people who built the wonder of the pleasure pier to the ones who couldn't be bothered to repair it after a storm blew the end away?'

He paused as if expecting an answer and then continued, 'And look at this: "To get the best view of Snowdon eighty miles north of Aberystwyth, stand on the Prom outside house number 7."'

He looked at me in astonishment, silent, unable to find the

words to convey what that discovery meant. What did it mean? That a guidebook should actually put someone's address and tell you to go and stand on their doorstep to view distant Snowdon? Such a thing was inconceivable now. They'd call the police. A hundred years ago they would probably have invited you in for tea. And lent you a telescope.

'Barbarians in the citadel,' he said again.

'Where's the pyramid?'

He turned and pointed across the road at the Old College. 'There.'

It was a lovely building, but architecturally it was the equivalent of a kid in a fancy-dress costumier's who tries on everything at the same time. It had Rhineland castle and gothic turrets, battlements and mosaics, statues and garrets. It would have been absurd but for the warm yellow stone from which it was constructed. It soothed the incongruity and lent it a strange beauty. You could forgive a lot of architectural sins with stone like that.

'It didn't use to be a college, it was built as a hotel by the railway company.'

I understood his astonishment. It was impossible to envisage a modern railway company possessing the self-belief to build something like that. Nowadays they just unbuilded things. The old Great Western Region terminus on Alexandra Road got smaller every time you went; like a family of impoverished aristocrats who had closed down all the rooms and were living in the scullery. One day the train from Shrewsbury will arrive and find nothing there.

'You got a week's free bed and board if you bought a return ticket at Euston. Nowadays they can't even cut the grass between the tracks. You know what it is, don't you?' said Eeyore. 'It's like that movie with Charlton Heston about the apes. You know the scene at the end when he rides that horse along the beach and sees the torch of the Statue of Liberty projecting out of the sand? Suddenly he realises he's been on Planet Earth all along, after it has been taken over by apes. That's Aberystwyth.'

He shoved the book into my hands. 'You keep it, it just annoys me.' He tugged Ariadne's halter free from the railing. 'Barbarians in the citadel,' he muttered and led the troop away, on the never-ending traverse of the ruined Prom; the Ozymandias of Cardigan Bay.

I cast my gaze back down at the pages of the book and found the text that had most upset him; words of almost inexpressible poignancy. Aberystwyth, it said, was superior to many fashion-able continental watering holes in being entirely free of such meteorological nuisances as the mistral, the sirocco or dust storms. In fact, said Sir James Clark, the court physician, it was better than Switzerland.

The words stabbed the heart. Free from the effects of the sirocco, that hot dry desert wind that blows in off the Sahara and ruins your picnic. It was impossible to imagine a guidebook writer expressing such sentiments today; and there was only one reason the man fifty years ago could write them: it would never have occurred to him that his audience might laugh. And they for their part would never have dreamed of responding to his kindly homilies with such impertinence. And that was it, the essence of our malaise: our forefathers were entirely free of that despicable modern vice, facetiousness. I stood transfixed for a while, infected with Eeyore's melancholy. He had reached the Pier now, or what was left of it after the storm forty years ago: a dilapidated shed bathed in thin grey drizzle, and Matterhorned with seagull droppings; but still undisturbed by those hot, dry Saharan winds.

Chapter 10

THE NEXT DAY was Sunday and we drove to Lampeter, about half an hour's journey south-east of Aberystwyth. Calamity had spoken on the phone to Emily's roommate at the college and she was willing to talk to us. Her name was Eleri. On the way, Calamity tried to recap the case but there wasn't much to recap.

'We've got an old man dressed as Father Christmas. He goes to see the new Clip movie and afterwards gets whacked. Maybe intentionally, maybe accidentally.'

'My money's on accidentally. Could have happened to anyone – he just happened to be in the wrong place at the wrong time. Simple drive-by slaying.'

'My money's on that, too. The Clip movie was made from footage found by workmen rebuilding the Pier.'

'There was a druid inscription warning them not to open the room, so naturally they did just that.'

'The movie is about the Mission House Siege. Something bad happened there, so bad no one wants to talk about it, although they don't show it in the movie.'

'The army chaplain went mad.'

'A taxidermist saw the movie and hanged himself from Trefechan Bridge.'

'A guy called Elijah turns up claiming to be the brother of the dead Father Christmas.'

'We think the dead guy hid a ticket from the Pier hat-check office in the alley before he died. The item deposited is a photo of Butch Cassidy and the Sundance Kid. This angle is potentially very interesting.'

'Or it's a red herring.'

'I've got a hunch it's the key to the whole thing.'

'I've got a hunch you're only saying that because you're starstruck about the Pinkertons.'

'No, I'm not.'

'Believe me, there's nothing special about them. You may think so now, but one day when you run into one of them you'll realise he's exactly like anyone else: a tired, soul-weary, overworked guy in a crumpled suit, with a failed marriage and a suitcase in the attic in which he stores a load of dusty things that used to be the youthful ideals he started out with.'

Calamity looked at me askance. 'Sounds like you know this guy.'

'He's every man who got past thirty without making something of his life. That's most people in Aberystwyth, including me.'

She thought for a second and decided not to go down that route. 'What about the Queen of Denmark?'

'I've no idea.'

'Think she's for real?'

'No, but then the whole thing is so crazy maybe she is.'

'That's what I think. It's hard to believe someone would invent a routine like that if they were trying to trick you, because only someone really stupid would fall for it.'

'Which means she must be for real, because if she's not it means I'm really stupid.'

'Don't be like that. It means I'm really stupid, too.'

'That's all right, then. The odds against two people being so stupid are too formidable. She must be genuine.'

'You really think so?'

'I'm a hundred per cent certain she's genuine. All the same, if you get a moment, speak to Llunos about getting the calls traced.'

We reached Lampeter College and drove under a stone arch into an inner court yard. We parked and approached the first student we saw. They weren't hard to spot. They were all wearing the distinctive uniform of Lampeter College of Theology: a henna, beige and grey striped scarf over a tan duffel coat printed with a repeating pattern of crosses and coffins. The girl said Eleri was teaching Sunday School. Colleges don't normally teach children on Sunday morning, but this was no ordinary college. They took seriously the scholar's vocation of shining a light in the darkness. The girl walked us across a quad towards a low single-storey wing of the college, through an arched door into an old-fashioned schoolroom: rows of wooden desks scarred with years of wear and tear. Fuzzy yellow lights hung from the ceiling. It smelled of paraffin and that subtle mixture of sweetness and fart that collects around cloistered children. The children all stood up when we entered.

Eleri greeted us warmly and shook our hands. 'This is home economics,' she said. 'Just the basic stuff at this age: weaving fabric from cobwebs, making soap from grit, anthracite perfume, penny hoarding, a hundred uses for stale bread, fifty simple one-cauldron dishes, making shoes out of slate. You know the sort of thing.'

'It all sounds very impressive,' I said. 'My late mother, God rest her soul, always insisted on a traditional education.'

'I knew it the moment I saw you,' said Eleri. 'Come, let's try them with their catechism. You'll be impressed.' She turned to the class. 'Right now, girls, who can tell me how the Soldiers for Jesus were founded?'

Hands went up around the room and the teacher pointed. 'Yes, Meurig.'

'Ma'am, there were three sisters from Llandre and they were walking one day and they chanced upon a woman who later scholars have revealed to have been an apparition of the Virgin Mary.'

'Very good. And then what happened? Menna?'

'Ma'am, she was drinking holy water from a brown paper bag and her speech was slurred.'

'That's right. Now who can tell us what she said?'

'She revealed a sacred truth to the children.'

'And what was it?'

Some of the hands went down.

'Yes, Rhiannon.'

'Miss, she said human happiness was just a fleeting will-o'-the-wisp; the tap of the hand on the window of a traveller in the night.'

'A traveller who is running from the gallows, miss,' another child added.

'That's right, very good. And what else did she say? Yes, Meryl.'

The girl stood up and recited with the air of one who is very proud of the words but has never really reflected much on their meaning. 'She said that things are very bad, much worse than anyone thought. God didn't have the heart to tell us just how bad things are and this was because He was a typical man. "We arrive as penniless beggars and beg for milk; we waste our lives pursuing empty dreams, deluded by myths of love and romance; the only thing that sustains us is hope, dangling like a carrot, the biggest lie of all. For how can there be hope for a race who will end their lives in a gabbling madness of disease and senility? Bereavement and mourning, loss and decay and despair; childbirth and betrayal; drunkenness and abuse; infant mortality, disease striking out of a cloudless sky at anyone; no warning, no indication; too little money, too great a burden; this is our lot. Denied fulfilment all our lives; haunted by desires that can never be stilled; robbed in our final days of all shreds of dignity; and heading for death, which spares none. And beyond? Oh, don't even ask! It gets worse but I don't have the heart in me to tell you poor blighters." And they said, "Oh, go on, tell us, tell us," and they wouldn't leave her alone, so she vouchsafed them a vision of a Heaven which is like Blaenau Ffestiniog without the little railway: a lot of slate, and low cloud and drizzle, and a lot of gorse. The angels play tambourines and wear fustian. There's also a small gift shop.'

'That's excellent, Meryl. Now who can tell us what happened next?'

Another girl supplied the answer. Two of the sisters, overwhelmed by the majesty of their vision, founded the Church of Our Lady of the Paper Bag. But because many people were too ignorant to see the beauty of the vision and said it didn't sound very nice they needed to be forcibly persuaded for their own good, and thus was born the military arm of the Church of our Lady of the Paper Bag, the Soldiers for Jesus. Their job it was to open the eyes of the unbelievers. The third girl, seeing the message of the prophet as confirmation that all routes through this vale of tears are useless, took the third fork in the path, the route to Aberystwyth. She embraced the gaudy life and began to make seaside rock.

As Eleri showed us back out to the yard I said, 'That was quite an interesting vision of Heaven. I'd never pictured it like that before.'

She giggled. 'Yes, I expect you saw it more as angels and harps and puffy white clouds.'

'Isn't that how most people see it?'

'Well, I expect parts of it are like that. The bit revealed to us was just the Welsh section.'

'Do they have sections in Heaven?'

'Oh yes, they have to. You see, it used to be non-denominational but it caused too many problems. People felt short-changed when they arrived and found that all paths to God were equally valid. It just didn't seem fair if some people could wear brightly coloured clothes and take drugs and stuff and still get to Heaven, whereas people like us had to get fifteen hundred

Sunday School attendance credits and wear shoes made of slate, and every Christmas get a stocking filled with rotten fruit to stand a chance. Especially if someone you hate also gets to be with God and you know they didn't give a tinker's damn about Him when they were alive. Don't you agree? It's an outrage really – I mean, it makes you wonder why you bothered. So now everyone arrives in their own segregated cordons and has the satisfaction of knowing that, of all the faiths and ways of believing, the one they chose was the only one that worked.'

'How do you know all this?'

'One of our saints told us, Mrs Llanfihangel. She was ever such a holy lady, so when she died we made her a saint and she turned up one day at a séance and told us all about Heaven. She said for a while she thought the Welsh were the only ones there, until one day someone left the gate in the fence open and she wandered out and met some Amish.'

We strolled back across the quad towards the car.

'Do you know a girl called Tadpole?' I asked. 'She's a Soldier for Jesus, too.'

'In Aberystwyth, you mean? I've heard of her. I wouldn't say I knew her – I don't go to Aberystwyth very often, especially at this time of year. It's such a bother finding a hat to wear.'

'Why do you need a hat to go to Aberystwyth?'

'Oh, come on, Mr Knight, don't pull my leg.'

'I'm not. Plenty of people don't wear hats there.'

'Yes, but we're students, aren't we? What happens if we see a student from Aberystwyth and we're not wearing a hat? We won't have anything to doff.'

'You need to doff your hat when you see a student from Aber?'

'Of course. It's a college rule: we must always take off our hats when see a fellow scholar.'

I pulled a face and she continued, burning with conviction, 'Oh, come on, Mr Knight. Don't tell me you've never seen someone doff a cap before.'

'I'm familiar with the custom, but not in this context. The normal way to make a man remove his hat in that town is to punch him on the jaw.'

We arrived at a construction like a medieval well; it had a bell hanging beneath the little roof.

'This bell is from Patagonia,' Eleri explained with evident pride. 'It was rescued from the Mission House, and presented to us. It's one of our most treasured possessions.'

'What happened out there?' I asked. 'I hear things didn't go quite according to plan.'

Eleri looked sad. 'Oh. The Soldiers for Jesus had quite a difficult time of it, I'm afraid. The Indians had a vision of Heaven that featured orgies and human sacrifice and lots of cocaine. It was very hard to make them see that ours was better. Besides, their language didn't contain a word for gift shop.'

'Your version does sound a bit austere.'

'It's not really. Our Heavenly Father loves us, of course, but He also likes us to do what we're told. We step out of line and we get smote.

Oh God of remorse
In your heaven of gorse
Who sent Noah a boat
While the rest got smote.

'That's our best prayer.'

'And the Indians didn't like it?'

'They were strange heathens. They said, "In our heaven we've got Tequila and cocoa leaves and we have sex all day. And we eat people. What have you got in yours?"

'And we said, "Well, we get to sing hymns all day – what could be nicer than that?" But they just sneered, so the schoolmarm showed them a picture of Blaenau Ffestiniog. Of course, she tried to point out it was like that without the train but they wouldn't listen. They all pointed at the little steam train and said, "What's that?" And she said, "It's a puffing billy," and they looked at her blankly so she asked for a Welsh–Spanish dictionary and translated. "El gran tren del choo-choo," she said, and they all fell about laughing. Apparently, choo-choo is a very bad word in their language. After that news spread like wildfire: in the Welsh gringo heaven they have a big choo-choo. They used to come for miles just to laugh. The schoolmarm fainted when she found out what it meant.' She stopped and looked slightly embarrassed at the failure.

We tut-tutted sympathetically. At least, I did.

'I heard the chaplain went nuts,' said Calamity.

Eleri blinked in surprise. 'I beg your pardon?'

'We heard something terrible happened and the priest went bananas.'

'I'm afraid I don't quite—'

'Lost his marbles,' she explained. 'Cuckoo. We heard the priest went mad. Is that true?'

'I . . . I'm afraid I'm not allowed to discuss military matters.' Eleri had lost some of her composure and stammered slightly. 'But I'm sure that couldn't have happened. You must be careful about some of the things you hear. A lot of people are jealous of us and try to undermine our reputation with calumnious remarks.'

I changed the subject. 'Tell us about your studies at Jezebel College.'

'What's there to tell? It's really boring. We don't get cadavers to dissect or anything, like the guys on the undertaking course. It's just the usual stuff, mostly theory.'

'About what?'

'Oh, you know, about the differences between a trollop, a tart, a slattern, a flibbertigibbet . . . that sort of thing. It's very boring. Mostly textbook.'

'So why did Emily call us?'

'She did some work for the Santa Claus who got murdered in

Chinatown. He went to see her and she helped him with some stuff, trying to trace a child born out of wedlock a long time ago. Emily was good at that sort of thing – she understood about all these forensic techniques and things – but me, I never had the patience. She was into Kierkegaard as well – well, we all are of course – but Emily was nuts about the guy. The woman was called Etta Place and the baby born out of wedlock was christened Laura.'

'Etta Place was the girlfriend of the Sundance Kid,' said Calamity.

'Who?'

'You know, the Hole-in-the-Wall gang, the famous outlaws.'

'No I'm not familiar . . .'

'The movie – *Butch Cassidy and the Sundance Kid*.'

Oh, we don't watch movies. We have to study. Except Clip, of course. We all want to see that. Oh, but I'm forgetting my manners. You've come all this way, you must be waiting to see Emily.'

'We thought she was dead.'

'She is.'

We declined the opportunity to see the cadaver, and made our way back to the car.

Eleri held out a hand to shake and said, 'You really mustn't pay any attention to the bad things people say about the Soldiers for Jesus. It's just the idle tittle-tattle of gossips. You see, Mr Knight, we do a lot of good work here: we give the girls a chance that normally they just wouldn't get. For many of them Sunday School is the only way out of the ghetto.'

'One other thing,' I said before closing the car door. 'If you qualify for a reward for the help you've given us, do you want the Lego?'

'The what?'

'The Lego. You know what that is, I take it.'

Eleri looked slightly hurt. 'Don't be silly. Of course I do. It's Latin for "I build", isn't it?'

Chapter 11

THE OLD MAN Elijah was waiting in the office. He was sitting peacefully in the client's chair with the serene air of a Buddhist monk or a man for whom waiting calmly is a skill honed during a lifetime's practice. The *Cambrian News* was on the desk in front of him, folded to display the story covering Emily's murder.

I took off my coat and slung it on the hatstand. I glanced at the newspaper and said, 'You predicted it and you were right. Now what do you want? We're fresh out of medals.'

'You know what I want. You found it in that alley.'

'Finders keepers.'

He smiled thinly. 'Yes, but isn't there also something in that ditty about weepers?'

'Suppose you tell me who killed her?'

He took a slow deliberate breath. 'You killed her.'

'I'd never even met her.'

'You need to be introduced first to kill a person?'

'Spare me the wisdom.'

'I see her name on your incident board, and yet you say you do not know her?'

'I said I'd never met her, and it's true. I could put up the name of the mayor of Gotham City, it wouldn't mean we were acquainted.'

'Then maybe he, too, would die.'

I sat in my chair and laced my fingers behind my head. 'Talk plainly or get out.'

'It is my belief that a parasite has taken up residence in your neighbourhood.'

'You mean like rats in the attic?'

'I do not refer to that, although I don't deny the possibility that you have them, too.'

'A parasite?'

'It is known as a Pieman.'

'A what?'

'You have a Pieman.'

'I have a Pieman?'

'I am sorry.'

'This comes as quite a shock.'

'It normally does. Naturally, you will say you do not know what a Pieman is.'

'Why bother to such a sharp guy like you? Feigning ignorance of a Pieman is a difficult stratagem to master.'

'That's for sure.'

'We have a guy across the road who eats a lot of pies,' said Calamity.

'Ah yes, you joke. Of course you have a guy across the road who eats pies. He is the Pieman. Or one of them.'

'You mean he's killing these people?'

'Not personally. He supplies the names of the victims, and those he gets from you, from your incident board. If I am not mistaken you will find the Pieman resides across the road in one of the top-floor flats—*don't look*!' His face flushed with fury. 'Don't look, you fools!'

Calamity and I both arrested the movements of our heads with a strange air of guilt.

'Louie watched him being winched in,' said Calamity, making a great pretence of not looking out of the window.

'If you were to visit him you would find a lot of pies and a thirty-five-millimetre camera with a long-focus lens trained on this room. On his wall will be a replica of your incident board.

The moment you put a lead on your board he takes a snap, develops it in a tray next to the camera, and twenty minutes later pins up the gleaming wet black-and-white photo. From this he harvests the names, which are smuggled out to the assassin in the empty pie boxes.'

'That's absurd.'

Elijah smiled. 'On the contrary, it is a most wonderful development. For the first time in perhaps twenty years Hoffmann has made a mistake. He has exposed himself. I cannot tell you how excited this makes me.'

'You mean Hoffmann is behind the Pieman?'

'Who else? Who else would go to such lengths to protect himself? And yet, paradoxically, in choosing to protect himself in this manner he may have fatally compromised himself. It is a wonderful development.'

'But why would anyone do such a crazy thing?' said Calamity.

'It is a venerable and ancient assassination technique, developed many years ago by Welsh Intelligence. The beauty of it – and this is partly why the Welsh thought it up, because their espionage budget has always been severely limited – the beauty of it is its cost-effectiveness. The Pieman, you see, is a crude although effective form of custodian, a keeper of secrets, a protector or gate-keeper, if you will. He is enlisted to eliminate people who pose a threat to whatever needs to be protected. And the great thing is, he is very cheap because he rides piggyback on someone else's investigation – in this case, yours. You do the legwork while he sits on his arse all day and eats pies. Hence the Pieman. Ingenious, don't you think?'

'Yeah, we're overwhelmed by his cleverness,' I said.

'That's if we believe you,' added Calamity.

'Trust me, I have better things to do with my time than make up stories like this.'

'So you say.'

'I guess we'll just have to go round and speak to the Pieman,' I said.

'That is what you must on no account do. Categorically not.'

'Why?' I sneered. 'Because we'd find nothing there except a guy who likes to eat pies, and no camera?'

'You really are very stupid, aren't you?'

'So you keep telling me. I'm getting quite tired of it, to tell the truth.'

'Just suppose for the sake of argument that I am not lying. What will happen if you go up there? You will find the Pieman and he will close down his operation. And what will you have gained? You will have killed the parasite. But what of Hoffmann? What of him? He will be long gone, and perhaps it will be another twenty years before he is heard from again. Perhaps it will never happen again. This one occasion is all we are given, this one chance, this unique moment in the annals of espionage. And you threaten it with your intemperate curiosity.'

'All right, I've supposed that. Now you suppose this. Just suppose for the sake of argument there is no such thing as the Pieman. We walk around all day taking ridiculous care not to look up at the window across the street and not putting things on the incident board, and all for what?'

'Exactly! All for what? What possible reason could I have for inventing such a story? It would make you look stupid, for sure. It would make your lives more difficult to a very slight degree; but neither of those two goals is of the slightest interest to me. Why would I care?' He paused, then added thoughtfully: 'Tell me, did a tradesman come round a few days ago selling AGC?'

'What's AGC?' I said.

'Anti-glare coating for your incident board.'

'Yes,' I said just as Calamity stammered 'No.'

She and I exchanged glances. Elijah smiled and looked at the incident board. It was as if the gods had been waiting for this moment: the clouds parted and a blade of fierce sunlight stabbed the gloom in the office and bathed the incident board in bright golden light. And yet, glare-free, not a single detail was obscured.

Whatever the salesman's motives, you couldn't help but admire the quality of his AGC.

'It is a common m.o. for a Pieman to employ,' said Elijah with studied nonchalance.

'So what do we do, then?' I asked, hating myself for being sucked into his absurd charade, but unable to resist. What if he was telling the truth? What if there really was a Hoffmann and, by compromising the Pieman, I blew the only chance to catch him that had presented itself in twenty years?

'What you do,' continued Elijah, 'is absolutely nothing. You carry on as normal – sticking your leads up on the board and doing nothing to indicate that the Pieman's cover has been blown.'

'But what if more people die?'

'Certainly more people will die. Do you think this is a game? More people will die, many of them innocent. But their deaths are of no consequence when set against the greater prize, Hoffmann.'

'We can't do nothing.'

'What are you talking about? Can't do nothing? Of course you can. Doing nothing is one activity that falls within the power of just about anybody. Even a nincompoop like you can do nothing. If I asked you to undertake some strenuous or difficult mission you might be justified in complaining, but here I am asking you to do nothing and you act as if it were an endeavour entirely beyond the wit of mortal man. You can certainly do nothing, and that is precisely what you must do. In the meantime I will speak to my organisation and seek instruction. A Pieman is a difficult infestation to deal with. It demands patience, and guile, and, above all, subtlety.'

'Can't we just follow the boy who delivers the pies?' asked Calamity.

'You think he won't be waiting for that? You think the Pieman is a fool?'

'Aren't you worried?' asked Calamity.

'About what?'

'If a name goes up on the incident board, the person gets whacked, right?'

'That in broad outline is the essence of a Pieman manoeuvre, yes.'

'What if we put your name on the incident board?'

He paused. A look of mild panic discomposed his features and his skin drained of colour. He swallowed. 'Little girl, I must ask you not to joke about such a thing. That would be tantamount to murder. You would be assassinating me.'

'Doesn't sound like such a bad idea,' I said. 'Tell me who Hoffmann is, and maybe we won't do it.'

'You joke.'

'No. It seems an excellent idea.'

Elijah opened the desk drawer and pulled out a bottle of Captain Morgan.

'Help yourself,' I said.

He unscrewed the cap, took a drink straight from the bottle and said, 'Hoffmann is a man who once stole a coat.'

The old man stared at the bottle, swirled the rum arond, deep in thought. We waited. Nothing happened. A lorry passed by in the road outside, making the windows rattle.

'Is that it?' I asked.

'Was it a nice coat?' said Calamity.

'In terms of tailoring I think it was undistinguished. At least, as far as I recall, neither the cut nor the quality of the cloth has ever been a feature of this case.'

We nodded. Calamity wrote down in her notebook, 'Not the quality.'

We waited for a minute or so but there was no more.

I said, 'Your name is Elijah, right?'

'Yes, you may call me that.'

I pulled out an index card and began to write. 'That's good. I'd hate to kill the wrong man.'

'W-what are you doing?'

'What does it look like? I'm putting your name on the board. See? Elijah, brackets, infuriating jerk. That's you, Pumpernickel, you in the silly hat.'

He slammed his hand down on top of mine. 'No, please. Please, you mustn't.'

'Start talking, then. A bit faster this time. And forget the Talmudic mystery tour.'

He took a gulp of rum and began again.

'The coat belonged to a man called Caleb Penpegws. It was stolen from him as he lay on a stretcher in the infirmary recovering from his wounds after the Mission House siege in Patagonia. You are familiar with that terrible conflict?'

'Yes, we've heard about it.'

'But of course the coat did not originally belong to the young soldier. He bought it from a woman, a Mata Hari, so they say, who stole it from the reading room of the Buenos Aires public library.'

Calamity jotted that down.

I asked, 'Is Caleb Penpegws the one who was tortured and used to cry out "Hoffman!" in his nightmares?'

'His nightmares are not a feature of the case but it is quite possible. As a wearer of the coat he would certainly have been tortured.'

'Who by?'

'Members of a secret organisation known as ODESSA, which you may have heard of. Created during the final days of the Second World War, its aim was to help high-ranking members of the SS escape from Europe. The usual route was through Switzerland, to Italy, from there by boat to North Africa, and from there to Lisbon before embarking for South America. To many countries, but predominantly to Argentina – it was run at the time by the Perón government, which had some sympathy for the Nazi fugitives.'

'And why were they interested in Caleb Penpegws's coat?'

'Because, of course, it was not his coat. He bought it from the Mata Hari and she had stolen it from the reading room of the library. It originally belonged to a man called Ricardo Klement who owned a dry-cleaning business in the city.'

'Why did ODESSA want his coat?'

'Because Ricardo Klement was not his real name. His real name was Adolf Eichmann, one of the most high-ranking Nazis to evade allied capture in 1945. You may know what happened to him. He was kidnapped in 1961 by the Israeli Secret Service, outside his house in Garibaldi Street in the San Fernando district of Buenos Aires. From there he was taken to Jerusalem and tried and eventually executed for crimes against the Jewish people. All this is a matter of historical record.

'During interrogation Eichmann told his captors about an item in his possession, one of truly epoch-making significance; so much so that it has since been eagerly sought by just about every intelligence agency in the world – by Mossad, and ODESSA, and the CIA, and M15 and Welsh Intelligence, and countless others. I am not at liberty to disclose the precise nature of this item, except to say it was in the pocket of the coat the day it was stolen from the reading room of the Buenos Aires public library; stolen by the Mata Hari, if she existed.' He paused as if reflecting, then said, more to himself than to us, 'Because I have my doubts; the long toll of the years has eroded my certainty in certain aspects of Eichamnn's testimony. He claims she seduced him, that it was a honey-trap, and that she took him to an apartment opposite the railway station where she prepared a dish of lamb and cheese for him. Can such a thing be possible? Lamb and cheese?'

It sounded like the traditional Welsh dish known as *cawl*; the recipe for which could be obtained from tea-towels sold at the tourist information shop. I didn't tell him; I decided to hold that card close to my chest. It might be useful if Odessa ever showed up.

'Where do you fit into all this?' I asked.

'I am here because of a promise I made to my dear mama on her deathbed: to find the two lovely sons she lost to Hoffmann. Two brothers, the like of whom the world will never see again. Little Ham, the youngest; we lost him to Hoffmann many years ago, somewhere – who knows where? – along the labyrinthine spoor left by this phantom. And Absalom, the man they found slain in the alley wearing the bright red robes of Christmas . . . For years he had been searching for Ham, and now alas he also has met his doom.'

'But what's all this got to do with Butch Cassidy?' said Calamity and then slapped her hand to her mouth in horror. It was an unusual slip for her and I put it down to the excessive excitement generated by her Pinkerton mania. I felt sorry for her.

'Shit,' she said.

Elijah allowed a sly smile to animate his features. He paused for a beat or two, allowing the import of her words to be felt, and then said, 'Oh dear, oh dear!'

Calamity looked at me, squirming.

I forced a laugh. 'Forget it, kid. It was nothing.'

'We all make mistakes,' said Elijah in a voice that made me want to punch him. 'But we can easily overlook it. All you have to do is give me the item you found in the alley. The one which rightfully belongs to my people, and which, I suspect, makes some reference to the celebrated outlaw Butch Cassidy.'

I picked up the index card. 'No, I think instead we'll just put your name on the board. That's a much better idea.'

'Then I am truly sorry.' He stood up with exaggerated weariness, walked over and stood behind Calamity. He placed a gentle hand on her shoulder. Then took out a gun and held it to her temple. She froze. We all did.

'There's no need for that,' I said in a cloyingly reasonable voice. 'No need at all. We can work this out.'

'Really? There's been so much time to work things out but here we are with everything still unworked-out.'

'Don't give it to him,' said Calamity.

'Don't be daft,' I said. 'Of course I'll give it to him.'

I raised my hands and moved towards him. 'Don't do anything sudden, Elijah. I have to get past you to get the item you're looking for.'

He caught my glance and I saw a sudden fear flash through the pools of his eyes. At least, I thought I did.

'You're scared of me? You think I will hurt your little girl? You don't understand . . .' He looked bewildered and puzzled. 'My people have suffered so much. You could not begin to imagine it— No, don't move!'

I was almost on him. Just another step and I would be there.

'And yet you look at me with that fire of condemnation in your eyes, as if . . . as if . . . Don't you see? It is we who were slaughtered. We're not the wolves, we are just the lambs . . . Oh God. *Oh God*! Have we become no better than our oppressors?' It was as if he was talking to an angel standing behind me in the room. Doubt clouded his gaze. He let the hand holding the gun fall to his side and began to sob. I made a grab for the gun; it slipped out of his hand and fell to the floor with a clatter. Maybe I should have noticed how ridiculously easy it was. Maybe I should have reflected on the fact that Mossad are not renowned for employing cry-babies. But I didn't. I dropped to the floor and picked up the gun. Calamity jumped clear and I shoved Elijah, who was old and frail, and crying, and not very hard to shove, up against the wall and pressed the gun barrel into his eye. The lid closed round it, the faint grey lashes fluttering like butterflies. I gave the barrel a slight twist and he groaned.

There was a pause, the moment when I was supposed to tell him what a dirty low-down dog he was, that I would shoot without giving it a second's thought. But that would have been a lie and we all knew it. Instead I was overcome by disgust. Nothing I could say would sound convincing; it would just sound like something on the TV. The moment had passed. I felt like Hamlet. I pulled the gun out of his eye and removed the magazine. I emptied out the cartridges and let them clink and dance on the table before gathering them up and putting them in my pocket. I slotted the magazine back in with a snap and returned the weapon. He took it without a sound and walked out, still sobbing. I felt sorry for him, sick in the pit of my stomach. But that was because I didn't know his bitter tears were just a lousy act and what I should have done was reload the magazine, stick the barrel back in his eye and pull the trigger.

Chapter 12

IT WASN'T THE first time someone had pulled a gun in the office, but it was the first time someone had pulled a gun and then burst into tears. You never stop learning on this job. I spent five minutes reassuring Calamity about the Butch Cassidy slip; it was the sort of thing that could happen to anyone. We arranged to meet later at Sospan's to review the Hoffmann case and discuss tactics for dealing with the Pieman. In the meantime I had an appointment with Police Commander Llunos. He'd asked to see me, in the strangest of places: St Michael's Church.

He was sitting in the back pew, looking unhappy. He always looked glum, but this was different: not the usual world-weary existential disgust of the long-serving cop, the one that comes as standard issue along with the sarcasm and the stained raincoat; today he just looked unhappy.

I slid into the pew alongside him. 'Come to take Him in for questioning, eh?'

'Who?'

'God.'

'My mother's sick,' he said. 'She's had a minor stroke.'

'Oh, I'm sorry.'

'Yes. I've had to take some leave.'

'I guess it's pretty serious?'

'They usually are, aren't they?' He considered with a puzzled look. 'I don't understand the human body. Normally it's so tough, it never fails to surprise you what it can do. People who should be dead hang on for years purely out of guts or will power, you know. And yet a stroke, it's just a vein popping in the brain, isn't it? You'd think something like that could wait till after Christmas.'

We both said nothing for a while. When the silence got too oppressive I said, 'I ran into your replacement at the Chinese. Nice fellow.'

Llunos made a slight upward jerk of his head in acknowledgement. 'Yes, nice. He loves you.'

'I noticed that.'

'He's not the sort of guy a smart guy makes a monkey of, so the first thing you do is make a monkey of him.'

'Did I do that?'

'And a monkey of me, too.'

'I don't know what you're talking about.'

'Erw Watcyns,' said Llunos. 'He's from the Cardiff Sweeney, which means he thinks everyone else, including me, is a bumbling, carrot-crunching amateur. He's especially fond of private detectives, particularly smart ones like you.'

'I didn't say a dickey-bird to him. Isn't this a strange conversation to be having in a church?'

'This building is about the only place left where a conversation like this might do any good.'

I couldn't think of anything to say to that.

'You think us cops are really dumb, don't you? You hide it well most of the time, but things like that have a way of revealing themselves.'

'I'm sorry about your mum, but giving me a hard time won't make her better.'

'I told him you were OK, I tried to protect you, but you had to go and do it, didn't you.'

'Do what?'

'How long have you been working in this business? A long time, right? And you know better than anyone that there are certain things I let you get away with and certain things I don't. Not because I'm an asshole but because I've got bosses to watch out for, too. And one of the things you don't get away with is working a murder case. Finding lost cats or cheating spouses, even missing persons, I don't care. Help yourself: you'll be doing me a favour. But murder? That's different and you know it. But I know you have to make a living, and I know sometimes you start a case that looks like a lost cat and before you know where you are you're embroiled in a murder enquiry. It happens a lot in this town. You don't seek it; it seeks you. I understand that and so from time to time I pretend not to notice. You don't shout about it and I'll just carry on thinking that's a lost cat you're looking for. Plenty of times I take heat to protect you and you never even know about it. Sometimes I've even come close to losing my job because of you. A lot of the big guys in the Bureau don't like peepers. They dislike them with an intensity that is frankly not healthy, especially for you. But you still go on practising, and on more than one occasion the reason is I protected you. And all I ask is you don't go around sticking your snout into murder cases and when you can't avoid it you don't advertise the fact. So what do you do? You put a fucking ad in the paper.' He turned to me with a withering look. My stomach bubbled as I realised what he was driving at.

'Llunos, I didn't publish that ad.'

'No, I know. It was the Queen of Denmark. Soon as I saw it I knew this would be your final joke. You can take the piss out of me and live to tell the tale. But not this guy. Not Erw Watcyns. He may be crazy, but he's not stupid. He's had plenty of run-ins with private operatives like yourself. Most of them are now ex-private operatives, and some of them are ex-human beings. So he knows the score. He knows all about this crap you lot come out with about protecting client privacy. That's the bit we hate most, you see. It's not enough that you have to trample all over the crime scene, contaminate evidence and break the law to get to witnesses before us; you have to tell us to sod off as well when we come along and say pretty please can you tell us who you're working for; not because we're nosy but because it might have a material connection with the dead guy. He knows all about that. If I hate it you can rest assured he is extremely unpartial to it. So hey! what do you do? You set the scene up. Oh yes, you're just itching for that moment, aren't you? When he asks you for the name of your client. He asks even though he knows you won't give it, but he still has to ask. But this time is different. You say, "Of course I'll give it to you, I'm a law-abiding citizen and it is my duty to assist the police. I'll tell you who the client is. It's the Queen of Fucking Denmark."' He shook his head in sad disbelief. 'When you placed the ad you probably didn't know you'd be dealing with him. That's where being smart gets you. That's one scene I'm glad I won't have to watch. The final act of Louie Knight. It's been a good show but it's over now, folks, back to your lives.'

'I'll keep out of his way.'

'It's too late for that, my friend. Too late. He'll be on his way to get into your way pretty soon, I'd guess. Just as soon as he sifts through the witness statements and finds out they were in your office a few days ago.'

'Who?'

'The Moth Brothers.'

My stomach churned again but it had gone ice cold.

'Or rather the two layabouts formerly known as the Moth Brothers. They were dragged out of the harbour last night. They'd been for a bit of involuntary scuba diving.'

Llunos's beeper went. He glanced down, grimaced and said, 'It's the hospital; I've got to go. If I were you I'd make my peace with the bloke who owns this place. He's the only friend you've got now.'

I watched him leave and pondered his parting words. I thought about the Soldiers for Jesus and their vision of Heaven – like Blaenau Ffestiniog. No one wants a God like that. God is Santa Claus for grown-ups, not a misery-guts, not an asshole; we've got enough of those in town already. I didn't believe; but the guy I didn't believe in wasn't like that. He was a warm, smiling chap, overflowing with benevolence; someone you looked up to with the same bafflement and confused wonder and absolute trust that you had for the giants who put you on your potty when you were two. He was a nice guy who would make it all right; who understood; the one guy you never had to explain your screw-ups to. He smelled good, too: of pews and old hassocks, floor polish and musty velvet drapes, of candle wax and mildewed pages. He resided in the tranquillity that can fill even the heart of an unbeliever in old churches, where the eye and the spirit are soothed by the flicker of golden candlelight and the gentle but vivid hues from the stained-glass good guys above the altar. And the great thing about Him was, He was human. You could feel sorry for Him. I knew there could be only one reason why He let us suffer like this: He can't find a way to stop it. Like a roller-coaster ride that gets too scary, there's no way off. He set it in motion and now He's as helpless as the rest of us.

I wandered down to Sospan's, still dazed and pained by Llunos's words. Calamity was there and recommended the special.

'It's the Paddington Bear,' said Sospan. 'A special all-in-one breakfast ice based on the morning ritual of the eponymous bear. Marmalade and cocoa.'

I ordered one.

'I think now is definitely time to call in the Pinkertons,' said Calamity.

'I had a feeling you might say that.'

'They'd have the resources to deal with something like this – that's the beauty of a preferred associate relationship.'

'I've got the resources to deal with a Pieman: a pair of shoes.'

'What does that mean?'

'Pair of shoes. That's all you need to walk up a flight of stairs and kick a man's backside.'

'Are you mad? You can't just barge in on a Pieman.'

'Why not?'

'Didn't you hear what he said?'

'Oh, I heard what he said. It's just I didn't believe all that much of it.'

'You don't believe we've got a Pieman?'

'I believe we've got a man across the road who eats pies; I saw him get winched up and I've seen the pies. If the act of eating pies makes you a Pieman, then, sure, we've got one. I don't believe he's a spy or an assassin or a custodian or whatever nonsense that crazy Jew said. It's just a set-up.'

'Set-up for what?'

'I don't know. I have no idea; but I do know I don't trust a single word that crazy man says. If he told me he was standing in front of me talking to me I wouldn't believe him.'

'Why don't we just take a look?'

'The same reason I don't take a look when someone tells me there's a ghost in the room: I'm not giving him the satisfaction. Especially as I have a feeling he wants us to go across there for reasons of his own, which will probably get us into trouble if we fall for them.'

'Boy, it's a good job the Pinkertons can't hear you talking like this.'

'They'd probably agree.'

'Shows how much you know.'

'And you know better?'

'I've been reading about it, about their m.o. They wouldn't just barge in and frighten Hoffmann off. They're smart.'

'And I'm not?'

'I'm not saying that. All I'm saying is they'd never do that.'

'What would they do?'

'The first thing they'd do is do nothing. That's rule number one. Whatever you do, don't make it worse. Then you consider your options. Maybe case the joint. I was thinking we could buy time by staging an argument in front of the incident board – you throw a tin of paint at me, and it goes over the board. That way we can take it down without arousing his suspicion.'

'Why don't we forget about the Pinkertons for the time being?'

'After what the girl in Lampeter said? She practically confirmed it. Absalom was trying to find the granddaughter of Etta Place and Sundance. In Aberystwyth! How can you say just forget about it?'

'Please give it a rest. This isn't their case, it's ours; and despite the generous measure of autonomy I give you, I'm still the boss.'

She opened her mouth to protest but saw my expression and thought better of it.

Eeyore turned up a few minutes later and seeing the look of pain on my face, asked, 'What's up?'

Calamity, misunderstanding, said, 'We've got a Pieman.'

'What's that?' he said and so she explained.

'I don't think I've heard of one of those before,' said Eeyore.

'That's because they're pretty rare,' said Calamity. 'We have to proceed with great subtlety; otherwise you can frighten the Pieman off. The best way to handle a Pieman—'

'The best way is to walk right up there and kick his ass,' I said.

'Don't be crazy!' said Calamity. 'Do that and you'll ruin everything. You'll spook Hoffmann and then we'll never find out who . . .' The words petered out.

'Who what?'

'Nothing.'

'Who what?'

'Who . . . who Hoffmann is.'

'I know what you were going to say. You were going to say "Butch Cassidy" or "Sundance" or something.'

'I wasn't.'

'You were. I thought I told you not to mention the Pinkertons again, but all I've heard from you on this case is Butch Cassidy this and Sundance that.'

'Louie, that's not true.'

'You just couldn't do it, could you?' I was still upset about Llunos and the Queen of Denmark. But as so often in life it is someone else who pays the bill. This time Calamity.

'Louie, I—'

'You just wouldn't listen. You had to go on and on. Well, let me tell you something. When you set up your own outfit you can be associate partners with whoever you want, but for the time being it says "Louie Knight" on the door and the only associate partner we've got is Captain Morgan. I'm sorry if it cramps your style, but those are the rules and if you don't like them you can always walk away.'

'Right,' said Calamity. She looked at me, mouth clenched tightly, eyes smarting with the beginning of tears. 'Right, then, I will.'

We watched her walk up the Prom towards the office and Sospan said, 'Don't worry, Louie, things will be better around here once he comes.'

I said nothing and then, as the import of his words made an impression, asked 'Who?'

'Our redeemer.'

I looked at him with a mixture of disbelief and anger. 'What are you talking about?'

'When he comes to redeem us.'

'Who's going to do that?'

'Who do you think?' Sospan shrugged slightly as if to disassociate himself from the words. 'That's what people are saying, isn't it? He who is coming to save us. . . . Hoffmann.'

'Hoffmann?'

'It means Hopeman in German, you see. That's what folk are saying. They've worked it out. It's a message to us. He's coming.'

'Hoffmann's coming?'

'He's going to redeem us, Louie. Hopeman. Everything is going to be all right.'

Chapter 13

TINKER, TAILOR, Patagonian sailor, ex-Nazi . . . Hoffmann. He's coming to save the townspeople. Hopeman. A false prophet, cut-price Messiah . . . the man they send when the town clock forgets to tick.

The people who sit on my client's chair, who are they?

In books the first thing the PI says is 'I don't do divorce stuff.' But that isn't right. Does the greengrocer say, 'I don't do potatoes'?

I'm thinking of changing the name on the door. Pandora Inc. That's what I'm thinking of calling the place. I'm tired of the Knight Errant nonsense. It gives a false impression. It leads the unwary to believe I might be able to help. Pandora Inc on the frosted glass. That way they'll know what they're letting themselves in for. I can find out the truth for you but it won't set you free.

The people who sit on my client's chair, why are they there? It's because everyone wants to run to teacher when things go wrong.

I tell them about two men I once knew. The two men I pity most in all the world. One was Sospan's friend: a bald chap, a bit on the short side, but he never let that get him down. For a while he was the happiest man alive. Had everything anyone could want, always smiling and waving, the most popular guy in the street; never a care in the world. Then one day it all changed. Cut a tooth and needed to be weaned. They moved him on to solids. Poor guy never recovered. With time you learn to deal with the vicious blows life metes out. But not that one. Ask Sospan, he'll tell you.

His brothers and sisters didn't even try to hide their glee at his fall from grace. What? You thought it was going to be like that all along, did you? Welcome to life. First thing you learn, milk isn't free. You can never really trust anyone after that. You just lie there in the cot trying to work it out. The betrayal. All the time we were doing that 'never a care in the world' routine, she must have known. She knew and she never said a word. Wormwood on the nipple. No wonder babies cry so much. And the other guy? Ah, you don't want to know about him.

We stood stiffly in the early-morning frost, our breath visible like dragon smoke. Above our heads the Pieman's light burned, a dark orange star; neither of us looked up.

'Well, I guess this is it,' Calamity said, the fingers of her small hand, clad in pale-blue fingerless mitts, twitching on the handle of the suitcase. 'Thanks again for everything.'

'Nothing to thank me for, it's . . . it's been great. I'm sorry you're going.'

'I think it's for the best. I was thinking about the things you said . . . I feel I have to see the Pinkerton thing through; otherwise I might regret it one day.'

She wore a drab military green parka with the hood up; fake grey fur framing her face in a sweet oval.

'Louie?'

Like a vignette from the old-time photographers who used to be on the Pier.

'Louie? Are you listening?'

'Yes. Sorry, I was looking at your hood.'

'I was saying I could regret it otherwise.'

'Yes.'

'You don't often get a break like this.'

'No, you don't. Have you got an office?'

'I'm using my auntie's front room in Prospect Street for the time being, until I can find somewhere more permanent.'

'You don't want to rush it; the right office makes all the difference.'

'That's what I thought. I'll probably need to talk to the people in LA about it, anyway.'

'Yes, they'll have some ideas. What about the anti-glare acetate – do you want to take that?'

'Don't you need it?'

'I've managed without for most of my life.'

'I was thinking it might be smarter to leave it; that way the guy might come back and try and sell me some stuff in the new office. Might be able to get a better look at him this time.'

'That's a good idea.'

We stood and stared at each other. Calamity's fingers still twitched on the suitcase handle. In the sharp early-morning cold her skin glowed and her cheeks were crimson like a carol singer's in an illustrated Christmas card.

She held out her hand. 'So long, then.'

We shook.

'So long. Just call if you need anything.'

She walked off down the street towards the library; flakes of snow fluttered down from the grey dawn. I turned and walked up the stairs to the office, sat down with a sigh, and put my feet on the desk. I pulled open the drawer and took out my associate partner, Captain Morgan.

The phone rang. I picked it up at the wrong end and got the flex tangled round my hand. Fixing it meant using the other hand but that would mean relinquishing my hold on the bottle of rum, which wasn't a great idea. I leaned forward across the desk and grunted into the phone.

'Gloria in excelsis Deo!' said the voice. It was the Queen of Denmark.

'Not round here, it isn't.'

'Oh dear, have I caught you at a bad time?'

'The odds were in favour of it.'

'I'm sorry?'

'It was statistically inevitable that you would, sooner or later.'

'You've been drinking, haven't you?'

'Don't tell me you don't approve.'

'It's not even nine thirty.'

'I bet the Vikings never worried about things like that.'

'Oh dear.'

'Stop saying "Oh dear."'

'Goodness!'

'I'm not a fan of that expression, either.'

'No? How about this one: go stick your head up your ass!' She hung up.

I went down to the Spa to buy some liquor. When I got back the phone was ringing. It was the Queen of Denmark.

'I'm sorry I said that.'

'It wasn't very queen-like.'

'We don't always do it like the ones in Hans Christian Andersen. He was Danish, too, by the way.'

'Or maybe you're not a queen.'

'What am I, then?'

'That's what I don't understand. Someone who's got it in for me, maybe. You know, it never occurred to me, but putting that ad in the paper has sure landed me in a lot of trouble with the cops.'

'Is that what this is about? The ad?'

'It's about lots of things.'

'Why don't you go home to bed and put your head under the pillow and make the bad world go away.'

'I might just do that?'

'They told me you were a man.'

'They lied to you.'

'Clearly.'

'They always lie; it's the only thing you can count on.'

'You're really feeling sorry for yourself, aren't you?'

'If you were me, you would, too.'

'Aw, diddums!' She hung up again.

I put the cap on the bottle and drove home to my caravan in Ynyslas. Sometimes it's good to put your head under the pillow and make the bad world go away. But there are times when the balm of sleep won't come, and then you need stronger medicine. Eeyore gave it to me once; the bottle lies under the bed in my caravan. Toulouse-Lautrec's favourite tipple: absinthe. The green goddess, green as the sea when it snows in February; it turns milky in water like the eyes of a blind girl I once knew. I sat at the caravan table, drizzled the liquor over a spoonful of sugar and incanted my favourite poem. It's called 'Ingredients'. Angelica, hyssop, melissa, lemon balm, veronica and cardamon, liquorice root . . . such beautiful soothing names, like girls we once loved on summer days . . . angelica, melissa, veronica . . . and wormwood. The bitterest substance known to man. In Ancient Rome the victor in the chariot race had to drink a cup to remind him that life had its bitter side, too. As if anyone needed reminding. Wormwood on the nipple: that's one hell of an overture. How could life disappoint after a start like that? Poor old Juliet.

Never blame the parents, though. They do their best to make it up. They give you childhood. It wears them out but they don't complain. Every child starts life on the stage and never notices Mum and Dad running back and forth, wheeling on the sets, wheeling them off. Stage managing. Two big productions every year: summer holidays and Christmas. Payback for the wormwood.

They take you to the seaside to live in caravans: tin boxes painted hospital green, bathroom blue and lemon curd; with chintzy curtains and bad TV reception; rooms synonymous elsewhere with failed lives but which for a while become palaces. Set in dry scrubby land on breeze blocks, amid sandy spiky grass that not even camels could eat. The tea tastes of plastic cups; sand in wasp-tormented jam sandwiches grinds against tooth enamel; the milk comes warm from a shop that smells of inflatable plastic trash. The sun never shines and the sea is the same colour as the run-off from a washing machine. Every morning the inside of the caravan drips with condensation, and yet it is all so unutterably lovely.

For Christmas they slave all through autumn, taking in extra sewing, to give you a cornucopia. Your heart's desire. Just ask, and you get it. It defies all the rules you are later forced to learn about life. You never see how tired those grown-ups are. Is there something they aren't telling you? There are tell-tale signs, of course. There's something odd about Santa's beard; it doesn't look real. And he smells. You don't expect that of someone from Magic Land. Half the stuff you want doesn't turn up and they say it's too expensive, but how can that be if Santa's paying? But kids are smart. They know it's better not to enquire too deeply about some things. They know better than to look behind the sets. The crucial thing is not to let inquisitiveness jeopardise the coming miracle, the one compared to which later ones, such as first love or the miracle of birth, are but pale shadows: that delirious ecstasy of an empty pillow case left overnight that fills through some magic parthenogenesis with spontaneously generated presents, each wrapped in paper, bright blue or red, bearing repeating motifs – holly and berries, bells, cartoon reindeers – images sweeter than a mother's face, which are torn apart amid a blizzard of fake snow. Flakes from a can drift and pile up inside the house and smell, inexplicably, of pine bath salts. They gather on the tree, the cards, and on the bauble that contains the uncomprehending face of a boy in pyjamas. Two flash-lit eyes, bright pinpricks of bafflement in a nimbus of coloured lights that twinkle as if a rainbow had been sawn up into logs, and ground to dust. There he lives for ever imprisoned in a silver bubble of memory, the boy that was me. The irises of his eyes darken across the years as the photographic dyes slowly age and the snow deepens, until one day it sets loose in the heart an avalanche of melancholy which nothing can assuage.

All men collaborate in the noble, selfless counterfeit. It's a code even criminals honour. Murderers, tyrants, footpads ... they never let on. They keep mum. Only a very few, the sickest sociopaths who have to be locked away in special wings to protect them from the wrath of other prisoners, are exempt. So every time you wander back, get too close to a cardboard backdrop, there is a kindly guiding hand, a policeman, old lady, or bank robber, to push you gently back towards the footlights.

Until the day you slip away; wander past the two-dimensional scenery flats and see them from the other side. See the carpenter's tools and tins of paints. The wires and pulleys. The discarded manikins and cups of instant coffee. Back into the bowels where all is painted black, down the stairs through the door marked Exit, into the cold wet street. Drizzle, gasometers, factory hooter. Newspaper gusting down the street. Life ...

The long walk to the client's chair.

Next morning I stepped gingerly over the empty bottles that rolled around the floor with unpleasantly amplified sounds. I fried some eggs, drank some coffee, and drove to town taking care to avoid my face in the driving mirror. The office was as I'd left it; smelling faintly of rum but probably not as much as I did. There were no messages and no indication that anybody had called, or cared, which didn't greatly surprise me, so I went for a walk. I had no goal in mind but my steps took me along the Prom towards the harbour and then I turned in after the castle and walked past the Castle pub. Another block and I was in Prospect Street. I didn't remember taking any decision to go there but here I was. The curtains of Calamity's office in the front room were closed but a light indicated she was open for business. I went to the front door and stood for a while, my hand in my pocket forming a fist to knock on the door. Then I walked back to the office. It seemed bigger. And emptier. Captain Morgan stared at me from the bin; he'd lost the power to spell the world away; the flames of the torch had gone out and the wolves howled. I spent the next three days like that. I walked along the Prom and down to the harbour, and back via Prospect Street, where I always paused but didn't knock. A couple of times I thought I saw the man in the fedora, but I couldn't be sure.

On the fourth day I passed a vagrant playing a violin on the pavement outside the entrance to the Pier. There was a hat at his feet but nothing in it. The familiar words passed through my head in accompaniment to his playing. 'Brightly shone the moon that night, though the frost was cruel. Then an old man came in sight, gathering winter few-oooh-el.' I stopped. The man was Cadwaladr, the old veteran of the war in Patagonia. He stopped playing and said, 'Bring me flesh and bring me wine, bring me pine logs hither.' I showed him a bottle of rum in my Spar bag and he packed up the violin.

'Follow me,' he said. 'I know just the place.'

We walked down towards the harbour.

'I thought you were painting the railway bridge across the Dovey estuary.'

'I was.'

'You said it was a job for life.'

'It was. Finish one end, and time to start again at the other end. Like Sisyphus, only better scenery.'

'What happened? Get tired of it?'

'Nope. They invented a new kind of paint. Lasts ten years.'

'I'm sorry.'

'They gave me redundancy money – I bought a van. See.'

He took me to a van parked on the Prom across from the Yacht Club. It looked like a superannuated ambulance or a furniture van or something. It looked like a lot of the vans that got parked here: mobile homes for people whose dogs had string for a leash. The poor man's Winnebago. He opened the back, pulled out a folding table and two matching chairs and set them up on the pavement. I put the bottle down and sat.

'What was it before, a furniture van?'

'Mobile library. Cost me two hundred quid.' He brought out two cups and we sat on the Prom, drinking rum in the dim light of midday.

'Mobile library.'

'I like that. There's an air about it, hard to define, an air of learning, of scholarship. And a hush like you get in a proper library.'

'You got a bed in there?'

'Got a bed and a cupboard and a primus. Got some water and some candles. Got some petrol. Got everything I need. Might even try a different country in the new year.'

'Still got the hush, huh?'

'I know it sounds strange.'

'I don't think it does.'

'You going to the carol concert this year?'

'Hadn't thought about it.'

'They say Myfanwy won't be singing.'

'Doesn't look like she will. She's lost her voice.'

Cadwaladr leaned back in his chair and stared at sea darker than an evergreen tree. 'Won't be the same.'

'She knows that.'

'Every year Myfanwy is the high point.'

'She knows that. I think the pressure of expectation is part of the problem.'

'Won't be the same, even if Hoffmann does turn up.'

'You think he will?'

'Me? No. But everybody else does. Tickets are already sold out. Doesn't matter to me one way or the other. I gave up hope of redemption many years ago, after I came back from Patagonia and found that no one would look me in the eye. The way I see it, we've done nothing to deserve our fate in the first place. We shouldn't even be in this position. If God wants to redeem us, he can just go ahead and do it. No need to make us jump through hoops first.'

'This Hoffmann stuff is pure craziness. It's a word written by a dead man in blood. No one's going to come and redeem us.'

'Your dad's supplying the donkey.'

'He supplies the donkey for the nativity scene every year.'

'They're going to have a torchlight procession led by Clip.'

'Is it true something terrible happened in the war—'

'Of course.'

'I mean at the Mission House siege. They say the priest went mad.'

Cadwalader rolled a cigarette. 'That definitely didn't happen. He was mad before he went.'

I touched the violin. 'Did you learn to play this in the war?'

'Learned as a kid. Do you know what the secret of a Stradivarius violin is?'

I was about to tell him but then I thought better of it. The world is full of smart alecs. 'No, I've no idea.'

So he told me.

'I always think of that story at Christmas. Those spruce trees growing slowly somewhere far away in the Alps. No noise at all, just silence and the sound of a tree growing slowly. Sounds mad, doesn't it?'

'No.'

'That's all there is. Just emptiness, bright grey light; the sound of snowflakes landing, the rustle of sifting snow. The tiny noise of a wolf's paw in the fresh snow. Must have been beautiful. Maybe far off there is a post horn, if they had them then. Two travellers, perhaps, wandering lost in the blizzard, calling with their horns.' He paused and looked sad. 'The man who told me that story about the violins used to make rocking chairs.'

'Yes, I met him. He once asked me if I'd ever ridden on an escalator.'

'They found the poor chap dead in the snow above Talybont yesterday.'

'The rocking-chair man is dead?'

'Someone smashed his head in with a tyre iron. They found him in the trees behind his house. Never had an enemy in the world, that bloke. Just a mystery.'

'He was a nice old man.'

'Every Christmas I'll think about him, too, from now on. The wolf, the post horn, and the rocking-chair man face down in the snow.'

They say the human heart is a mansion with many locked rooms and wings which are closed to the public. All the nice furniture is in the parlour at the front; the one that gets plenty of sun through those fine bright Georgian windows; the one that looks out onto a gravel forecourt and beyond to neatly clipped privet hedges and topiary.

This section is open to the public.

Towards the back there is a roped-off section, leading to stairs and a labyrinth of dim corridors. The sun doesn't shine here; the doors are locked; the furniture is covered in sheets. Sometimes at night you can hear moans and cries echoing down the empty corridors, the cries of long-dead people. And you can see an ancient white-haired servant taking a tray of food and collecting an empty one. He has a key to the final set of locked doors at the corridor's end. Someone lives there, someone they would rather you didn't see. A man in a tracksuit. The school games teacher.

Reluctantly, I decided it was time to pay a visit to the circus. If I was lucky maybe I could get in and out during the strongman's performance. I would not have to meet my former games teacher. But I needed to speak to his moll, Mrs Llantrisant. For years she had swabbed the steps of my old office in Canticle Street, and had given every indication of being a dim-witted, gossiping busybody in her headscarf and curlers; we were later surprised to learn that she was a criminal mastermind at the top of the hierarchy of druid gangsters. As such, unless she had lost her power it was inconceivable that the Moth Brothers could have done a hit on Santa without her foreknowledge or consent. Unless it was an opportunistic slaying, but even then she would know about it. Although the chances that she would tell me what she knew were small.

If you are leaving town, the road east along Llanbadarn is not the prettiest, but it gets the job done. You drive past some nice houses for a while, then follow the floodplain of the Rheidol; before long you begin to climb through ancient hills where the eternal contours are obscured by undifferentiated rows of Forestry Commission conifers. The dark rows between the trees flicker past at the periphery of your field of vision, dark enchanted aisles into oblivion. The manufactured uniformity of the trees is unpleasant and conceals like a cheap suit an immemorial world; ancient stone hills criss-crossed with the tracks and the stone remains of our ancestors. The world here is old and misty, always misty, and it feels pagan. Somewhere beyond Ponterwyd you fall off the map into a desolate place designed for fugitives to hang out in and slowly starve; the sort of land where someone on the run would eventually get so spooked by the emptiness that he would turn himself in, even if it meant going to the chair; because the touch of the man who applies the electric conducting jelly to your temples is still a form of human contact.

I drove onto the grounds of the circus and parked behind some bales of hay. A passing dwarf pointed out the trailer belonging to Mrs Llantrisant. I went over and knocked. Her voice, thin and feeble, bade me come in and I found her lying on a bed, propped up by pillows, and watching a small portable black and white TV. Her hair was loose and fell across her shoulders in drab grey skeins like darning wool. On her forehead in the centre was a livid red sore.

'I wondered how long it would be before you showed up. I said to Herod, "You mark my words, he'll be here before Christmas."'

'You were right.'

She pulled her glasses higher on her nose and scrutinised me. 'You've lost weight around the jowls. And your hair is thinner, and I can see some grey.'

'That must be me getting old.'

'You don't know the meaning of the word. You've still got that pleasure to look forward to.' She reached out, pulled back the curtain, and sighed with exasperation. 'Mist still hasn't lifted.'

The Perspex window was so scratched it was difficult to tell whether the mist had gone or not; but I didn't say it.

'You can take some lion droppings home if you want, put them on your garden. Not that there's anything worth growing this time of the year. I've always hated winter. It's the spring I like. But will I see another one?'

'You should go home, where people can take care of you.'

'I'd rather die out here than be in prison.'

'I haven't come to turn you in.'

'It wouldn't be up to you.'

'If you're sick—'

'What I'm dying of no hospital can cure. There's a hex on me.' She touched the red spot on her forehead, uncannily close to the place where Tadpole's mum had stuck her pin. She took a glass of water from the side table and drank slowly, making loud gulping sounds. From far away there came the sound of cheers and gasps. An elephant trumpeted in vain for the far-off plains of Africa.

'Do you believe time is an illusion, Mr Knight?'

'I don't see how it could be.'

'Some people say so. All the moments of time exist at once, like the different cards in a deck. The sequence is a human construct. Do you believe that?'

'It means nothing to me.'

'Me neither.'

The hand holding the glass fell to her chest, as if the effort of holding it was too great.

'I know why you're here. It's about Father Christmas. You want to know who killed him.'

'I know who did it: the Moth Brothers. I want to know why, who authorised it.'

'No one authorised it.' She sighed. 'Yes, I see the doubt in your eyes.'

'Father Christmas has always enjoyed immunity in this town.'

'You think only I could give permission to change that. You think his death means I'm losing my power. Rest assured, Mr Knight, my sceptre is not broken, despite the scene you see before you. The people who did it have been punished.'

'I know. They were found in a fishing net.'

The elephant trumpeted again and there were more thin, distant cheers. Mrs Llantrisant's attention was diverted for a second.

'He'll be on soon. You shouldn't hang around, Herod won't take kindly to seeing you here.'

'I have no more quarrel with him.'

'Is that why you knocked him out of the plane with a cricket bat?'

'My lawyer says he jumped for the ball.'

'Don't joke with me, Mr Knight. You've never understood how much it grieves him, have you? It crucified him, that boy not coming back from the cross-country run. He never got over it.'

'He got over it the same afternoon.'

'That's how much you know about it. I hear you've raffled the cricket bat.'

'No, I lent it to the Rotary Club just like I did last Christmas. You pay fifty pence to take a swing with it; the money goes to the deaf school.'

'Who'd pay fifty pence for that?'

'A lot of men in this town passed through his games lessons over the years. They still remember. It's surprising how many want a go with the bat. They bought a new adventure playground with the proceeds last Christmas.'

'They should go down on their knees to thank him, not mock him.'

'Thank him for what? The nightmares?'

'For preparing them for life. It's a teacher's job to prepare the child for what he finds beyond the school gates. It's not a bed of roses, in case you haven't noticed. You need guts and vim in the heart. He gave them that; he didn't like it, but he knew where his duty lay. Nobody would have thanked him for turning out milksops like you.'

'This is Aberystwyth not Sparta.'

She snorted.

'I think it's time I went. Are you going to tell me why the Moth Brothers did the hit?'

'There's nothing to tell. There's no mystery. They did it of their own volition, without authority. For kicks, I suppose. Well, they won't do it again.'

'Is there anything you need from town?'

'Nothing that lies in your power to give.' She took her eyes off me and spoke to the ceiling. 'You know, I expected disillusionment at the end of my life. But I thought it would be better than this.'

I bought a ticket and took a seat at the back. Herod stood inside a large cage placed in the centre of the ring, wearing a leopard-skin suit. He was in his sixties now and the leonine locks that were part of his act were stained with dark dye. Thick mascara lent him a freakish aspect like Bela Lugosi in some long-lost silent horror movie. Torn-up telephone directories littered the sand around his feet. He preened and displayed his muscles while a smaller cage was rolled into the arena and wheeled into the bigger cage containing Herod. Inside, asleep, was the Methuselah of tigers. The fur round his muzzle was snow white with age, and elsewhere his coat was ragged and threadbare like a boarding-house carpet. One ear was missing; the tail was half the length it should have been; ribs poked through the skin. There was a roll of drums, the door to the cage dropped open with a dra-matic clang, the crowd gasped, and nothing happened. Herod walked over to the cage and bent down to pick up an iron stick. Despite his age his body seemed in good condition and probably had many more telephone books left in it. But you could see the real toll of his life was on the spirit. It showed in every sinew of that bear-like body.

He jabbed the iron stick through the bars at the tiger's rear end. The beast stood up, took a lazy step forward and slumped down again. Herod jabbed again, harder, and with a growl of irritation the tiger rose with great weariness and hobbled forth. He walked on all threes and kept one hind leg aloft betokening some injury or thorn contracted years ago and never removed. The crowd held its breath and the tiger continued to walk straight ahead towards the bars of the big cage, towards the audience. They began to pull back in fear, even though a wall of iron staves stood between them. The tiger walked straight into the bars and growled once more in irritation, taking a lazy swipe with a paw. It was clear he was blind. He lay down to sleep and Herod walked over and grabbed him and started wrestling. The tiger permitted this latest indignity with an air of weary submission. Perhaps he was too tired of the routine to care any more. Herod performed a judo throw and thrust the big cat down hard onto the sand of the arena. The crowd gasped again. The person in front of me turned to his companion and said, 'They can smell fear, you know.' But it was not clear whether he was referring to tigers or games teachers. Herod stood victoriously with one foot on top of the inert animal and preened to the crowd. I left my seat and made for the exit. The last I saw was Herod bending down, with a worried look on his face; pressing his ear to the tiger's chest, checking for a pulse, and then applying mouth-to-mouth resuscitation. The crowd hissed its dissatisfaction.

Chapter 14

I SPENT THE NEXT few days in my caravan, immersed in a cocoon of camping-gas warmth, swimming in the amniotic fluid of tea laced with rum. The weather had warmed up slightly and turned to sheets of rain that approached from across the Irish Sea in thin bands like interference on TV. I stared out at a sodden world: through smeared and scratched Perspex windows onto a bleary grey watercolour wash of wet dunes and beach and, beyond, the deeper grey of the sea. On the fourth day, in the fading light of late afternoon I saw a figure walking through falling rain which whipped against the window with tiny drumbeats. I watched for a while until I became aware that the figure was moving towards the caravan. The form took more distinct shape and I realised it was Myfanwy.

She came in, wiped her feet on the mat and said, 'Surprise, surprise!' She was holding a brown paper bag from the Chinese takeaway and the smell of hot food, sweet and sour and soy sauce and pineapples, filled my nostrils.

'It's a bit cold but it won't take long to warm up.'

'Shouldn't you be in the nursing home?'

'What sort of greeting is that? Aren't you pleased to see me?'

'Of course I am, I'm just worried.'

'I discharged myself.'

I stood behind her and rested my face on the back of her hair, feeling the warmth of her pressed against me.

'I was listening to them talk about how brave you were, how you risked your life for me and I felt so bad. I thought—'

'Myfanwy, please don't say anything about that.'

'But I—'

'You don't have to. I don't want you to say anything.'

'OK.'

She turned from the stove and looked up into my face. She put a hand on my cheek.

'You look a mess.'

'I am.'

'Everything smells of rum.'

'Must be the mince pies – I like them strong.'

She started to grin but stopped halfway as she saw the mirthless look on my face. 'I heard Calamity left.'

'Yes, she's going to try some sort of associate partnership with the Pinkertons.'

'Why did you let her go?'

'I couldn't find a pair of small enough handcuffs.'

'Louie, don't!'

'Because I love her.'

'But you two were such a great team.'

'It was good, but nothing good ever lasts.'

'How can you be so cold about it?'

'I'm not being cold. Calamity leaving me is a car wreck, but it's one I knew was coming. Everyone has to leave the nest.'

'No, they don't, that's crap. Kids and stuff, of course, but she was your business partner.'

'She has to make her own way. I would never stand in her way.'

'But, Louie—'

'Look, stop it! Why say all this to me? I'm not the one who left. I'm still in the same old office staring at the same old boring ceiling.'

She kicked a bottle on the floor. 'This won't help, you know.'

'I'm not trying to help. Are you going to stay here?'

'I thought I would for a couple of days, if that's all right.'

'Then what?'

She avoided my eyes and began to stir the food that was heating on the stove.

'Then what?'

'I . . . I might go to my auntie.'

'Which one? The one in Llanrhystud?'

'The one in Shrewsbury.'

'Oh. When?'

'After the carol concert.'

'I thought you couldn't sing.'

'I can now. My voice has come back.'

'That's good. I told you it would.'

'Of course, if you say I can't go—'

'You know I'd never do that. I just want what's best for you.'

She nodded sadly, stirred the food. And then brightened. 'We'll have our Christmas now. Have you got anything other than rum?'

'I haven't even got that. It's all gone.'

'I want wine.'

'I'll get some.'

'No—'

'I'll drive down to the village and get some.'

'Don't be long.'

The rain had gathered strength and I drove with extra care, terrified of ending up in the verge on this night of all nights. The ones you never planned always turn out to be the special ones. Cars overtook and hooted their horns in derision. It's strange how angry you can get about someone driving slowly. Move over, Granddad. I usually did it myself. When Eeyore was driving I cringed with embarrassment. But tonight I was the slowest of them all.

When I got back she was sitting on the sofa looking glum; someone else was stirring the food. It was Tadpole.

'What are you doing here?'

'Oh, hi, Louie. You're back. We were starting to wonder where you'd got to. Sweet and sour, my favourite. Must have known I was coming, huh?' She started rummaging around in the kitchen looking for something, as if she'd been here many times before. 'Honestly, Louie, this place is a mess. You need someone to look after you. I guess this will have to do.' She pulled out a bucket and filled it with water. She put flowers in and arranged them.

'You'll be in trouble when the doctor finds out you're here,' she said over her shoulder to Myfanwy.

I looked at her sitting on the sofa, her face a picture of desolation.

'We had a great time the other night, didn't we, Louie? That's one of the best dates I've ever been on. And I've been on a few, I can tell you.'

She took the pan off the stove and started scraping the rice out onto three plates. We both watched with mesmerised helplessness. She brought them over and put them on the table, then fetched cutlery. She sat down and looked at us invitingly, saying 'Aren't you going to open the wine?'

I didn't move.

Tadpole lowered her head and intoned, 'Oh Lord, all we ask for is a stale crust and a few cobwebs and yet You give us Chinese. Truly we are not worthy of the bounty. Amen.' She paused as if to give the Lord chance to deny the compliment. He said nothing and Tadpole began eating.

'What are you doing here?' I asked.

'I was in the neighbourhood.'

'Carrying flowers?'

'Honestly, Louie! Give a girl a break. You want me to stand on a box and shout that I brought the flowers specially?'

Myfanwy was avoiding my gaze, looking away into the middle distance. Rain pattered on the window and the wind began to pick up, acquiring an eerie quality like a woman softly weeping. I tapped Myfanwy gently with my foot under the table. She looked at me and I made an exaggerated frown at the top of Tadpole's head. She sniffed and turned away.

'So,' said Myfanwy, injecting an artificial warmth into her voice, 'you two had a date.'

'We went to see Clip.'

'How nice.'

'You should try and see it.'

'It wasn't really a date,' I said lamely.

Tadpole shot me a look of angry consternation and said, 'Don't you hate it when they do that? We've been seeing each other for a while now.'

'That's nice,' said Myfanwy. 'I didn't know.'

'Have we?' I said.

'He really knows how to charm a girl. Trip to the cinema – tickets to see Clip, of all things. Champagne and roses; holding my hand; whispering sweet nothings. Oh, my head's still swimming.'

Myfanwy stared down at her food. After a while she swung her arm out, brought her wrist up to her nose, and peered at her watch in the familiar dumbshow of someone who is going to announce a pressing need to leave. 'My goodness! Is that the time?'

'Do you have to go?' asked Tadpole.

'No she doesn't.'

'Yes, I think I do. It's getting late.'

'No it isn't,' I said. 'It's not even seven o'clock.'

Tadpole had finished her plate of sweet and sour and was looking hungrily at Myfanwy's. 'Aren't you going to eat your food?'

'No, I've lost my appetite.'

'Pity to let it go to waste.' She picked up Myfanwy's plate and held it above hers. She was about to scrape it onto hers, but I stopped her. I took Myfanwy's plate off her and put it back down in front of Myfanwy.

I said, 'What are you doing here? Myfanwy and I are supposed to be having dinner together.'

'I'm not stopping you, am I?'

'Yes. Now, why have you come?'

'Oh God, Louie. Don't be so dense, will you?'

'What do you mean?'

'You know why I'm here. Don't make me say it in front of Myfanwy. I'll die of embarrassment.'

'Say what?'

'You know. About our little secret. Spare a girl some blushes, please.'

'I have no secrets from Myfanwy. State your business and go.'

'Oh, Louie, please don't make me say it, please don't. I'll go red. I hate it when that happens.'

'Just say what you have to say.'

'I've come to collect . . . you know . . .'

'What?'

'Them.'

'Them what?'

'Oh, Louie.'

'Stop saying, "Oh, Louie." It's driving me nuts.'

'All right, you asked for it. I've come for my pants.'

What?

'I think I left them here the other night.' She stood up surprisingly quickly. 'No, don't you two move, I'll get them. You just enjoy your dinner.'

She rushed up to the other end of the caravan and whipped back the bedclothes. There lying on the sheets on one side of the bed, just below the pillow and about as wide, neatly laid out, was a pair of pants.

'Oh, here they are. How embarrassing.' Tadpole scooped them up and stuffed them into her pocket.

I looked at Myfanwy. 'You're not buying any of this nonsense, I hope.'

Myfanwy glared at her food and refused to look at me.

I stood up and walked over to Tadpole and took her by the

wrist. 'Come over here. I want to tell you something in secret.'

I took her coat off the hook, thrust it into her hands and pushed her to the door.

'What are you doing?'

'Throwing you out.'

I opened the door and pushed Tadpole onto the step. 'Now push off,' I said.

'But, Louie—'

'Get lost!' I closed the door. I walked back to Myfanwy and sat down.

Tadpole appeared at the window. Her fist was in her eye and her mouth contorted into that familiar figure-of-eight on its side; she wailed. I mouthed my parting words through the Perspex and she wailed even more. I drew the curtain across. There was silence for a second and then the sound of a pudgy fist beating on the side of the caravan and a voice crying, 'Let me in!'

I put my arm round Myfanwy.

'Louie it's so awful. Why won't she leave us alone?'

'Don't worry, she'll soon get tired of banging on the wall. Eat your dinner.'

There were tears in her eyes; she sneezed them back and picked up her fork. She started moving the food around the plate. After a while the banging ceased. Myfanwy stopped playing with her food and we sat there waiting, holding our breath, silently praying that Tadpole had finally given up and gone home. We sat still as statues, listening. All we could hear was the thin tap of rain on the metal skin above our heads; and distant creak of the Lyons Maid sign outside the newsagent's. And then beyond that a soft roar as the wind picked up. I wondered what made caravans so cosy. Maybe it was the very thinness of the membrane protecting us from the wilderness. Out there beyond that line, the little crooked rectangle of white pebbles taken from the beach, you could die. You could wander onto the sands, oblivious in the night, and never return. You last memory would be the sea; the dark salty glugging liquid forcing its way into your mouth and nose and ears.

Myfanwy sank into my side; I nestled my chin on her head and rested my gaze on her hair, the colour of conkers. Some girls try to buy it in a bottle, but all they buy is a colour, and colours on their own are nothing: flat expanses of undifferentiated hue, like a song with only one note. In truth the colour we call chestnut is really a swirling sea of many different hues: of mahogany and umber and sienna; faint swirls of black; and lighter russets like the flecks in a tawny owl's eyes. . . . As a child in autumn I knew the secret; when I prised open the lime-green thorny shell and popped from the moist sucking socket an egg of wood, it's shine so deep I saw my own puzzled tiny face staring back against the backdrop of the wide unfathomable sky. You can't buy it. It is a gift from your ancestors. You have to be born in these parts and inherit the green-grey eyes and the fair skin, lightly speckled with pale freckles like eggshell. Or you have to imprison it in the bars of a song. They used to specialise in it: those bards and ovates with their long oaken tables, clanking jugs of ale and rustling chain mail. Bring on the minstrel! the poet! bring on Taliesin and sing to us of this girl's hair while the wolf howls and we quaff. They've all gone now; the bards, the warriors and, saddest of all, the wolf. What was it the poet said? Driven from their halls by brambles. But the beauty they sang of, the ancient beauty of the hills and feral sky, you can still see it in Myfanwy's face.

There was a loud clunk against the side of the caravan. We froze. There was a pause; and then the rhythmic scraping sound of boots on the rungs of a ladder. Seconds later the noise was above our heads, as if the caravan was at the bottom of the ocean and a deep-sea diver in lead-soled boots was clumping across the roof.

'Oh, my God, she's on the roof.'

'Louie!'

'Just sit there. Don't do anything.'

I stood up and from the air vent at the other end of the caravan came Tadpole's voice, slightly warbled and distorted as if she too were under water.

'Looooooouie!'

'Look here, you!' I shouted up at the vent.

'You shouldn't have done that. I'm angry now. You shouldn't have made me angry, Louie.'

'Get off my roof.'

'Or you'll do what?'

'I'll come out and drag you off.'

'I'd like to see you try.'

'If I come out there I'll break your goddamned neck.'

'I'd soon sort you out. I've been trained by the Soldiers for Jesus.'

'We'll see about that.'

'Send Myfanwy home and I promise to forget what you did.'

'Are you nuts?'

'Don't upset me any more. I'm plenty mad now, Louie. Send her home and I promise no one will get hurt.'

'You can spend the whole night on the roof, for all I care.'

'Don't make me do it.'

'Do what?'

'Don't make me use my Soldiers for Jesus techniques.'

I paused and looked around. Lying on top of the cupboard above the stove was a spray can of oven cleaner. I picked it up, aimed at the vent and squirted. There was a squeal, followed by a backward clumping sound on the roof towards the edge. Then a second or so's silence, because even Tadpole doesn't make much sound when falling through the air. There was a thud and more silence. Myfanwy watched me wide-eyed with terror.

'It's OK,' I said, trying to sound like I thought it was.

I walked to the door, gingerly opened it, and peered outside. Tadpole was slumped on the ground at the other end of the caravan. I walked over to check. Her head was wedged awkwardly against a concrete gatepost. It was slicked with her blood but she was still breathing. I went to the kiosk on the main road to call an ambulance.

Chapter 15

I SPENT THREE MORE days drinking before going back to the office, late in the afternoon. The car with the Swansea plates was parked outside when I arrived. Erw Watcyns, the out-of-town cop who hated people to crack wise, was sitting placidly in the driver's seat, a copy of the sporting newspaper spread across the wheel, a half-eaten sticky bun in his hand. It was not a heart-warming sight and my instinct told me to run, but he probably wanted me to do that, and where would I run to? I walked across to the driver's window. It wound down with a smooth electric purr.

Erw Watcyns looked up at me. 'We found the Moth Brothers, Snooper. They weren't looking too good. Care to come down the station and have a chat?'

'Not really.'

'It wasn't a request.'

I walked round and climbed in the passenger side. Erw scrumpled up the newspaper and thrust it in the well between the two seats, then eased the nose of the car out into the traffic stream. He steered with one hand, the one holding the bun. As he drove he took bites from the bun and steadied the wheel with his elbow.

'They were face down in the harbour. Know anything about that?'

'No.'

'Tyre-iron marks on their heads. Know anything about that?'

'No.'

'Witnesses saw them come out of your office a few days ago. Know anything about that?'

'No.'

'I didn't think you would.'

The stone steps that led down to the basement of the police station had that same old gritty sound: that oh so familiar rhythmic, plodding, forlorn scraping like a steam train chuffing sadly on its way to the wreckers' yard. The walls glistened with the same municipal cream paint, applied to the same uneven brickwork, wet with the same saline condensation and the same all-pervading rheumatic dampness. The air was laden with the same stale cooking smells, from a canteen where food is assembled from kits. There were dull thumps of things being moved around, a few floors up; and the awareness of a presence: inaudible, odourless, below the threshold of any sensation; but there, somehow, all the same. A far-off susurration . . . it was the subliminal register of the sea coming in and going out. It seemed to me I had been making this journey all my life, like those people who take their vacation in the same spot every year. The ones who book the same caravan and come not because they want a change but because they don't. Life is too hard if you have to think about it. Aberystwyth police station: our cell is marked with an X. The food is a bit greasy, but the weather has been nice. We get regularly beaten. Please send a lawyer. Wish you were here. The light was as yellow as egg yolk.

We turned left at the bottom of the stairs, into D section: a short corridor with four cells up one side and wall-to-ceiling bars like in the cowboy films. The deputy showed me to my room. There was someone already in it. Miss Evangeline. She was sitting on the bed, staring ahead with the fixity of purpose that rabbits in headlights are said to display. She flinched when the door slammed and the key went clickety-click like the bolt being pulled back on a rifle. Tadpole had been kept in the hospital overnight with mild concussion and released next morning. That was two days ago. She'd been busy in the meantime: this was her revenge.

'Miss Evangeline, what are you doing here?'

'I've been arrested. Oh dear Lord above!'

'For what?'

'The charity disabled boy outside the Pier, the one made of fibreglass, someone broke his box open and took the money. They say it was me. I wouldn't do a thing like that.'

'Of course you wouldn't. It must be a mistake.'

'They found some money in my handbag. But I don't have any money.'

'What were you doing at the Pier?'

'I was with that nurse.'

'Tadpole?'

'Yes. She took me for a walk along the Prom, it was so nice of her – normally she never bothers. When we got to the Pier I lost her and the next thing I knew there was a consternation and they were accusing me of stealing. Oh Lord!'

Erw appeared in the corridor. I walked over to the bars, we stood face to face.

'Let her go.'

'Can't do that, Peeper, she's a felon. Damaging council property, theft, can't let her go.'

'She's blind, for God's sake!'

'So is the law, Shamus, so is the law.'

'She didn't do anything and you know it.'

'Do I know that?'

'She was set up.'

'Who by?'

'Tadpole.'

He pretended to consider, then shook his head with incredulity. 'No, not Tadpole. She'd never do a thing like that. She loves those old codgers up there.'

'Like hell she does.'

'It broke her heart, it did, having to turn Miss Evangeline in. You should have seen the trouble I had getting her to fill out the witness statement.'

'And I bet she's the only witness, too.'

'I've got a witness and the evidence of the stolen money. I've got enough to be going on with. She'll get her day in court. If she's innocent, if it's all just a terrible miscarriage of justice – and let's be honest, these things do happen now and again – then she'll walk.'

He flicked open a notebook and consulted his notes. 'Now, suppose we forget the bleeding-heart stuff and concentrate on the matter in hand, namely the nature of your connection with the two deceased Moth Brothers. Tell me what they were doing in your office. And please don't pretend they weren't there.'

'They came to confess to the murder of Father Christmas.'

'That was nice of them. Now, why would they do that? As opposed, for example, to confessing to the proper authorities, i.e. me.'

'I don't know.'

'I don't like that answer, Louie.'

'I don't like it, either.'

'OK. Suppose you tell me the name of your client.'

'Her name's Margrethe Glücksborg.'

'Margaret . . . ?'

'Glücksborg. With an umlaut.'

'With a what?'

'Two little dots above the u.'

'You think I don't know how to spell Glücksborg?' Something flashed in the pools of Erw's eyes when he said that. It could have been the shiny silvery belly of a trout dashing through the sun-dappled waters, but I didn't think so. I think it was the switch-board sparking angrily when no one is in attendance; the dancing blue flame that says this man is totally mad and is capable of killing someone over the perceived insult of not knowing how to spell Glücksborg.

I said, 'Sorry, of course you know.'

'Where can I find her?'

'Copenhagen.'

He paused to reflect, made a slight nod, and wrote it down in his book. 'And what does Margaret do?'

'She opens shopping malls.'

He nodded again and enunciated the sentence as he wrote it down. '. . . shop . . . ping . . . malls. Excellent. We're almost finished. You've been very cooperative. Now, just one more question, merely routine. 'Opening shopping malls isn't really a job, is it?'

'Not really, no.'

'If it was, I wouldn't mind doing it myself. But the thing is, normally they get important people to do it; do you see where I'm heading? So be a sport, tell me who she really is.'

'She's the Queen of Denmark.'

'Wonderful.' He wrote it down. 'Queen of Denmark. I think that covers all the formalities.' He snapped the notebook shut and handed it to a deputy. 'Get that typed up.' He watched the deputy depart, then turned back to me. We were alone now, just the three of us.

'Speaking off the record, I have a little problem. I don't like your Queen of Denmark story. You know? Somehow it doesn't ring true. When you've been a policeman as long as I have you get a sort of instinct for these things . . .'

'A hunch?'

'Exactly. A hunch. And mine tells me the Queen of Denmark story is all poo. Do you feel like changing or adding to it?'

I said nothing.

'Not feeling talkative? That's OK. In my experience peepers are never the most chatty of people, but I have a way of dealing with that.' He walked over to a cupboard and brought out a monkey wrench. A big one. The sort mechanics use to loosen the wheel nuts on giant earth-moving machinery. He waved it in front of me and rattled the bars with it. The muscles of my groin tightened and I took an involuntary step back from the bars. He laughed and walked over to the radiator. He put the wrench on the valve and began twisting it shut. After he had finished he did the three others along the corridor. Then he brought out a long hooked pole and opened all the skylights. The cold, damp air swirled in and the temperature plunged.

'Brrrr!' he said.

Miss Evangeline began to shiver violently.

'Oh yes, I do so like to hear people chattering.'

'Look,' I said, 'this is between you and me. Let Miss Evangeline go, or take her to a warm cell. She doesn't have to suffer this.'

'Tell me who your client is, you asshole peeper, and we can all go home, including ... Miss Evangeline.' He put on a silly accent to say her name and I knew then that it was hopeless. There was no point appealing to his better side: he didn't have one. He was made from the same stuff as Tadpole: industrial waste from the arsenic factory. He walked to the wall and unhooked the fire hose.

'OK, I'll tell you,' I said.

He grinned and aimed the fire hose at me. 'Shoot!'

'She's ... er ... he's ... it's ... oh, what's the point? You won't believe me.'

'Try me.'

'It's someone – I don't know his name, we meet in secret – but it's someone from the police, undercover, some sort of secret investigation.'

He laughed. I would have laughed, too; it was pathetic.

He brought the fire hose up and said, 'Yeah, well, I'll check that out. In the meantime we're going to play a party game called Pass the Pneumonia. You can tell me in the morning who your client is.'

'Oh, Mr Knight, I'm so cold!'

I took my jacket off and slipped it over Miss Evangeline's shoulders. It was the stupidest thing I ever did.

It took him the bat of an eyelid to work out the implications of my chivalry. Longer than most people would have taken, because he couldn't understand from personal experience why anyone would want to comfort another person like that. But he knew an opportunity to twist the knife when he saw one. You could trace the progress of the penny dropping by the speed of the grin stealing over his face. He turned the hose from me to Miss Evangeline and turned it on. It knocked her off the bed, and by the time I reached her and tried to shield her she was drenched. He turned out the lights and left. I shouted after him: obscenities, and threats, vile insults to wound his manhood, to goad him into returning; but it was no use. He was wise to that one, too. So I shouted at the skylight; shouted until my voice gave out; hoping to alert someone passing by. But the sound of a man's cries coming from the police station window is not unusual. Only when it goes suddenly quiet is it really scary.

I read somewhere that an Eskimo who falls through the ice into the water in Greenland has only one chance of survival. He has to run; anywhere will do as long as he runs. If you stand still you freeze to death in under a minute. I didn't know if it was true; I would have to ask the Queen of Denmark next time she called. I looked at Miss Evangeline shivering and knew she wouldn't want to run anywhere. At such times you realise how many simple facts about this world there are that you should know but don't. Is it better to keep your cold wet clothes on or take them off? But the point was academic, I knew she wasn't going to be taking them off; so I did my best to hold her and keep her warm. She soon lapsed into delirium. She spoke about the horse in the paddock for a while, and gained more lucidity and spoke of the child they took away from her.

'It was a little girl,' she said.

'That's nice.'

'I wonder how she's doing.' And then: 'You could find her, couldn't you? You're a detective.' She paused to collect her breath and control the shivering, as if summoning up the strength for one last important task. 'Couldn't you?'

'I suppose . . .'

'Find her for me, please, Louie. Tell her that her mum didn't want to give her away, tell her there wasn't a day when I didn't think about her. Will you tell her?'

'Yes,' I said.

'It doesn't have to be now. Not tomorrow. But one day.'

'Yes. One day I will find her and tell her.'

'Thank you.'

It was about 2 a.m. when she died.

The next day Calamity bailed me. It was a bright sunny day: the sky as pellucid and blue as a china doll's eyes. We stood at the sea railings, leaning against them, hair ruffled by a soft sea breeze, our faces gilded by the watery sunlight. On such days it was a joy to wake up. Sometimes you had to wonder what the gods were playing at.

'You shouldn't be worrying about me, you've got your own business to run now.'

'We go back a long way, Louie.'

'That's true.'

'No way I could have left you there. You wouldn't have left me.'

'No, but I don't want you . . . you know, to let things slip. You need to work hard to build a business up. How's it going?'

'Oh, pretty slow. Still waiting to hear back from the Pinkertons; can't really do much until then. Sorry I wasn't in when you came round.'

'I haven't been round.'

'Oh. Someone told me they'd seen you knocking on my door.'

'No.'

'Must have been someone else.'

There was a pause and we were distracted by a man in a sandwich board walking past. 'HOFFMANN IS COMING,' it said. The End was, it seemed, no longer nigh. The Apocalypse had been postponed. Calamity made a slight, embarrassed shrug, as if the world had gone to pot during my night in jail and she was somehow to blame.

'There are a lot of rumours going about,' she said. 'They reckon he's coming. Some say he'll turn up at the carol concert.'

'Pure craziness.'

'I know. Who would fall for a thing like that?'

'Who?' Who indeed, I thought. Tinker, tailor, Soldier for Jesus, gaoler . . . Take your pick. The people in the client's chair have one more stop on the run from the wishing well to the priest.

'Where did you get the money for a bail?' I said.

'It was only fifty quid.'

'I know. Where did you—'

'Oh! Before I forget,' said Calamity, 'I need to tell you . . . I did something . . . I did a tail job on the boy who collects the pies. He takes the empties to Erw Watcyns.'

'Really?'

'Yes.'

'That's very interesting. Where did you get the fifty quid?'

Silence.

'Calamity?'

'Oh, you know . . .'

'Oh, no! You didn't . . . Not the book . . . ?'

'It's OK.'

'You haven't sold it?'

'I pawned it. I can get it back if you don't jump bail.'

'That's good.'

'Yes.'

'I'm going to jump bail.'

'I know.'

*   *   *

It's the one thing they never tell you about in the movies: the hard manual labour. You see people walking around all the time – shaking martinis, playing tennis, clutching long cigarette holders – but they never tell you about the problems you get when you kill one of them, when you take away their means of self-propulsion. It's a can of worms. It's like having a dead cow in the living room. And then there's the mess. That's another thing they don't talk about. When people can still move about they have a thing called delicacy. They go to secret places to empty themselves. It's not the same when they're dead. They don't care any more. They're just offal. They spill themselves all over your carpet. You can spend all morning mopping up the blood, but a lifetime is not enough. The forensic boys will come along and laugh at you. They spray the room with special chemicals and turn on an ultra-violet light and hey presto! the stains are back, shining in glorious Technicolor. The floor is as clean as a new pin and guess what? Something red seeped through the gaps in the floorboards. All you did was give him a little bang on the head; you put news-paper down; there was no mess. But it forms an invisible aerosol cloud and floats around unseen like a thought bubble; ten million microscopic droplets. They only need to find one and you're off to the chair. The forensic boys laugh at you; they love you; they eat you for breakfast.

What are you going to do with all that meat, anyway? All that gristle and cartilage, and bone, a stomach full of undigested food and an arse full of shit? Where are you going to put it? What are you going to use? Kitchen utensils? It's like demolishing a piano with a pair of scissors. The only one that's any good is the ice-cream scoop to take out the eyes. And even then one of them rolls under the sofa and won't turn up again for years. And boy, do they struggle! They flail and scratch and gurgle; they bite and kick; they stick a finger in your eye and pull your hair . . . Those poor crazed African dictators couldn't take it any more. Just couldn't watch. They came up with a better idea: put two people in a cell with a sledgehammer and tell them to sort it out between themselves. One of you goes free. You decide. And hose the place down afterwards.

It's the one thing they never mention in the movies. We're too effete these days: we don't have the strength. Just ask old Doc Sawbones in his frock coat and blood-spattered top hat how hard it is to remove a limb: he'll tell you. Try using an axe. Chop, chop, chop . . . They'll still get you. You'll run out of bin bags. Or a bit of bone goes in your eye and turns sceptic. The surgeon who takes it out is an amateur sleuth. The worst sort. Sticks it under the microscope and knows it all: it's amazing what they can see. Young female, early twenties, five foot six in her socks, blonde hair, blue eyes, twenty-six-inch waist, had cornflakes for breakfast. All from a splinter. OK, Louie, let's go through it again, and this time skip the fairy stories. How did you get DOA's thigh bone in your eye? I don't know, I keep telling you, I was chopping wood and I must have slipped. How do you explain the cornflake? It's from your packet, the lab boys gave us a perfect match . . . Yes, it's the one thing they never mention in the movies. You can't burn them, you can't hide them, you can't cut them up; you can't do anything with them. They're made from the toughest substance known to man: man. In case you're wondering, it's why I will never kill Erw Watcyns.

Chapter 16

BESIDES THE CHAPLAIN there were four mourners at Miss Evangeline's funeral: the director of the nursing home, one of the patients, a woman from the social services, and, standing some distance away, Lorelei, the one-eyed street-walker who used to visit Miss Evangeline. A small lane runs through Llanbadarn cemetery, and in the late afternoon gloom the streetlamp was already lit. She stood like a sentinel under the lamp, surrounded by swirling white moths of snow; her mouth a scarlet fissure across the powdery moonscape of her face. It was as if she was reluctant to get too close, as if a life being made to feel unwelcome at any sort of respectable gathering had led to ingrained habits that were hard to dissolve, even for the funeral of an old friend. We stood together and listened to the drone of the chaplain's words. Watched them lower the coffin into the ground. Listened to the thud of dirt on hollow wood. When there was nothing more to watch we walked down Elm Tree Avenue together and on down Queen's Road to the Prom.

We went to the Cliff Railway station café and ordered two teas just as they were closing. Teas served with sullen ill-will because the appearance of two customers at this hour would make the woman late closing. Lorelei took out a metal flask and poured shots of whisky into the tea. The woman closing up with unnecessary bangs and accusatory crashes threw a look of dis-approval. This was an unlicensed café, I could lose my licence. The last train of the evening clanked down to rest on the buffers. No one got off, no one got on. On a night like tonight there was no point trying to escape. Better to drink. To wassail.

'Not much of a turn-out,' said Lorelei.

From the radio in the kitchen came the haunting anthem of all troubled Christmases: *Silent night, holy night. All is calm, all is bright.* The simple ditty that made the soldiers in the Great War lay down their arms and play football. Then pick them up and start shooting each other again. There is no better cameo in all the annals of human history for demonstrating the futile insanity of war.

'Mind you, I'll be lucky to get four turn up when I go.'

I squeezed her hand in an attempt to reassure. 'Does it really matter, once you've gone, who turns up to the funeral?' I said.

Lorelei considered. 'We were quite close in school. Then we lost touch.'

'How long have – had you been visiting her at the nursing home?'

'About ten years. I left town for a while, then when I came back I heard about her from someone, so I started going to see her.'

'She kept talking about a child.'

'Yes. I never knew about it at the time.'

'I promised her I'd try and find it.'

She nodded.

'Was I wrong, do you think?'

'It's not for me to say.'

'A dying woman's wish. I could hardly say no.'

'No, I suppose not. That Erw Watcyns . . . Someone should do something.'

I asked her if she had heard of a soldier called Caleb Penpegws, because all boys who fought in that war, as in all wars, must have passed on their way to the front through the arms of someone like Lorelei.

'There were so many boys,' she said. 'I never remembered the names. But there's a man at the Pier, Eifion. He might know.'

I paid for the teas and just before we stood up to leave Lorelei said, 'Will you kill Erw Watcyns?'

I looked at her in surprise, unsure whether she was asking me to do it or asking if I planned to. She saw the look on my face and nodded and said, 'It's all right. I know. I'm sorry I said that.'

We walked out into the falling snow; the Prom was hushed and filled with a soft luminescence. Light was a thing you had to be very wary of. In summer it flashed in strange, haunting fashion off the hot chrome bumpers of distant cars turning at Castle Point. All cars have chrome, so why should a flash like that stop you and make you long for things you cannot name? We stood at the brim of the Wishing Well, maintained by the Round Table, and heavily padlocked against wish-thieves.

'Make a wish,' I said.

'I could do with some shoes that don't pinch.' She looked down at her feet, clad in old grey vinyl trainers, the ones put out by one of the high-street chains in a forlorn attempt to imitate a famous brand.

'That Salvation Army shop has plenty on display.'

'Army Surplice? They always charge me double.'

'You never find charity where they advertise it.'

'Oxfam are nice enough.'

I threw in a 50p piece and made a wish about Myfanwy and Christmas and snow.

Son of God, love's pure light, and then the line I liked best: *Sleep in Heavenly peace*. But only children know the secret of how to do that. It's a different country when you grow up.

An old man approached the Wishing Well and stopped when he noticed us. I could understand; being caught making a wish is undignified, like reading pornography. It was Elijah and he was crying. Instinct or tact made Lorelei step away into the shadows.

Elijah said, 'I am sorry about your little girl, what I did: pulling the gun.'

'It's OK.'

'I am astounded at what has become of me.'

'You just got carried away.'

'That is what astounds me most. All my life I have made it a point of principle not to get carried away. Giving in to passion is for fools.'

'And for human beings.'

'This, you see, is the poison of Hoffmann. May the ever-merciful Lord blight and curse that fiend.'

'They say he is coming. They say the name means Hopeman.'

Elijah scoffed. 'They! Who are they? The peasants of Aberystwyth? What do they know, the poor ignorant fools? They see a word painted in blood and they think their troubles are over.'

'You don't think he'll come?'

'You ask that of me, a man who has spent a lifetime searching for this chimera? You think this ignis fatuus will just turn up and sing "Away in a Manger"?' He scoffed again.

'If that's the case, why don't you give up your quest? Can it really be so important now, after all these years? Surely most of the people involved must be dead?'

'Two brothers I have lost to this cause. Two lovely brothers, two of the noblest men ever to walk the earth . . . First there was delightful Ham the poet; and then delicate Absalom, the prophet and scholar. I never knew a human heart so little visited by the vice of pride as Absalom's. He was willing to wear the ludicrous red robes of a Christian icon and work in a department store in order to fill his belly with bread – honourable bread – rather than shame his family by begging. Both those boys were superior to me in so many ways. Sometimes I wish God had taken me in their stead. You ask me to give up my quest, after such a price has been paid? After my family has lost so much? I should pack my bag and go home to the grave of my dear beloved Mama and tell her I could not save her sons; I could not find them because I lacked the strength to carry on when so near my goal? You ask me to do that? You ask me to dishonour myself.'

'But if he's not coming . . .'

'Did I say that? You asked if I thought he would turn up and announce himself to the people of Aberystwyth and I said no. But all the same I feel that he is here. And so must my brother Absalom have felt it, too. Otherwise, why would he have come?'

'But Absalom came in search of Ham.'

'Yes, and Ham was seeking Hoffmann. By finding one you find the other. Such are the perplexities that confront me. And yet you could so easily lift my burden by telling me what your girl found in the alley.'

'Why don't you lift my burden and tell me what was in the coat pocket, the one stolen from Eichmann?'

'You offer to trade?'

'That's fair, isn't it?'

'The item in the pocket was the list of names of people who attended Eichmann's weekly card game.'

'Just a list of names?'

'Ah, but think who would be on that list. Think who would want to see it. Every Nazi fugitive in Patagonia would be on it. What wouldn't the Israeli secret service give for that information? What wouldn't Odessa give to see that they did not get it?'

'So why did the Americans want it?'

'Because the Israelis wanted it. And the Russians wanted it because the Americans wanted it.'

'Who is killing all these people?'

'The Pieman.'

'Who does he work for?'

'Hoffmann.'

'And who does he work for?'

'Welsh Intelligence.'

'Do they also want the list of names?'

'Oh yes, they want it more badly than any of them.'

'Why?'

'Because the people on that list were witnesses to the commission of an evil crime.'

'What sort of crime?'

'One so grave it caused a priest, so they say, to lose his wits.'

'Yes, but what was it?'

'I don't know.'

'Hey! We're supposed to be trading ...'

'Truly, I don't know. I haven't the faintest idea. It's your turn now, anyway.'

'The item we found was just a picture of Butch Cassidy and the Sundance Kid.'

Elijah's face flashed with anger and disappointment. 'Even now he mocks me. After I treat fairly with him, he cheats me, the *Gonif*.

'It's true.'

'Oh yes, it's true! A picture of Butch Cassidy and the Sundance Kid? You like to swindle me, heh? You ... you ... *moyshe Pupik*! You ... you *chiam Yankel* ... with your *Shikseh* from the *Shandhoiz*!'

'But it was! Truly!'

'Of course it was a picture of Butch Cassidy. But what else?' He threw his hands up in weary despair and walked off, shouting, 'I throw salt in your eyes! And pepper in your nose, you *Kucker*!'

Lorelei and I walked the length of the Prom. She was taking me to see an old soldier called Eifion, one of those sad, benighted fools who are addicted to the Laughing Policeman machine. It was too early to find him and we headed for the Castle for a drink. At the shelter overlooking the crazy golf course a man stood on an orange-box preaching to a small crowd. It was the army chaplain, the one who left his wits behind in Patagonia. His voice drifted over and we stopped to listen.

'. . . and yet, like many here tonight, they had no stomach for the truth. They expected me to pull a rabbit out of a hat and say, "It's not really happening; you're not really ensnared in a tragedy from which the only escape is the grave; you're not really about to die in a cause that no one here can remember any more the point of." I tried to show them, to make them see how little a thing to be feared is death. I said, "Why do you fear to die?" And they did not know. The fools did not know why. I told them. We fear death because in looking upon it we contemplate our non-existence and see how utterly the world will be unchanged by our absence from it; and, even more terrifyingly, how little difference it would have made to the world if we had never existed at all. A few minutes is all it would have taken at the dawn of our life for us never to become even a spark in the eternal night. Imagine it! He who was to be your father comes home and pauses to scrape some dog poo off his shoe. And lo! the universe is different. He does not mount that woman who would have been your mother; that night they watch TV instead. Their first child, the one that is no longer you, is conceived the following night. So easily could you not have existed. And therein lies our salvation, because if that is the case, if our existence is really such a trivial accident, what pain could it possibly cause us to end it? This I said to them and they repudiated me for it.'

The chaplain paused to catch his breath; his brow was glistening with sweat.

'It is a curious thing that a man mortally wounded on the battlefield, when he knows his end is near, will cry for his mother. I used to walk among them and say, "Oh yes, now you cry for your mummy, you big baby, you big ninny, you hopeless cissy! Have you never considered how little she would have noticed if you had not been born? And yet here in your final moments, with the last of your strength, you cry to her!"' He paused again and said softly, more to himself than to the assembled crowd, 'What a fucking nightmare. Let us pray.'

*   *   *

The bar was gloomy, illuminated only by flashes of colour from two fruit machines against the wall. I used to like playing them in the days when you just pulled a handle and no other input was needed. But I didn't understand them any more. Nowadays you needed a pilot's licence to operate them though it was difficult to see why: for all the extra sophistication the outcome never changed. How could it, since it was fixed by law? Perhaps it was all just a metaphor, an easily understood parable for the citizens of the town, which illuminated the cruel but strangely popular Calvinist doctrine of predestination. For reasons we can only guess at, it is said that God decides before we are born which of us are to be saved and which consigned to eternal damnation; and not just before we were born, but before anyone was born. Before He started work on the universe, before He had even laid the first brick, it had been ordained who would be lost and who would be saved; and which of us would serve our time in Aberystwyth. Nothing we do on this earth makes a blind bit of difference. God pulls the arm, the wheels spin, we are damned or saved. All you can do is hope He gives better odds than the publican.

A figure detached itself from the dark and walked over to our table. A man's shadow spread across Lorelei's white, powdery face. We looked up. It was Erw Watcyns.

'This is a nice surprise,' he said with the air of one who doesn't like surprises. 'Two of Aberystwyth's noblest professions sharing a drink. The whore and the shamus.'

'Now you're here, we've got the set,' I said.

He laughed. His eyes were glittering from the effects of drink. 'Enjoy your jokes, Shamus, I'm not interested in you tonight.' And then to Lorelei, 'It's you I want tonight, hotpants.'

She raised her eyes in an understanding that took me a second longer to grasp.

'She's done nothing . . .' I began, but the sneer on his face told me that this was not about what she had done; but about what he would make her do.

'Not yet she hasn't; but she will. Get your coat.'

She stood up with the weary air of a prizefighter who had hoped the referee would count her out. 'Please, Louie, pay no mind. I'll be back in twenty minutes.'

I sat and drank my pint along with the handful of people who were in the bar that night; people for whom drinking was less a pleasure than a ritual which imposed structure on the terrifying abyss of time stretching between now and the grave. I thought about the people in my client's chair. What did they expect? Why did they come? Because nothing ever turned out they way they hoped. Really? What were you hoping for? I don't know, it's so long ago now. I was seventeen. Full of bubbling expectancy, latency for things I couldn't name. I just assumed something would turn up. Guess what? Nothing did.

The people in my client's chair.

Have you thought about a Promised Land? That often helps. Patagonia is one, but there are plenty more to choose from. Just follow the Yellow Brick Road. Can't miss it. It snakes over hill and dale, curves and wriggles over the landscape and round church spires, and is lost somewhere in the gentle mauve haze of evening. The Promised Land. The address is easy to remember: yonder.

I looked at my watch and slid off my chair. I walked out into the cold night air and stood in the porch of the pub, a three-sided alcove with three doors as if ingress to the sanctuary was of vital importance and no time could be lost admitting the patrons. Across the road, beyond the railings, the sea roared with the usual muted thunder, like a storm beyond the hills. There was a scrape of shoe sole on gritty pavement, the sort of sole that my ears, with that otherworldly intensification of the senses which sometimes happens in nights like this, detected as belonging to sensible shoes; ones worn by nuns and district nurses and the terminally insane. A face popped out of the darkness into the light of the the porch, like the ghost train at the fair; a bright moon of a face, tear-stained and with eyes shining in fear like those of a colt disturbed in a byre by a thunderstorm. Crowning the face, across the forehead, was a dishevelled bandage. It was Tadpole, looking like Frankenstein's monster. I jumped back, startled, half-expecting a bolt of lightning to hit the spire above the pub and fill Tadpole's veins with current. She looked deep into my face, breathing heavily, features wild. Neither of us spoke and then just as suddenly she darted away across the road. A car driver hit the horn and swerved, tyres squealed, but she reached the other side and banged into a lamppost, ricocheted off and gathered a momentum which took her to the railings. She rebounded off them like a wrestler off the ropes and fell to the ground in a misshapen sprawl. Her sobs resounded across the tarmac, adding a sad harmonic to the thunder from the beach. I walked across and knelt down beside her, put my hand on her back. She throbbed like a frightened animal. It was the easiest thing in the world to despise someone like Tadpole. But was she responsible for being despicable? She just played the hand she was dealt, like the rest of us. Could Myfanwy take credit for being beautiful and beloved? If she burned her face badly in a car crash, would she still infect people with the joy that accounted for her popularity? Tadpole was one of the most unpleasant girls I knew, but also the unhappiest, and these things are not disconnected.

'I know what you're thinking,' she snivelled, 'about Miss Evangeline. But it wasn't me, it was Erw Watcyns. I know what you think, I know you hate me . . .' She sobbed into her hands.

I made no attempt to deny that I blamed her or hated her. Maybe she was telling the truth, but I knew that if she was guilty she would still be here lying about it, saying: 'it wasn't me'.

'I was going to tell you, at the caravan. When I came round for my pants, I was going to tell you.'

'Tell me what?'

'About Hoffmann. I know who he is. You'll be amazed when you find out. I was going to tell you and then, and then . . .' She collapsed again into convulsions of sobs. I waited. 'All I wanted was for you to like me. All that stuff, it wasn't true. I said it to impress you. I haven't really had lots of dates. I ... I've never had a boyfriend. Only once, some lad took me on his motorbike and ... did it in the hedge. He left me there. Now all his mates point at me when they see me. No one liked me in school, no one's ever liked me.'

'I like you,' I said.

'No, you don't. You're just saying it so I'll tell you who Hoffmann is.'

'I'm not. I don't give a damn. Honest.'

'I had some whisky.'

There's nothing wrong with that. I drink, too, when I'm unhappy.'

'They say you shouldn't.'

'Sure.'

'I don't usually drink. It made me feel sick.'

And then she was. I tried to reposition her so she could throw up over the ledge of the pavement, onto the beach, but it wasn't easy. She didn't have the will to try, so the stuff flowed down over her shoulder. I took out a handkerchief and wiped her mouth. I brushed a wet straw of hair aside; her tear-stained cheeks glistened in the streetlamp.

'Better?'

She nodded. 'Louie?'

'Yes?'

'Kiss me.'

I tried not to react.

'Just for Christmas. A Christmas kiss. I've never had one. Please.'

I bent forward into the fumes of her ammoniac breath and gave her a peck on the corner of her mouth.

She smiled. 'Thank you.'

I helped her to her feet, rearranged her coat, like a mother getting a kid ready for school.

'Louie, let's go away.'

The sinews of my body stiffened.

'Take me away, now, tonight. We could go to Shrewsbury, or London. I've got fifty pounds in the bank. You can have it . . .' The words trailed off. 'Louie.'

'It's not possible.'

'Why?'

'It just isn't.'

'You said you liked me.'

'I do.'

'It's because of her, isn't it? Myfanwy?'

I thought for a second. I was about to deny it, but that felt like a betrayal. 'It's because of her and lots of things. I said I liked you, that doesn't mean—'

She jerked herself away from me and said, 'I was going to tell you about Hoffmann, but I'm never ever ever ever going to tell you now, you bastard. Never.'

She waddled drunkenly off along the sugar-white railings of the Prom, that railway line where they shunt human woe all through the night.

When Lorelei returned she looked stricken; maybe that was normal after a trick. She gave me a slight nod and we left. Outside the Old College she said, 'Hang on a sec,' and pulled an eye dropper from her bag. She tilted her head back and let some drops fall onto her glass eye. 'Artificial tears. My tear ducts don't work – it's called Sjögren's syndrome.' She strode off, newly wetted eyes glistening like a rain-slicked street after a storm. I followed thinking, In Aberystwyth it's not just the harlot's smile that is bought.

Chapter 17

I T WAS A QUIET night in the Pier arcade. The machines flashed unattended. The evening bingo had finished and the midnight game was still a couple of hours away. The money-changer girl sat in her booth, watching a portable TV that had once been a prize in the bingo. We walked past her, past the video games, towards the back and the more traditional machines. A lone man sat on a stool in front of a glass case, inside which sat a crudely articulated doll of a policeman. You put in a shilling and the doll became animated and laughed. The laughter was staccato and unconvincing, the movement not much more than a shake, the eyes blue and wooden; and that was all. After a minute or so the laughter stopped and you put in another coin.

The man who sat on the stool wore a cloth cap and a tan tartan scarf like the coats that pampered lapdogs wear. His raincoat was old and greasy. He was thin and hunched on the stool, his expression blank like the face of a statue in a public square whose features have been worn away by wind and rain. The only part of him that moved or exuded a sign of warmth or ability to emote was white and protruded from the breast pocket of his coat. It was a mouse. When the policeman's laughter reached its zenith the man would look down at the mouse and the mouse, whose eyes were glittering with enjoyment, would break off gazing at the policeman and peep up at the man and there passed between them a look of complicit understanding; as if there was a secret to this pastime, a layer of meaning which was unavailable to people like me, but which would, if only I possessed the key, unlock a rich seam of humour hidden away in the pantomime.

Or at least it must have been something like that since the laughter of policemen on its own has never in my experience been a source of entertainment to the recipient. It is usually sarcastic and sneering and hopelessly narcissistic and worlds away from the genuine variety that makes the eye twinkle.

We stood and watched for a while. When the laughing ceased the man dug around in his coat pocket and found another coin to reanimate the doll. He did it without visible sign of pleasure, or of having had to deliberate. It was automatic: the action of a man who has no choice, like a chain smoker who starts the next cigarette before the current one is finished. Once he had found the coin and allowed the evident relief to shimmer around the edges of his mouth, he looked up and offered a look of polite enquiry to Lorelei.

'This is Louie. He's asking about a man called Caleb Penpegws. Louie this, I believe, is Eifion and Tiresias.'

There was a pause, slightly awkward, because protocol demanded that the man on the stool speak but he didn't.

I tried a light-hearted comment. 'Which one's which?'

The man looked annoyed. 'You should read your Greek tragedy, then you wouldn't have to ask.'

'You're probably right, but they refuse to give me a ticket at the library.'

'Tiresias was the blind soothsayer. Do I look like a sooth-sayer?'

'So you're Eifion.'

'Yes.'

'Is the mouse blind?'

'All mice are practically blind, but Tiresias has sinus problems which means he can't smell very well; if you're a rodent, not being able to smell is like being blind, isn't it? That's how they find their prey.'

'And their cheese.'

'It's a myth that mice love cheese.'

'Can he see the future?'

Eifion furrowed his brow in mild annoyance and looked at Lorelei.

'I'm sorry,' I said. 'It's not important. I wanted to ask you about your buddy from the war, Caleb Penpegws.'

Eifion slipped off the stool and walked past us and out onto the Prom. I said goodbye to Lorelei and followed him home. He lived in the old hall of residence at the end of the Prom, the one earmarked for demolition. He walked round the side of the ugly grey building to the entrance that would have been called the tradesman's entrance in the days when tradesmen knew their place. He knew I was following him but made no attempt to stop me. A piece of composite board hung across the back door. He pulled it aside and walked through. I followed. He walked across floors covered in cement grit and dusty, fallen roofing joists. Here and there my foot detected in the darkness the smoother traction of municipal floor tiles. The only light came from holes in the roof and the sheen of street lamps outside squeezing past the boards that had been nailed over windows.

He climbed the stairs, rising flight by flight, until he reached a final landing and then walked down a corridor past a kitchen where now only ghosts wrote their names on the cartons of milk in the fridge. He stopped outside a room that had a padlock on the door, unlocked and went in leaving it open for me to follow.

Inside, he flicked a lighter and began to light a forest of candles glued by spilled wax to the surface of a coffee table. The golden light warbled and made the shadows dance. There were some beaten-up easy chairs, rescued from a dump, perhaps, and now spilling their horsehair innards onto the floor. There were bottles and plates and silver trays of take-away food. Pet food for the mouse spilled out onto the table top. On the floor there were saucers of what had been milk but that had been licked away by a small tribe of cats which peered from the shadows, their eyes gleaming like pale green candle flame. In the corner was a dirty mattress lying on the floor. Cobwebs brushed my face. It was grim, but probably no worse than in the days when the place had been a hall of residence.

Eifion motioned me to sit and I eased myself gingerly into an armchair.

'Aren't the cats a threat to Tiresias?' I asked.

He shook his head. 'I've brought them up to respect the sanctity of all life. That's a lesson I learned in the war.' He took a tin of throat lozenges from his pocket and prised off the lid; but carefully, as if he was worried he might spill the contents. I peered forward and he held the tin out for me to see. It contained dead flies. He picked one out with a pair of tweezers and went over to feed a spider. 'Come on, my beauties,' he said. 'Dinner time.'

'What about the sanctity of the fly's life?'

'The flies aren't real. I make them out of soya.'

I watched as he worked. It wasn't easy to get the dead 'fly' to balance on the spider silk, but he was methodical and patient; soon he had fed his entire herd of spiders.

'Caleb Penpegws,' I said, feeling a great weariness manifest itself in all my limbs.

He sat down and said in the dreamy tone that sometimes accompanies reminiscence but more often play-acting. 'Yes, I seem to remember a man of that name, but it's all so long ago, you understand.'

I sighed; the weariness was now so great even sighing felt like weightlifting. 'Yes, I understand. This is the bit where you have trouble remembering and I say, "Oh maybe a five-pound note will help you recall," and miraculously it does for a while. But then, once we get halfway through your story, the lights go out again and I have to put some more money in the meter. And so it goes on until a few simple pieces of information – the sort which a normal person would be only to happy to volunteer – end up costing me twenty quid. Yes I think I know how this story goes. It has a depressingly familiar ring to it; perhaps it's déjá vu, or perhaps it's . . . What do they call it? Reincarnation? Or is it transmigration of souls? . . . As a classical scholar you will surely know . . . Yes, something like that. Maybe we met in a different lifetime; you were a priest officiating in a minor temple beside the Nile and I was a palace shamus working for King Otephep III or something. Or maybe it's not that at all, maybe it's just I've spent way too much of my shitty life playing this scene: sitting in a filthy pigsty room with lowlife nobodies, asking simple questions and getting in return wisecracks or a feigned amnesia that slowly lifts; or just gouts of infuriatingly imprecise Talmudic wisdom; when all I asked for was a simple sentence composed of easily understood English words. I don't know, it feels like I've spent my whole life doing this and know the script off by heart.

'But tonight it's going to be different. I'm sick of that story; I'm re-writing the script. I'm tired of risking my life on behalf of the people of Aberystwyth; trying to help them; trying to bring justice to birth; trying and failing – but failing heroically – to somehow wrest the tiller from the hands of fate once in a while and make things better than they should be, or than the people of this town ever have the right to expect; and doing it all for so little money I'd be ashamed if people found out. Tonight is not going to be like that. Tonight I'm going to ask you a civil question and you are going to give me a straightforward answer; the sort you would give to your mother if she asked you what you wanted for your tea. And the reason you are going to do it is simple. You will do it because it's the right thing to do; because it's the decent thing to do; because two men who have no reason to hate each other should be able to sit in a room and have a nice conversation, one in which the one helps the other for no other recompense than the joy that comes from offering a hand of help to a wayfarer lost in the gloom of this world.

'You're going to do it because of all these things I have mentioned and because you are a good person underneath it all, a man who has suffered for sure, but still a man. I can see that from the very fact that you are here in front of me today. You are a man who fought and looked into the abyss in Patagonia, where many men forfeited their wits; and yet returned, it seems to me, with most of them intact. Thus you are a man, but being a man entails certain duties and responsibilities, chief of which is to bear your suffering well and sort it out alone; and never make it a burden to another man, who will assuredly have pain of his own in his soul which decency forbids him from showing you. You must, alas, shoulder your cross and not whinge. It is not easy, but being a man is not easy. For all these reasons you will help me here tonight and for one other reason, which I hoped I would not have to name, but I see alas! from the look in your eye that I do; namely this: you will help me, because if you don't I'm going to make you eat that mouse.' I finished and exuded a long, long sigh, almost completely enervated by the effort of what I had said.

There was silence for a long time after my speech ended. I smiled. He said nothing. I smiled again. He chewed a nail and looked at Tiresias; kissed the little rodent. He picked up a box of fire lighters and made a small fire in the grate. It gave me an idea what I might do if he refused to co-operate. It wasn't a nice idea and made me hope Tiresias wasn't blessed with the gift of prophecy. It never does you any good, anyway. Ask Oedipus. Finally, Eifion spoke.

'Caleb Penpegws and I were wounded at the Mission House siege. We lay side by side on stretchers in the field hospital. One day some men turned up and took him away. I didn't see him again until five years later, back in Barmouth. He told me they tortured him for a week about some coat they said he'd stolen. They wanted to know about this Hoffmann guy who everybody's talking about. I said, "Hey, great to see you again, buddy," and all that. I could see he wasn't happy, so I suggested we go on the

Fairbourne railway together. Thought it might cheer him up. We used to love riding that train. But he didn't seem interested. He went all sort of misty and stuff, and said, "What's the point?"'

Eifion looked baffled. 'I guess it must change a man being tortured.'

'Where can I find him?'

'Not in this world, that's for sure.'

'Dead?'

'For many years now.'

'Is it true an angel appeared on the eve of the battle?'

He picked up the mouse and held him in one hand and stroked with the other. 'Yes, it is true'

'You really saw it?'

'I really saw it.' He put the mouse down and rested his chin in his cupped hands.

'There was a little girl up in the mountains, a little goatherd. There was a spring up there, where she used to water the herd. The angel used to appear there to her and tell her stuff. She was famous and the peasants for miles around would go to see her and listen to her describe her angel. So me and some of the guys went along and spoke to the girl. We told her how scared we were and could she ask her angel to watch over us during the coming battle. Because, you see, we all knew the mission was madness. We knew none of us would come back alive. The little girl said she would ask her angel. And lo! on the eve of the battle she appeared among us, riding a shining white horse. It could have been a different angel, but what are the odds of there being two of them in Patagonia at the same time? Beautiful, she was, all shining white and pure and holy and all sorts of shit. Looking at her was like . . . I don't know . . . It was like how you feel as a kid in church on Christmas Eve when you looked at the beautiful image of Christ in the stained-glass window. As a kid you're not listening all that closely to what's being said, but at that moment you look at Him in the window and you hear the words,

"Once in Royal David's City" or something and you just feel for that moment that there really is a greater Father who loves you and will make it all right in the end.

'That's what it was like looking at this angel on her horse. She stirred up our hearts and filled us with courage, and I suppose you could say she filled us with the Holy Ghost – all of us, the non-believers, too. At that moment our fear evaporated like dew on a summer's morn; death no longer held terrors for us. What would it mean, other than a transition to the state of Grace the angel had given us a glimpse of? How could a man whose life is normally full of trouble and vexation fear such a thing? The next morning we arose at dawn and went out to fight with the hearts of lions. Nothing could dismay us.' He paused and wiped the back of his sleeve across his nose. I realised he was crying silently in the darkness. His cheeks glistened with silver snailtrails in the candlelight. He snivelled and spoke in a voice that warbled out of control.

'What the fuck was she thinking?' He shuddered as sobs swept through him. He repeated the words, but this time in a pitch nearer that of a whining dog. 'What was that angel thinking?'

I sat and watched the man weep into his hands. Tiresias climbed up his sleeve and put a tiny mouse paw of comfort on his finger, but to no avail. I stood up and said, 'Is that what made the priest lose his wits?'

He shook his head behind the hands and said in a muffled voice, 'No, it was what came next.'

'What did come next?'

He opened his hands and looked through them at me. 'I can't tell you; my lips cannot utter it. All I can say is this. If I was that angel, I would never have gone back.'

Chapter 18

THE DESK DIARY said today was the shortest day: the moment the tide of light changed from ebb to flow, the highwater mark of night. It must have been tough working it out in the days before desk diaries, but nothing was more important. They had good reason to fear the dark, huddled together for warmth in their wooden halls. It was full of terrors. The evil men who had been cast out from the bosom of society and lived in the dark forests grew leaner and more desperate; travel was treacherous. Malevolent spirits, incorporeal, came out at night and waltzed through the wooden walls and locked doors and took away whoever they wished. No one was safe, but the old people, those whitebeards over twenty-five, had most to fear. They sat awake at night, too frightened to close their eyes; sleep, the one balm, now a Judas. They huddled together and threw great logs of oak onto the fires and licked the grease from their fingers. They put their best priests on the task of measuring the lengthening night; augurers who divined the year's pulse in the sweat of the gravedigger's brow, and the fat on the ribs of his children. When they pronounced the moment had arrived, the morning after the longest night, it meant the worst was over; the time had come to bring in the Yule log, and to wassail. You had passed the halfway mark, there was hope. You could maybe make the long run in till spring. All you had to do was get to the end of the shortest day. Piece of cake.

*　　*　　*

Myfanwy was leaving.

She stood in the middle of the office, as if reluctant to come in too far, anxious not to make it last longer than necessary. She did not want a cup of tea.

'I think it's best this way.'

'Uh-huh.'

'I'll be leaving on the bus to Shrewsbury tonight, after the carol concert.'

'OK.'

'I'll stay with my auntie. Maybe I can help out in the shop – you know, start a new life.'

I sat at the desk, resting my head on the palm of one hand. I felt grimy and unwashed, unshaved; mouth filled with old beer; teeth gritty with old rum and not enough food. My head ached. I dragged my head up from staring at the desk and said, 'Help out in the shop? That's a great idea.'

'Don't make it difficult, Louie.'

'You're a singer. Your place is in Aberystwyth . . . singing. We need you.'

'I just don't feel I can do it any more.'

'You can't go.'

'Please don't try and stop me; you said you would never stand in my way—'

'When did I say that? I never said that.'

'In the caravan.'

'I said I wouldn't stand in Calamity's way.'

'Because you love her?'

'Yes.'

'So you don't love me.'

'Myfanwy, what's happened?'

'Tadpole has explained everything. I—'

'Tadpole!'

'Please don't make this harder than it is. You needn't try to explain.'

'There's nothing to explain.'

'No one's to blame, these things happen. It's not a crime to fall in love.'

'It ought to be if this is what you have to deal with.'

'I hate it when you get like this.'

'Like what?'

'Bitter and dark.'

'You're walking out on me, what did you expect?'

'I think that's a bit rich in view of what you did. Oh, don't say anything, please! I don't want it to be like this. I didn't come here to end in recrimination. It's not your fault, I know. She told me. Told me how it was, and that you never meant it to happen.'

'Myfanwy, this is all fantasy. She only joined the nursing home a few weeks ago. She's a screwball.'

'Is she? I think she's been very brave.'

'Brave? Climbing onto the caravan roof?'

'She let you go, Louie.'

'How did she manage that?'

'If only you knew how hard it was for her. You were the first man she ever loved, did you know that? If only you'd seen her, Louie, how noble she was to let you go like that, if you'd seen how much she cried.'

'I've seen her cry. She does it all the time.'

'But of course I wouldn't hear of it.'

'What are you talking about?'

Her cheek muscles quivered. 'It's no good, Louie. I love you and always will but I'm going to leave because it's for the best.' She turned her face away, towards the window, the drab morning light causing her eyes to glisten. 'We can't argue with the iron laws of fate.'

I stared, mesmerised, at the edges of her eyes, two soft lanterns in the darkness of my life. Pure, soft translucence. 'Did she tell you that?'

'Oh it's too hard, I can't . . . I can't . . .' She wiped her hand roughly across her cheek, as if swatting a fly. The tears ran unheeding.

I sat, unable to think of the words to say, that might make her stay.

'I just wish you hadn't . . . I could forgive everything but that . . . just wish you hadn't given them to her. That's all.' She turned to the door, with her knuckles digging into her eye.

'Given her what?

'M . . . my records.'

'Huh?'

'See! You thought I wouldn't find out, didn't you?'

'But, Myfanwy, I d-didn't. I'd never do such a thing!'

'Don't make it worse by lying, Louie. She's got them all. And you've scribbled my name out and written hers on the l-l-label.'

Myfanwy ran out the door, slammed it behind her. High heels clattered down the bare wooden stairs. I stared at the closed door. I sat there strangely inert, drained of energy. I looked out at the garret across the road. The Pieman's light was still burning. Maybe he would know what to do about Myfanwy. I put on my hat and coat. The phone rang.

'I've named an inlet after you.'

'Lucky me.'

'In Greenland. Louie Knight Sound. Just below Van Hoegafhgaaerden's Land, a hundred and fifty miles south of Ultima Thule. That's what I do, you see. Name inlets.'

'That sounds like my kind of job.'

'Trust me, you wouldn't like. There are so many of them, the whole coastline is perforated like the edge of a postage stamp.'

'Couldn't you have named it Louie's Gulch?'

'What's a gulch?'

'I don't know, but all the tough guys get one named after them.'

'It doesn't sound very Greenlandy.'

'Not to worry. I'm not feeling very tough today.'

'How's the case going?'

'Oh, pretty good. It's largely solved, just tidying up a few loose ends. I was going to send you a report in the new year.'

'I'll look forward to it. Any chance of a heads-up?'

'It's all very complicated and not easy to reduce to a few sentences, but I think we have narrowed the field of enquiry down to a couple of main theories. Theory 1: the dead Father Christmas was a former Mossad agent gunned down because of historical links with Odessa and Butch Cassidy and the Sundance Kid. Or . . .'

'Yes?'

'Or theory 2: he was just an unemployed guy who took a seasonal job and happened to be in the wrong place at the wrong time and got gunned down; and all the rest is moonshine.'

'Hmmm. Quite different sorts of theory. You seem to have covered both ends of the spectrum.'

'It's a special technique I've devised. Start with two theories, the mundane and the outlandish, then work inwards. Never fails.'

'Butch Cassidy and the Sundance Kid eh? I loved that movie.'

'We all did.'

'Sure hope that part of the theory comes good.'

'We're all keeping our fingers crossed on that one.'

'Must go now, I've got "thank you" letters to write. I'll send you some more money for what you've done, and we'll talk after Christmas.'

'OK. Thanks for the inlet.'

'It's nothing.'

The line went click. I replaced the receiver with exaggerated care, anxious not to disturb the silence with an upsetting clack of Bakelite. I don't know why. There was no one here to disturb. I sat and thought about that other guy I pity, the twin of the one who was weaned. He's lying there staring at a bare ceiling. Nothing to look at except discolouration in the distemper.

A strange word that means a dog's disease and cheap municipal paint. His teeth are in a glass on the bedside cabinet, next to the panic button. They keep him drugged because it's cheaper than pictures or ornaments. Everything would be fine but for one thing: he's not stupid. They haven't found a drug that will do that yet. Or, rather, the ones that do can induce unacceptable side-effects such as euphoria and happiness. When the nurse puts her head round the door every morning he knows it's only to see if he's still alive. He can feel the impatience, like the chambermaid's when you stay in your hotel room past noon. In front of other people she adopts a phoney cheery tone of voice, is nice to him in a patronising way. But it's different when they are alone.

He feels like a dog being given a bath by a technician in an animal lab. In the periods of clarity he thinks of how things were many years before in Ynyslas. He digests the honeycomb of happiness gathered long ago and stored in his heart; subsists on it like a chick in the egg devouring the rich protein of the yolk; except he will never break out of this shell. Will fade away and dissolve to nothing in the sea of albumen. Sky, dunes, marram grass ... A train like a tiny blue and green caterpillar far off crawls across the estuary, over a bridge of lollipop sticks and treacle; the estuarial waters glistening and sliding. The train glides without sound as in a silent movie towards Barmouth, along the coast, round the gentle curves, so close to the water you could lean out of the window and catch a fish. The train ducks into a tunnel and as it emerges into the bright summer sun the sea glitters and a party of heliographers in the lead carriage flash their mirrors in unison. He thinks of these things before the drugs kick in and the lids fall. He thinks of the sand dunes, the estuary, a girl with chestnut hair, chasing into the sharp, cold sea; hot breath of an embrace in the foam, her hair wet and sticky, goose bumps flickering along her salty arms ... He winces at the sweet agony of remembrance, the gathered honeycomb of a life. She was a nightclub singer, the one whom the whole town loved, but whom no one loved more deeply than he did . . . What was her name, now? The last ceiling he'll ever see; the last human touch, visits from Nurse Tadpole. She comes in one day with a marker pen and unbuttons his pyjama top. She's giggling, he can smell liquor. He watches, too frail to intervene, as she holds the thick pen like a child and draws on his old white belly. A smiley. Then buttons him up and walks out snorting with suppressed laughter. Is that how it ends? At least I've got an inlet. Myfanwy is leaving. It's time to talk to the Pieman.

Empty pie boxes were strewn outside his door. I knocked and waited. I knocked again, listened, pressed my ear against the door and listened harder. I went in. A small attic room. Bare floor-boards, a reinforced iron bed, a chamber pot filled with yellow liquid, an incident board, a camera on a tripod, and various dark-room paraphernalia. And a fat man was staring out of the window with his back to me. The incident board was similar to ours except for one significant detail: it looked like someone had thrown a fruit pie at it – raspberry or strawberry. But when I looked more closely I saw it was not a fruit pie but the Pieman's brains. One side of his head was missing and on the other side, corresponding to it, was a hole. I was no expert but I'd say he'd been shot. At close range. I touched his clammy skin. It was colder than a bathroom floor in winter. A floorboard creaked and I spun round. Erw Watcyns was standing in the doorway.

He smiled. 'Lousy weather we're having, isn't it?' He walked into the room and looked around. 'I'm glad I found you. I've been looking all over.' He wandered round and pretended to be taken by surprise at the mess on the board, but he said nothing. It was too droll for words. He bent forward, peered at the dead Pieman and said to me, 'What's up with him?'

'I don't know. He hasn't said a word the whole time I've been here.'

'He's probably shy.'

'That's probably it. I knew there'd be an explanation.'

'Some folks are like that, they clam up in company, they don't feel at ease in social situations. You shouldn't hold it against him.'

'I don't.'

'It's psychological.'

'That's OK by me. A man has a right to remain silent if that's the way he feels.'

'That's about the way I see it, too.'

'Most people don't understand. They encounter a silence and they can't resist filling it. They don't care what they fill it with as long as there's some noise.'

'You and me, we think alike. I'm a quiet type. I reckon if you don't have anything worth saying it's better to hold your peace.'

He peered closely at the hole in the Pieman's head. 'Yeah, I sure do like a man who can keep his peace.' He touched the hole with his finger. 'So what do you think you'll be doing for Christmas? Going anywhere special?'

'Oh, I hadn't really thought about it. The usual, I suppose.'

'Stay at home? Yeah, that's the best. Get a few bottles in, stoke up the fire, watch the Queen on the telly.'

'Why did you want to see me, anyway?'

He shrugged dismissively. 'Oh nothing much, just paperwork, really. Someone tried to fence a stolen library book – it came from the police library. It's probably a case of mistaken identity, you know how it goes, but you have to follow these things up.'

'Library book? That sounds serious – you could throw the book at me for that.'

Erw Watcyns became convulsed with fake laughter. 'Hey, that's very funny! You should be on the TV. Oh yes, ha ha! Throw the book at you.'

'I'm always happy to oblige the police.'

'I've noticed that.'

'Anything they want, I'm there to help.'

'You're a model citizen. I wish there were more like you.'

'The thing is, I really don't remember taking out any library books.'

'To tell the truth, we don't think it was you. We think it was your father. As I say, it's purely routine.'

'This wouldn't be a book about the Pinkertons would it?'

'Yes, I think it might be.'

He walked over to the incident board and examined it. 'You've got a board like this in your office, haven't you?'

'Ours doesn't have the fruit pie filling all over it.'

'Is that what this is?'

'I've no idea. What does it taste like?'

He ran his finger through the goo and tasted it. 'It tastes like that stuff coming out the side of his head. It's not fruit, more like meat. Do you prefer sweet or savoury pies?'

'I can go either way.'

'Me, too. Depends on my mood. You know, there's something about all this that isn't quite right.'

'Really?'

'I can't put my finger on it but I have this strange feeling – call it intuition if you like – that I've seen a man who was strangely silent like this before. Only I can't recall where.'

'I hate it when that happens. It's on the tip of your tongue, but the more you try to recall, the more it eludes your grasp.'

'This is driving me nuts. Where've I seen a guy like this before?'

'Take your time, it'll come to you. How did you know I have an incident board like this in my office?'

'I was there a while back looking for you.'

'I see.'

'That's where I saw the library book. Police property, you see, I always notice.'

'Don't they have a statute of limitations on things like that?'

'Of course not. It would encourage people to hang on to the books wouldn't it?'

'That's true. What made you go round to my office in the first place?'

'I wanted to talk to you about a blood-stained photo of Butch Cassidy and the Sundance Kid you removed from the Pier cloakroom. Whoever deposited it left some blood behind on the register; seems it matches the blood of the poor Santa Claus who was so cruelly murdered in Chinatown. Remember us discussing that case a while back?'

It was as if the temperature in the room had dropped ten degrees. People often report feeling like that when a ghost is present, and maybe one had just turned up. Or maybe it was the realisation that his question earlier about where I would be spending Christmas was the first part of a little joke which had as its punch line the sure fact that I would be spending it not watching her Majesty on TV but enjoying her hospitality. You could tell he'd spent all yesterday working it out.

'Bingo!' Watcyns cried in pantomime joy. 'I've got it! I've suddenly remembered where I've seen a guy like this before. In the morgue. Because he was dead.' He turned towards the dead Pieman and shouted, 'I think he's dead!'

'That's right,' I shouted back. 'Someone has blown his fucking brains out.'

'Oh, look over there!' he shouted. 'A gun!' He walked across to the side of the bed. On the floor was a gun. 'Do you suppose it could be the murder weapon?' He threw a sick smile. 'That would be a stroke of luck, wouldn't it?'

The temperature dropped another ten degrees. The gun was the same one, or I guessed it was, that Elijah had pulled on me and then let me take from him; and here it was with my prints all over it.

Erw bent down with that world-weary puff of air of a man who is not as sprightly as he used to be. He pressed a hand onto his thigh to support himself and took out a pencil with the other hand. He lifted the pistol by the trigger guard and put it into a clear plastic evidence bag that he just happened to have handy.

'If we can find some prints on this, we might be able to find out who shot this man. Wouldn't that be a stroke of luck!'

He was kneeling with his back to me. A couple of feet away was the corner post of the bed. Reinforced iron ending in a globe of steel the size of a melon. I looked at the hard metal ball, I looked at the soft flesh and bony globe of Watcyns' head, and back at the ball. I thought about Myfanwy packing her case. I contemplated Christmas in jail. I remembered Miss Evangeline. I looked at the ball of iron and at Erw Watcyns' head. I realised I had so much to do today, and yet it was the shortest day. I lunged forward, grabbed the collar of his coat and yanked. His head hit the globe with a mixture of sounds: a boing, a crunch and an oh! He slumped to the floor, rivulets of blood matting and darkening his hair; blood and tissue were on the bedstead. I paused. I had a number of options. I could wipe the prints off the gun, or I could simply remove it. But the sight of Watcyns' own police-issue revolver peeping out from the folds of his jacket gave me a better idea.

I walked over to the incident board, on which the Pieman's gore was congealing. I peered closely and, helped by the swirling patterns of splattered blood that led me to the epicentre, I located the bullet embedded in the wall. I prised it out with my door key. Then I removed Watcyns' gun and walked up to the Pieman. I put the muzzle of the gun into the hole the first bullet had made, pulled back about six inches, and fired. There was less gore thrown against the wall this time round. But the slug went home accompanied by a plop of flesh, like a spoonful of jam catapulted by a naughty child. I stood for a second, entranced by the ghoulish abattoir on the wall, amazed at what I was doing. I could have gone a stage further and shot Watcyns with the other gun and put it in the Pieman's hand. But that would have been gilding the lily. Besides, that would have been murder, assuming he wasn't already dead. Whereas shooting the Pieman, a man who had already been shot and was assuredly dead, was simply a misdemeanour. This was better. The slug in the wall, which ballistics would eventually identify as matching Erw Watcyns' gun, was a slow-burner. I took out my handkerchief and wiped the gun for prints, then put it back inside Watcyns' jacket. I picked up the other gun and wiped it. I cast a glance down at Erw: he didn't look very well. I had no idea what to do next so I decided to listen. There were four sounds in that room: My breathing; the tiny tick-tock of a travel alarm clock; the noise a dead man makes; and, from the door, the cough of a man who wasn't me.

Chapter 19

H<small>E STOOD IN</small> the doorway, leaning casually against the jamb. A man I thought I'd seen a number of times recently: once on the Prom; once underneath a street-light holding a match to an unlit cigarette; once hurrying away from Sospan's; and once in the shadow of an arch when the light was especially bad. The sort of man you try and dismiss as a mirage brought on by the dark fear of walking these streets at night, just a phantom invented by your own paranoia. You try and dismiss it and you could, but for one thing: the fedora hat.

I raised the gun and pointed it at him. It didn't seem to worry him. He looked with mild interest at the dead Pieman, and then turned his attention to the Pieman's brains disfiguring the wall. He didn't seem perturbed by that, either. He had the air of someone who has spent a lifetime standing in the doorways of dingy rooms where dead men sit slumped in the chair, their brains on the wall; a man wiping off a gun in the other corner of the room. He was about fifty-five or sixty, filling out round the waist but with an air of physical hardness about him. His face was expressionless but not cold; it was the absence of expression that professionals acquire, the habit of not judging; worn by people who have seen so many things in life that expressions of shock or disgust become merely a chore. It could have been a cop's face if it had been colder.

'Two handkerchiefs are better for wiping it off,' he said.

I stared at him blankly.

'That way you don't miss anything. Doing it with one looks slick, but it's more of a party trick, like striking a match on your chin.' He smiled. His voice was soft and relaxed, with a gentle American drawl. I couldn't place it, but that was no surprise: everything I knew about America came from the movies.

I stopped wiping and considered. 'I could always use it to shoot you.'

'That's not a bad idea.'

I tapped my jacket pocket. 'Looks like I'm out of second hand-kerchiefs.'

He took one out and threw it across the room. I caught it, wiped both guns more thoroughly, and replaced them.

He asked, 'Is he still alive?'

'I didn't hit him that hard.'

'Often you don't need to. Maybe we should go for a walk; if he's not dead he'll come round soon.'

'I have this thing about going for walks with strangers.'

'Sometimes events don't leave you much choice.'

We left together and walked across the road to my office. I poured two shots of Captain Morgan and began collecting things: car key, papers, money. It was a routine I had often prepared for. The man sat in the client's chair and drank rum.

I stopped gathering and said, 'Are you Hoffmann?'

He laughed. 'No. Are you?'

'So tell me why you're following me.'

'It's a long story.'

'I'm patient.'

'You have to be in this line of work, but I was thinking more about our friend across the road. Maybe we should go some-where more discreet.'

'I'm not leaving here with you until you tell me what your angle is.'

He swirled the rum around in the tumbler and stared at it. He raised his eyes and smiled. 'Once upon a time there was a man called Ricardo Klement – just an ordinary guy with a small house on Garibaldi Street in the San Fernando district of Buenos Aires.

He ran a laundry business. To the neighbours he seemed respectable enough. Kept himself to himself, but that's not a crime. Then one day they watched in astonishment as a car turned up and four tough guys jumped out. They bundled Ricardo Klement into the back and drove off. A few weeks later they saw his face spread across the front pages all around the world. He'd changed his name to Adolf Eichmann, and was on trial for his life in Jerusalem.

'By all accounts he was surprisingly co-operative, almost pathetically eager to please his captors. It was hard to believe that this polite, well-spoken, respectful man was the same one who had sent millions of innocent people to the gas chambers. They had to keep reminding themselves that the man before them was a monster. They asked him about a document they were interested in. He told them it had been stolen from him by a woman he met in the reading room of the Buenos Aires public library. He said she seduced him and they spent a night in a pension nearby. He had left the document in his coat pocket and she stole the coat after their night of passion. A classic honey trap, he said. His captors were dubious; it seemed like he was just spinning a yarn. But they managed to track down the woman and she confirmed his story. She said she had sold the coat to a soldier on leave from the front, and had never once looked in the pocket. The soldier was called Caleb Penpegws. Now, there's a funny thing about spooks: for people who spend their lives veiled in secrecy they're hopeless at keeping secrets. At any given time you can guarantee half of them will be working for both sides. The other half forget which side they're working for and swap; after a while they swap back. It's a merry-go-round; and the secrets in which they trade are the like the prize in the kids' parlour game Pass the Parcel. Sooner or later everyone gets to hold it. That's what happened to the story of the coat; it got passed around, and soon everyone was looking for Eichmann's coat.

'It just so happened that Odessa got to Caleb first. They wanted the document, too. They tortured him for a week and he told his interrogators that the coat had been stolen from him while he lay on a hospital bed recovering from surgery. Stolen by Hoffmann. Who was Hoffmann? No one knew, but they started looking for him, in all the usual places. East Berlin, Prague, Warsaw, Moscow, Peking, even Hanoi. And no one got so much as a sniff. Then one of the smarter spooks asked himself, how did Hoffmann know about Caleb and the coat? Answer: the woman must have tipped him off. So then they started searching for her, the beautiful Mata Hari who had sprung the honey-trap. All they knew about her was contained in the transcript of Eichmann's testimony. He met her in the public records room of the library. They didn't even exchange names, he said, because of the tacit understanding that existed between two lonely strangers who became lovers but knew in their hearts it would be but for one night. In the morning they would go their separate ways never to meet again on this earth. To introduce the sad wrecks of their lives into the romance would have spoiled it. Or so he said. It seems a bit convenient to me, and maybe his interrogators thought so, too. But he stuck to his story, and what sanction can you bring against a man who is going to the chair and knows it? But though he couldn't give her name he did say one interesting thing: she was researching her family tree. Her grandparents had been outlaws hiding out in Patagonia. Their names were Mr and Mrs Harry Place, names which meant nothing to anyone at the time. South America has always been full of fugitives of all colours and persuasions, including ex-Nazis. She showed him a newspaper cutting from the turn of the century about her grandfather and grandmother. The headline was *Pistoleros Norteamericanos*.

'As I said, the names didn't mean much at that time in the early sixties. No one apart from a few specialists had heard of Butch Cassidy and the Sundance Kid. Then in 1969 the movie was released. It won four academy awards and the whole world went to see it, including a young Mossad agent called Elijah.

You've met him, I know. He had been present when they inter-rogated Eichmann, and during one of those sessions Eichmann had used a certain Spanish expression. Years later, sitting there in that darkened movie theatre, Elijah heard the phrase again. *Pistoleros Norteamericanos*. It made the hairs stand up on the back of his neck. Suddenly he realised the woman who stole the coat from Eichmann must have been the granddaughter of Etta Place and Sundance. And, just as suddenly, he knew exactly what he must do. He had to seek out the world's leading expert on Butch and Sundance. Me.'

The man paused and refilled his glass. 'Bored?'

'No.'

'Don't you think we should be going?'

'Let them come. Carry on.' I stood at the window. Across the street two medics threaded their way through the crowd of gawkers towards the back of an ambulance. The body on the stretcher was too small to be the Pieman. It was probably Erw Watcyns, but I couldn't be sure; there was a sheet covering his face.

The man took another drink and tapped his hat on the desk: I walked to the door and said, 'Thanks, it was a good story, but I have something to attend to that can't wait.' I closed the door and turned the key. There was the expected sound of a chair scraping. The door handle turned and rattled a few times in its socket. 'Sorry about this,' I said. 'The cleaner will be along later.'

I ran down the stairs and out into the cold December air, my heart pounding as fast as if I were going on a date.

Llunos was slumped over a pint in the Castle, looking morose. I knew he would be. He was reading the sporting pages and on the seat next to him there was a bag from Lampeter House. He looked up at my approach, pulled out a chair and moved the bag to the floor.

'It's for my mum, a cardi for when she wants to sit up in bed.

They suggested I get it. Not sure about the size, though. Strange isn't it? Fifty years and I've never bought her anything to wear. You don't for your mum, do you?'

'Is she any better?'

'No, not really. This year won't be much of a Christmas, I'm afraid. What about you?'

'The way things are looking, I'll be spending it in jail.'

He didn't react. 'What you done this time?'

'I think I've killed Erw Watcyns.'

'Why are you telling me?'

'I'm turning myself in.'

'Why?'

'What do you mean, why? I just told you I think I killed a man.'

'I know. Why are you telling me?'

'I thought murder was against the law.'

He nodded as if the penny had dropped. 'Oh, right. Murder. And you're turning yourself in. Very noble. How did you kill him?'

'I was in the garret across the street from my office. There was a guy sitting there, dead. They call him the Pieman. I had nothing to do with that, but Erw Watcyns was going to pin it on me. I don't know what happened; I panicked and banged his head on the bedstead. I didn't intend to kill him or anything, just give myself a head start while I got out of there.'

'What do you want me to do now?'

'Run me in, I suppose.'

'Run you in? Trouble is, your story doesn't ring true. Why would you kill someone and then immediately turn yourself in? You've forgotten the bit where you run and hide and we chase you. There's always that bit. If we didn't have that I'd be out of a job. We could just have, what do they call it? An honesty system. We leave a book out on the desk at the station, and you fill it in yourself. Just take a key from behind the counter and choose a cell.'

'Hey! I killed someone, let's all have a laugh.'

'You're having a bad day, Louie. We all do; get over it.'

'It's more than that.'

'Is it? Call it a bad week, then. Who cares? So you killed someone. The way you describe it you won't do the maximum. You'll get twelve to fourteen. Out after ten. How old will you be then? Fifty-five or so? You'll be laughing. My mum probably hasn't got a month – in a cardigan that's too small or is the wrong colour.'

'As if that matters.'

'That's just the point, it does. That's always the worst thing – you go up there and see them wearing clothes that they hate, and would never have worn when they were able to take care of themselves. But they're too meek to say anything to the nurses who dress them. You can see it in their eyes, though. They know.'

'So why didn't you get the right size? It's not hard.'

'Because I'm not a genius like you. I can't think of everything.'

He sighed. 'Louie, I can't arrest you . . . because of a technical detail; it's a sort of legal safeguard to protect the innocent. Basically, you can't arrest a man for the murder of a man who isn't dead. I'm sorry.'

'He's not dead?'

'Nope.'

'He looked pretty dead to me.'

'It's a trick, Louie. He's pretending.'

'How can you know that?'

'What makes you think he's dead?'

'I saw them carrying him out – the sheet was up over his face.'

'Yeah, that's how we do it with murders. First thing we do is call an ambulance and take the DOA away. Other police forces, they like to do it by the book. You know, all that scene-of-crime forensic shit. Photographers and medics, and guys with latex gloves and little evidence bags picking up snot with tweezers and dating it. Not us. We're more streamlined. We just take the guy away, dig a hole and throw him in. Doesn't even have to be a hole. Sometimes we just leave him out with the bins.'

'You're still blaming me for the newspaper ad, aren't you?'

'You and the Queen of Denmark. She's in it up to her ears as well. Get out of here, you fool, before Erw finds you. He doesn't believe in legal safeguards to protect the innocent.'

I went over to the bar and fetched two pints. Sometimes quarrels are like that: if you leave halfway they'll never get sorted out.

When I returned he was calmer. He said, 'How's your dad?'

'Seems to be doing fine.'

He nodded. 'What about Calamity?'

'I'm not sure. She ... er ... she ...' It wasn't easy so say. 'She's trying things on her own for a while.'

'I had a complaint against her from Mrs Dinorwic-Jones, the art-teacher. Says Calamity's been shining torch beams into her bedroom window. What the hell's she playing at? You're supposed to be watching over her.'

I paused and wondered. Llunos twisted slightly in his chair. 'That's another thing I turn a blind eye to: kid not even eighteen acting as your sidekick. But I thought you were having a good influence on her.'

'She was doing some sort of scene-of-crime ballistics thing she found in a book. Stick knitting needles in the bullet holes in the wall; shine the light along them and you find out where they came from. That's the theory. She said it didn't work.'

Llunos's brow furrowed. 'That's interesting. The shots came from Dinorwic-Jones's apartment. Funny, she never mentioned hearing shots; you'd think she would if they came from her apartment.'

'Some people are hard of hearing.'

'Something about her has been bugging me for a while. It's not right all this trauma she says she's been suffering on account of the mutilation. She teaches life drawing and stares at naked men all her life. She draws the outline at the scene of crime and has been seeing chopped up bodies half her life. How come she's so upset now?' He paused and we drank in silence for a while. Finally he said, 'So, who's the Queen of Denmark?'

'I don't know.'

'I'm not wearing my copper's hat.'

'I know that. I'd tell you if I knew. All I know is, she sends real money; at least, it fools the people at the post office.'

'You really don't know?'

'I've got two theories. One is ... One is she's the Queen of Denmark. And the other ...'

'Yes?'

'Actually, I've got one theory.'

'Kind of hard to believe you don't know a thing like that.'

'You'd be amazed at the things I don't know. I don't know who Hoffmann is. I know who killed Santa but I don't know why. I don't know who killed the men who killed him. I don't know who the Pieman is or why he did what he did. I don't know who paid him or who killed him. It might be the guy in the fedora hat who's been following me but I don't know why he would kill a Pieman. And, to be honest, I don't know for sure if he really has been following me. Maybe he's just an ordinary Joe in a fedora hat. After all, someone has to be. I don't know who Elijah is; and I don't know who Erw is or was or what his role in all this is or was; but I know he has a role in it somewhere. I don't know why a dying man should write "Hoffmann" in his blood, or why he should say his life was fulfilled after seeing a movie about a dog. I don't know what happened at the Mission House siege. I don't know why the priest went nuts. I don't know who my client is, or even if I've got one. I don't know what I am going to do about Calamity. I do know Myfanwy is leaving, but I don't know what I'm going to do about that. That's why I'm here, I guess. I was hoping to spend a quiet Christmas behind bars and forget about it for a while.'

'Do you know what the drill sergeants say? When a man is done in, when he's reached the end of his tether and can't take any more, doesn't have an ounce of strength left in him, they say when he reaches that point he's usually got about another twenty per cent in the tank. Get your coat.'

'Where are we going?

'We're going to see the art teacher.'

Mrs Dinorwic-Jones sat clutching a mug of cocoa, dressed in a pale lemon housecoat, her grey hair in curlers beneath a hairnet and on her feet slippers crowned with a woolly bob. She stretched her feet out towards the gas fire.

'I don't mind telling you,' she said, 'it was a heck of a shock to me.'

'Yeah, we heard that,' said Llunos with a tinge of sarcasm that went undetected.

'I'm still a bit upset.'

'These things take time.'

'I've seen a few bad things in my time, doing the chalk outlines for the police, but this – the mutilation – well, that was different.'

'I expect the noise would have upset you as well.'

'Noise? What noise?'

'Gunfire. It never fails to shock me how damned loud a gun shot is. You, not being used to it, must have jumped out of your housecoat.'

'I . . . I don't know what you mean!' Her grip tightened on the mug of cocoa.

'Yes you do,' said Llunos. 'Those two goons, the Moss Brothers, were your nephews. They shot the guy from this room.'

'No they didn't.'

'Yes they did.'

'You're barking up the wrong tree. There were no guns fired from this house.'

Llunos picked up his trilby and spoke to the hatband. 'You know my mother, don't you? She's in Bronglais—'

'Yes, I heard. I'm terribly sorry.'

'You never liked her much, did you?'

'I . . . I . . . That's not true—'

'Yes it is. You never liked her. In fact, you were always sniping at her, weren't you? Always a bad word to say. I know all about you, you see. You're a bit of a busybody on the quiet. We've got quite a few in this town. And you're the Queen, the Queen of Fucking Busybodies. I see you in the early-morning queue at the butcher's or the baker's, when I drive past. I see you gossiping with the rest of them; and even though I can't hear, I know what you're saying isn't good. You see, that's the difference between you and my mum. She never has a bad word for anyone. Doesn't mean she likes everyone, she just doesn't say it, keeps it to herself. It's called manners. You don't need to pull a face, Mrs Jones, and you don't need to tell me it's not a crime to say bad things about your neighbour; even though you spend half your life sitting in church professing to love him. I agree it's not a crime; it's just a moral failing, I suppose, and I am the last one to lecture anyone on that. In fact, I'm only saying it now because she's dying, a good woman with a heart full of kindness who you have badmouthed for as long as I can remember. I never said anything before, but today I'm telling you. I'm here to ask some questions and I don't want you to lie to me or you'll find out what twenty years of pent-up contempt can do. Do you understand?'

Mrs Jones regarded Llunos with a look of defiance. 'I won't be intimidated into confessing to something that didn't happen.'

'I'm not trying to intimidate you,' said Llunos. 'I'm just clarifying the matter. I don't want you to be under any illusions that you have a friend in this room. You haven't.'

'Tell us about the phoney leg routine, Mrs Jones,' I said.

'What do you mean?'

'You spotted it straight away, didn't you? That leg facing the wrong way. After forty years drawing them in class and chalking round them on the tarmac, I guess it was pretty obvious.'

'You're talking in riddles.'

'Maybe, but I've got a hunch. It's been growing inside me, ever since I met a man called Elijah at the Wishing Well on the Prom. My hunch is this: the dead Father Christmas didn't plant a picture of Butch and Sundance in that alley. At least, not just a picture. Why should he? Elijah already knew about that angle – everyone did since the day the movie came out. He must have planted something else and someone switched it. But who could have switched it? My money's on you.'

'I didn't switch anything, I haven't a clue what either of you are talking about.'

'Would you care to take a polygraph test on it?' asked Llunos.

I looked at him in mild surprise, but fought it back so Mrs Jones wouldn't notice.

'A what?'

'A lie detector. We could sort this out in a few minutes.'

'I didn't think they were allowed in this country.'

'The American sort aren't, but this is a traditional type, the one they used to use to test witches. What we do is fill the bath with water and hold your head under. If you drown it means you're innocent and you will have our sincere apologies; if you survive it means you're guilty. It will only take a few minutes. I do it all the time; it saves paperwork.'

Mrs Jones's face drained of colour. 'You wouldn't do that to me!'

'I'm afraid I don't have any choice; it's my job.'

'But I can't swim.'

Llunos turned to me. 'Go and fill the bath, will you?'

'Hot or cold?' I said.

'Hot, of course. We don't want Mrs Jones catching her death of cold, do we?'

I stood up. 'Always happy to act as a midwife to justice.'

Llunos leaned towards Mrs Jones. 'You know, you could save us a lot of wasted time by telling us what happened in that alley.'

I watched the bath fill. 'It's about ready,' I shouted.

Llunos led Mrs Jones by the arm up the stairs. We stood crammed into a small bathroom.

'It's better if you kneel down,' said Llunos. 'Head at this end, or you'll catch it on the taps.' He placed a hand on her shoulder.

'Please don't do this, Mr Llunos.'

He pressed gently on her shoulder. 'If you're innocent you've got nothing to worry about.'

'Please don't duck me in the bath.'

'Tell us what happened and we won't have to.'

Mrs Jones burst into tears and through the sobs began to squeak. 'They weren't meant to kill the poor chap.'

'Who weren't?'

'My nephews. I just told them to put a fright into him so he went back from where he came from. But they went too far.'

'You mean the Moth Brothers?'

'Yes.'

'Why did you want to frighten him?'

'Because ... because ...' Mrs Jones wrung her hands and looked from Llunos to me and back to Llunos. 'Oh, dash it all!'

'Just tell us what happened, Mrs Jones. If it's like you say, if you just meant to frighten him, that's not so very serious. It's not your fault if those two goons went too far. I'm sure we could talk to the judge about it, but you need to tell us what happened.'

Mrs Jones continued to wring her hands. 'Nothing happened, really. I asked them to frighten him but they shot him ... a few times. They they went down with my bread knife and did the ... the ... you know.'

Llunos took Mrs Jones back downstairs and we sat again in front of the fire. She slurped from her mug of cocoa with shaking hands.

'Why did you want to frighten him?'

'Because he came to see me. A few weeks ago now. He wanted my help, you see, because of the work I do with the local history society. He asked me, "Have you heard of Butch Cassidy and the Sundance Kid?" and I said, "Well, of course I have, I'm not stupid you know." And he said, "Did you know that Sundance had a girlfriend called Etta Place?" and I said, "Yes, I saw it in the movie – she was a schoolteacher wasn't she?" So he told me that the disappearance of Etta Place was the great mystery of the Butch Cassidy legend and no one knew what had happened to her. He said she left Patagonia around 1908 and she was carrying Sundance's child. No one knew where she went, he said; they all assumed she went back to Kansas but he had found out that she caught the boat to Wales. He said she died on the crossing but gave birth to a daughter called Laura and this was Sundance's daughter, and he wanted to find out what happened to her. So naturally I agreed to help him; wouldn't that be a feather in my cap, I thought, if I helped find the Sundance Kid's granddaughter in Aberystwyth? Well, it wasn't too difficult to find out what happened to the girl – born out of wedlock wasn't she? I sent him to Jezebel College in Lampeter. They've got all sorts of advanced techniques for tracing girls like that.' She paused and took a breath as if the next bit was particularly difficult. 'A week later he came back with a photocopy from the workhouse records, and if a marriage register. He also had a photo of a grave. He told me Etta Place died on the voyage and her daughter went to the workhouse. When she left she married a plumber.' She stood up, went over to a sideboard and opened a drawer. She brought an envelope over and handed it to me.

'I found that chit to the Pier cloakroom in the alley, you see, and redeemed it. There were three photos, the Butch Cassidy one and these.'

I took two photos from the envelope. One was a picture of the simpleton at Tadpole's house. The other was a snap of a slate headstone: a plain mauve crooked slab of stone, surrounded by weeds, in a churchyard on a hill. The name was Laura Llantrisant. If it was the grave of Etta Place's daughter, it meant she must have married and taken the name Llantrisant. Her daughter – the Sundance Kid's granddaughter – was the woman who'd swabbed my step for twenty years, Mrs Llantrisant.

'I removed them, you see. Just left the Sundance Kid picture and re-deposited it, then put the chit back in the alley.' Mrs Jones's voice broke into a flood of tears. 'I had an arrangement with the girls out at Jezebel College. They were going to say it was ... it was me. ... Oh, it's just not fair! Why couldn't I be Sundance's granddaughter?' She sobbed into her hands. 'Why not me instead of that silly bitch? That awful, step-swabbing, holier-than-thou, gossiping busybody, Mrs Llantrisant!'

Chapter 20

THE MAN IN the fedora hat was sitting at the desk writing a report when I returned. His briefcase was open, papers spilling out. The bottle of Captain Morgan was hardly touched. He looked up and smiled.

'What happened, forget your umbrella?'

'Something like that.'

'I made a few calls, I've left some money.'

'There's no need; they're on the house. Always happy to help an operative of the famous Pinkerton Detective Agency.'

He pushed the papers away, leaned back and grinned. 'I knew you'd work it out pretty quickly.'

'It wasn't hard. As you said, Elijah went to see the world's leading expert on Butch and Sundance.'

'My name's Joe Winckelmann.' He held out his hand and we shook.

'That your real name?'

He laughed. 'One of them.'

'Care to finish the story?'

'There's not much more to tell. I was a junior at the time, just joined the Pinkertons and I started at the bottom – everyone does. It was my job to deal with the cranks who walked in off the street from time to time with some dramatic new lead on the Butch Cassidy case. We used to get one or two a month. So when Elijah turned up, they sent him to see me. But I could see straight away he was different from the usual nuts. For a start, he didn't give a damn about Butch Cassidy. He wouldn't have cared if Butch Cassidy had turned up and danced a polka on his head. He had a different bee in his bonnet. He had this Hoffmann thing and his point was simple. He reasoned it out like this. How did Hoffmann know that Caleb Penpegws had the coat? The woman who stole it from Eichmann must have tipped him off. How did she know it was of any great significance? She didn't, until the spooks tracked her down and asked what she did with it. She said she had sold it to a soldier, which was true. She said she didn't know who he was. Maybe that was true, maybe it wasn't. But she clearly wasn't stupid. After those spooks left she must have thought about it and asked herself, what could be so important about the coat that some spies would track her down for it? So she sent someone to get the coat back. She sent Hoffmann. That means the woman researching her family tree in the library must know Hoffmann. Therefore, if you can find her, the granddaughter of Etta Place, you can solve the Hoffmann mystery. But, equally, if you could find him you could find her – it works both ways. It was a strange sort of symbiosis. Of course, Elijah didn't deal straight goods with me; he didn't tell me all this at the time. But I was young and ambitious and keen to progress in the organisation and I knew there was no better way to make a name for myself than by solving the Pinkerton's most celebrated unsolved case. So I snooped on Elijah a bit.' He took another long drink of rum.

'I went to the hotel where he stayed and searched his room; listened in to his phone conversations; gradually built up the picture. Over the years we met a number of times. It was one of those strange relationships – I knew if he ever cracked the Hoffmann case it would lead to Etta Place; and he knew if I ever solved the Etta Place mystery it would lead to Hoffmann.

'And so the years passed and we both grew old. I worked on plenty of other cases, and no doubt so did he in his world of smoke and shadows. But it always haunted me, that Hoffmann angle; in my heart it kept on bubbling away. Then earlier this month a clipping bureau sent me the story from the *Cambrian News* about the dead Father Christmas. I knew instantly what it meant. Hoffmann had come in from the cold. The Pinkertons weren't going to fund any trips on this case so I put in for an extended Christmas vacation and came over. It's a personal thing, you see. I'm due to retire in the new year and it would be wonderful to solve the mystery of Etta Place before I leave – my first case and maybe my last. Here, have this.' He slipped a business card across the desk. It said, 'Joe Winckelmann, The Pinkerton Detective Agency, Los Angeles'.

'So who was Absalom?'

'I'm not sure. There have been a lot of spooks working the case over the years, so he could be anyone. Elijah says Absalom was his brother. It could be true.'

'Why would he come to Wales now, after all these years?'

'I don't know. I have a hunch it must be something to do with the movie *Bark of the Covenant*.'

'I had the impression you've been following me for about a week.'

'I have.'

'You didn't come because of the fax Calamity sent you, then?'

'No, no faxes. As I said, I'm not here officially. This is a private matter.'

I refilled his glass and poured one for myself. 'How would you like to meet the granddaughter of Etta Place and the Sundance Kid?'

He grinned.

'She's very old and frail. I'm not sure if she could take the publicity if this got out.'

'It wouldn't have to. As I said, this is a personal thing, the end of a lifetime's quest. No one has to know.'

'Have you got a manual in that briefcase?'

'What sort of manual?'

'You know, the standard-issue Pinkerton agent's manual. Art and praxis of the hunch, interrogative misdirection, that sort of stuff.'

He reached into his case and pulled out a book. 'Sure.'

'A recent edition?'

'The current one.'

'Can I have it? It's a present for someone.'

He slid the book across the desk. 'Be my guest. I can always requisition a new one.'

'If I take you to see Etta's granddaughter, will you do something in return?'

'If I can.'

'I want you to meet my partner Calamity Jane, she's only seventeen and four-fifths. She sent a fax to your organisation. Can you pretend you came because of the fax?'

He pondered for a second and a smile spread across his face. 'Sent a fax to the Pinkertons, huh?'

'Yes.'

'She sounds like quite a bushy-tailed sort of kid.'

'She's a great kid. Sometimes she's filled with so much enthusiasm I wonder she doesn't explode.'

'I used to be like that. Of course I'll pretend. Came here as soon as we got the fax. If she's looking to set up some sort of associate partnership, that would be just dandy. We Pinkertons have been looking for some representation in Aberystwyth for a while now.'

I had already begun to like Joe Winckelmann.

We picked up a video of the Butch Cassidy movie at a hire shop and drove out to Ponterwyd. I parked behind the caravan and left Joe Winckelmann in the car. I found Mrs Llantrisant where I had left her, lying on her bed watching a portable TV. It was a soap and she stared at it glassily as if the mini-dramas that are the staple of such programmes were an opiate for her troubled soul. She cast me a glance and said mechanically, 'He's not here, if you're looking for Herod. He's gone, for the carol concert.'

'I came to see you. I've brought a video for you to watch.'

She scowled. 'I never watch the things.'

'You'll enjoy this one. It features your grandmother, Etta Place.'

She looked thoughtful, the scowl melting softly at the mention of the name. 'My mother left me a Bible with a photo inside, a picture of Etta and those two cowboys in New York.'

'I've seen it.'

'All through my childhood I wanted to know who those people in the picture were.' She shuddered as a twinge of pain ran through her. 'Ooh!'

'Are you OK?'

'Just a twinge. I get them from time to time.' She reached up and touched her forehead. The red spot that had been there last time had opened into a sore. A pale orange excrescence dripped down.

'It's that woman, Tadpole's mum. Don't think I don't know. And I know who's put her up to it and all. That Dinorwic-Jones.'

I stood there helpless, wanting to scoff but rendered helpless by the evidence on Mrs Llantrisant's brow.

'I know you think it's all superstitious nonsense, but I've been around a while longer than you and I know about these things.'

'Have you had anything to eat today?'

'No, there's no point. Food won't help me if there's a hex on me.'

'What would happen if I found the photo and took the pin out? Would that help?'

'But how would you find it?'

'I know where to look.'

She made a sour expression, the look of someone who hates to concede ground, even when it's to her advantage. 'Well, it might.'

'Then you'll need food to re-build your strength.'

I slipped the video into the tape player and switched it on. 'Take a look at this while I drive to the village and get some hot food.'

I apologised to Joe Winckelmann, who was still sitting in the car, for taking so long. He waved it away. He had waited all his life for this, he said. What was an extra half an hour? I drove to town and managed to find a fish and chip shop open and returned about forty minutes later.

Mrs Llantrisant was sitting up, holding the remote-control like a sceptre and replaying the scene with the bicycles over and over again. Tears glistened on her drab white cheeks.

'Oh, Mr Knight! Do you know, I've never ridden a bicycle. My, oh my! And Sundance . . . He's so handsome . . . Who'd have thought it? My grandfather so good-looking he could have been a movie star.'

We ate our fish and chips and watched the movie to the end. Mrs Llantrisant's hand moved rhythmically from the chips on her knee to her mouth, accompanied now and again by the other hand dabbing away the tears. Yet at the end when her grandfather runs out into the market place, into a hail of bullets, and stands immortalised in a freeze frame that turns into sepia and then black, the tears washed down unabated. I let her cry. Like sleep, it's about the only thing that works.

She turned to me. 'There was a time I would have been ashamed – born out of wedlock like that. All my life I've looked down on such people; but it's funny, Mr Knight, today I see it differently. You know, I think I'm proud of them.'

'I would be, too.'

'You can tell Sundance loved her, can't you?'

'Yes, I'd say he loved her. He just didn't know how to say it.'

Mrs Llantrisant nodded. 'That's right. She was too hasty, the silly girl. I guess you can't see it when you're nineteen or whatever she was. When it comes to love and things, you can't see the wood for the trees; you get it all wrong. And yet at my age it all looks so obvious. When she tells him she's thinking of going back home she doesn't mean it, does she? You can tell she's just aching with every ounce of strength in her little young heart for him to say, "No, you can't! You mustn't!" And what does he say? He says, "Oh, all right, that's fine if that's what you want to do." But he doesn't mean it, does he?'

'No, I guess he doesn't.'

'Of course he doesn't. He's just another young fool who doesn't understand what's going on in his own heart. It's the disease of youth, and by the time age brings the cure, it's too late. He says, Go if you must, if that's what you want to do; I won't stand in your way. But what he means is, my life is nothing without you and if you go now I will die like a dog in a marketplace in an unknown town and strangers will spit on my corpse and throw rocks on my grave; and that will be my end; but I will never tell you these things because I love you. Even though I could never bring myself to use those words, you know I love you, and because of that I will never tell you what to do or where to go. If you want to go back to America I will let you, even though it will kill me. And the reason is this: all my life I have never been able to abide bars on a window or the feel of shackles on my flesh. The greatest gift I can give you is what I crave most, freedom. The stupid man. So typical. And so she doesn't tell him she is carrying his child and she leaves. But instead of going back home like everyone says, she finds herself on a ship to Wales. Oh, Mr Knight, I'm quite overcome. What a beautiful film.'

There was a bottle of sherry on the side table and I fetched two teacups from the kitchenette and brought them over. I filled them to the brim and handed her one.

'Happy Christmas, Mrs Llantrisant.'

'And a Happy New Year. Don't forget about the pin.'

'I won't.'

She drank the sherry in three greedy gulps and reached for the bottle. I passed my cup over.

'Pity we don't have any mince pies.'

'There are some in the cupboard.'

I walked over to fetch them and she continued, 'This reminds me of Christmas with Eichmann.'

She saw my expression of surprise and added hurriedly, 'Of course, I didn't know who he was then, did I? I'm not one of those Nazi sympathisers, if that's what you think. I lost a good cousin in North Africa to Rommel. He sent me a picture of him and his mates frying eggs on a tank. How we laughed. They all died, though, those boys.'

'Tell me about Eichmann.'

'I knew him as Ricardo. Ever such a gent, he was. Just goes to show, doesn't it? I never understood that thing with the Jews. We had one here once, the draper. Very respectable man.'

'And you met him in the library?'

'I was checking my family background. Of course, the names of Cassidy and Sundance didn't mean anything to me. I suppose you could say he picked me up. We had a tryst. I can remember every detail of it. It was a cheap hotel on the Plaza de la Constitución, across from the railway station. It was a corner room on the top floor with a rickety old bed with broken springs and a picture of the Madonna hanging over the bed. All through the night as he made love to me there were flashes like artillery shells from the trams passing outside the window, and I could hear the shrieking whistles of the engines in the sidings. I remember thinking that night, this is one of those times, one of those rare occasions . . . I don't know how to put it . . . you know even as you experience them, you sort of know how special they are.'

'I think I know what you mean.'

'Even when they are happening, you know they'll never come again. Do you get that?

'I've had one or two.'

'Yes. We all get one or two if we're lucky. Doesn't seem much, does it?'

'Why did you steal his coat?'

'I didn't steal it, Mr Knight. When those secret agents came after me I told them the same thing, but they didn't believe it. I borrowed his coat because it was raining, and the next day I took it round to his house to return it and that's when I saw them bundling him into that car. I was so scared I didn't know what to do so I sold the coat to Caleb Penpegws. I never looked in the pockets, I didn't think. So I don't know anything about this document they're all asking about. And as for Hoffmann, I don't know who he is, either. I sold it to that silly man and his stupid mouse.'

'Caleb had a mouse? I thought it was Eifion, his buddy, who had the mouse?'

'Oh no, Caleb was the one with the mouse. He's still got one. You can see him every night at the Pier watching that laughing policeman machine. That's what war does to you.'

I went out to fetch Joe Winckelmann and took him to meet the granddaughter of Etta Place and the Sundance Kid.

There was so much I had still to do, so much to undo, to set right, to fix; so many amends to make. Too much for any day, and today was the shortest day. I drove Joe back to his hotel and we arranged to meet later. I went round to Prospect Street. The light was still burning behind the curtain, and this time I rapped on the glass. The curtain was drawn back and Calamity stared out at me. It was one of those moments. The sort when you are not sure if there is any argument between you, even though you know things are not quite right. She closed the curtain and opened the front door. She invited me into her office.

'Good to see you,' she said.

'And you. How's it going?'

'Oh, pretty good, you know. Slow, but pretty good. I think we're making progress.'

'That's good.'

'Yeah.'

I looked around the room. There was an incident board but nothing on it.

Calamity followed my gaze. 'Actually,' she said. 'It's crap. I've been a real dope. Would you like a cup of tea?'

'No, I can't stop. I have things to do. Lots of things. I've just come to say . . .'

'Yes?'

'I need you to come back.'

Something flashed in the depths of her young eyes. 'Need me back?'

'Please.'

'Well . . .'

'Something's cropped up.'

'Really?'

'I can't explain now, I have things to do. But something's cropped up and I need you. I'll catch you later, OK?'

'Sure.'

'I just wanted to let you know, that's all.'

Chapter 21

I WASN'T SURE WHAT I was going to say to Caleb, but something would occur to me. It generally did. Whatever it was, his first answers would be a pack of lies. People never told the truth these days, it was a point of principle. But that didn't matter. I would find some way to bring truth to birth; I just didn't know what. Something told me Tiresias might help me. Maybe I would have to hurt him. I didn't want to. I didn't even want to be here on the last Tuesday before Christmas, walking along a near-deserted Prom, in the drizzling rain, the grisly cold wet collar scraping my chin and channelling clammy drops of rain into the precious hoard of warmth beneath. I didn't want to be here, but here I was, aware without looking, without the heart to look, that I was being watched by the old people in the front windows of the seaside hotels.

They were happy: in a room filled with warmth, stomachs full of too much lunch, and the faint tizzy feeling that comes from an afternoon of sherry. A real fire crackles in a real grate and Christmas decorations festoon a room that boasts a real Christmas tree in the corner. They're happy because they are here; on the other side of the glass; they have the money to stay in a decent hotel where the people will go to the necessary effort to make it Christmassy. They know a lot of other people their age are sitting at home with nothing because they don't have the heart any more to put up a Christmas tree; and its absence, even though they have decreed it with pointless Spartan austerity, rankles in their soul more than anything.

The old people, watching me through the windows of the

seafront hotel, they know it will never be like it was all those years ago. How could it? Christmas is defined by the poignancy of loss. But all the same they are happy in the knowledge that it is still pretty good and the next salver of sherry is just a raised eyebrow away. Oh yes, I didn't want to be here, walking along an empty Prom in the season when only the broken-hearted walk like this, but here I was, trying not to look, head bowed, ploughing into the icy rain.

A man put a hand on my arm. It was Eeyore.

'Come,' he said. 'Have a pint with your father.'

We went to the Marine Hotel and sat in the bay window. The room glistened with gold foil, paper chains and crackers, balloons, Santas, silver stars. It was awful, cheap, tacky kitsch . . . it was glorious. I loved it. There was an angel above our heads and I asked Eeyore if he believed in the story from Patagonia.

'Angel of Mons,' he said. 'That's what it was, the Angel of Mons.'

'I don't understand.'

'It's one of the great legends of the First World War. Mons is a place in Belgium, I think, or France or wherever it was all those poor blighters lost their lives. The story goes that an angel appeared to the troops on the eve of the battle there; an angel on a white horse, holding a flaming sword aloft.'

'You mean you think it was the same angel?'

'Of course not, son. Your dad's not that daft. But it is possible, I think, to use the one to explain the other. You see, it's a funny thing. Although the original story is a timeless myth, no one has ever been able to produce a soldier who claims to have seen the angel with his own eyes. Plenty of them knew someone who had been there but there was never a proper eye witness. In fact, the story seems to have originated not on the front but with a spiritualist in London, who claimed to have heard it from an officer on leave. Many people suspect this officer was involved in black propaganda. They made stories up, you see. There was one about a Canadian soldier crucified by German troops. And they planted a fake diary on a dead German soldier in which he described working in a factory that rendered the dead bodies of fallen soldiers for use as glycerine. You see what I'm saying? This Angel of Mons rumour appeared at a time when British fortunes were at a low ebb; morale on the home front was waning. There'd been a series of battlefield setbacks; poison gas and tanks had both been recently introduced. I reckon the story was concocted to boost morale.'

'Trouble is, with the Patagonian angel there are people who claim to have seen her with their own eyes.'

'That's right, but just think of it. As a military man General Llanbadarn would have known the story of the Angel of Mons. Maybe he went one better. He wanted to send the men out on a dangerous mission; there were rumblings of mutiny. An angel might have been just what the doctor ordered. He knew, too, about the story in the local papers concerning the goatherd girl and her visions. Maybe it gave him the idea. Maybe he thought, why not treat the lads to a visit from a real angel?'

'You mean, you think he actually had a girl ride a horse through the camp pretending to be an angel?'

Eeyore nodded. 'Why not? Soldiers are notoriously superstitious. It wouldn't be difficult to fool them. A bit of fancy dress, moonlight, a girl on a horse.' He paused and said softly, 'I'm glad you never had to go off to war, son.'

Caleb was asleep on a pile of empty liquor bottles. Tiresias was running in his wheel but stopped and stared when I walked in. It was his big day, but he didn't know it yet. Caleb snored. I shoved him with my foot and he rolled off the bottles; he snored some more. I glanced around the room and my eyes alighted on a hammer and some nails left behind by the council workmen who had boarded the place up. I picked them up and began nailing Caleb to the floor. Not through the flesh, because I didn't want to wake him, but through the fabric of his clothes. I'd seen this done before and knew that after a few nails it was impossible to get up without assistance. I put five nails into the sleeve of the right arm and moved over to the left.

He woke and blinked as he tried to work out what was happening. He tried to move but his right arm was pinned and I was sitting on his left, nailing it into the floor. He raised his legs and kicked but you need good abdominal muscles to keep that up and you don't get them from a lifetime watching laughing policemen.

'What on earth are you doing?' he said.

'I'm nailing you to the floor.'

'I can see that. What I mean is, why are you nailing me to the floor?'

'I always do this to people who lie to me.'

'Have I lied to you?'

'You told me your name was Eifion.'

'It is.'

'That's not what I hear. I hear your name is Caleb Penpegws.'

'Whoever told you that is a liar.'

'Well, that's possible. Everyone is a liar in this town; it gets on my nerves sometimes.'

'Why are you here?'

'To wish you a happy Christmas.'

'Sod off.'

'Yes, I'd like to. I really would. There's nothing I'd like more than to walk out of your sty and back down the Prom to my partner, Calamity, who I love dearly and who I have missed terribly. And then to take her and maybe that Joe guy, because I like him too, even though we've only just met, take them both down to the harbour to my father's house and eat some mince pies and, you know, generally wassail among friends. While Eeyore poured the drinks I would phone Myfanwy and tell her to come and join us because there's no one in all the world I would rather be with right now than her.

But alas! Here I am standing wet and cold in your filthy room and really not happy at all.'

I finished the left arm and moved on to the feet. After five minutes he was pinned down like Gulliver in Lilliput.

'Why don't you go and join them all, then? Leave me in peace?'

'Because of all the people who will be spending miserable Christmases this year on account of me. A nice family I met out near Talybont, for example. The guy there made rocking chairs for a living and now he's dead. Why is he dead? No reason that I can see apart from the fact that his name went up on my board. And there was this Absalom guy, lying dead, brutally mutilated, the Chinese meal still undigested in his stomach. Why is he dead? Someone knows, but I'm damned if I do. And there was a girl who answered an ad in the paper, a girl called Emily, a fan of Kierkegaard. I never met her because she's dead, too. I never met her, but she was probably a good kid. Studious and sober. I mean, when was the last time you met a trouble-maker who read Kierkegaard? Then there was poor Miss Evangeline. And so it goes on. The reason I am here and not enjoying the company of friends is all these dead people are dead because of something to do with me and a guy called Hoffmann; and something terrible that happened out in Patagonia, something so awful it made the chaplain lose his wits.'

'I don't know anything about nothing.'

'You mean you don't know nothing about anything. If that's true the next half-hour is going to be very painful for you.'

'What do you mean?'

'The best way to find out if someone's telling the truth is to hurt them very badly and see if they stick to their story. Never fails.'

'What are you going to do?'

'Don't be so impatient. you'll find out soon enough.'

'Go and fuck yourself.'

I laughed. 'You know, for a man nailed to the floor you've got a lot of chutzpah.'

There was a Pyrex salad bowl lying in the corner of the room. I'd seen it the first time I came and now as I looked at it a plan took shape in my mind. I ripped open Caleb's shirt and exposed a belly of quivering lard. Then I picked up the salad bowl and up-ended it, placing it firmly on his belly. The fat pressed upwards and sealed the bowl. I fetched some firelighters. Caleb followed me with his eyes.

'Watch closely, now, you're going to enjoy this.' I opened the door to Tiresias's cage and picked him up by the tail.

'What are you doing? You leave Tiresias alone.'

I lifted the salad bowl and popped the mouse under it then remade the seal. The mouse ran round in frantic circles in his new glass prison, occasionally jumping up and testing the glass walls with his paws.

'What are you doing?'

'You're a Classics scholar, you should know this one. I think the Romans invented it.'

I lit the firelighter and held it aloft, a waxy brick of greasy white chemicals which burned with a fierce but almost invisible flame. I put it on top of the dish. I took another firelighter and added it to the pyre. I rolled up my sleeve and placed my elbow on the Pyrex dish to test the temperature. It was starting to get hot in there for poor old Tiresias.

'I read about it somewhere so I can't absolutely guarantee it will work, but theoretically what is supposed to happen is this: the mouse starts to get hot and goes a bit nuts and then he starts to get very hot and tries to escape. And the only way out he can see is to burrow through the floor. Normally that's not too great a problem, but, as you will be aware, the floor in this case is your stomach.'

'You're mad. Tiresias would never do that.'

'You know him better than I do, but I wouldn't be too sure of his loyalty. Rodents can be very fickle. Rats, especially, who are but distant cousins to the mouse, are notorious turncoats when their life is threatened. They sail with you in the hold all the way from Byzantium; eat your grain and drink your water; and then the first sniff of smoke they're off down the gangplank.'

Caleb leaned forward and watched in horrified fascination. 'He'll never do it.'

'I've got ten quid that says he does.'

'He loves me.'

'Each mouse kills the thing he loves.'

Caleb glared.

'Anyway,' I continued, 'you mustn't take it personally. Instinct drives him to it. It shouldn't be interpreted as a waning of his love.'

We watched the mouse scurrying around frantically, trying to get away from the heat. Then he turned his attention to Caleb's belly. Caleb screamed. Who wouldn't? Mice have got sharp claws and sharp little teeth and Tiresios was gnawing Caleb's belly, his tiny muzzle already frothing pink with blood.

'Apparently they can gnaw through steel.'

Caleb yelled again.

It turned my stomach just watching, but I forced myself to appear unconcerned. A picture of nonchalance.

'What do you want to know?' he cried.

'What's the terrible thing that drove the priest mad?'

'I can't say.'

'You mean you won't.'

'All right, I won't. My lips are sealed . . . Oh!' he groaned at the pain.

'Who's killing all these people?'

'The Pieman. Please make it stop.'

'Who is the Pieman?'

'He's dead.'

'I know he's dead, you fool; this is not a good time to split hairs. Who was the Pieman?'

'Make it stop,' he screamed, 'and I'll tell you.'

I considered.

'Please!' he screamed.

I continued to consider. The mouse was tearing up strands of human tissue now, like a heroin addict whose stash has fallen between the floor boards. Caleb screamed again. I lifted the bowl and took out the mouse. I put him back in his cage. Caleb panted heavily as he tried to capture his breath.

'The Pieman,' he said, 'was one of us. There were five of us who survived the Mission House siege, me, Erw Watcyns, the Pieman and two others who have since died. We did something terrible – I can't tell you what it was – and we swore a vow of silence. We swore that so long as we all lived we wouldn't speak about the shameful thing we did. But because of this Hoffmann guy we keep getting people every now and again who turn up asking about what happened. Sometimes they're spooks or spies, sometimes Wild West nuts – you know the type: looking for the lost grandchild of the Sundance Kid. Erw and the Pieman were the assassins. Anyone who turned up and got too nosey, they took care of it.'

'You mean killed them?'

'Yes.'

'What was this terrible thing you did, the reason so many harmless innocent people had to die?'

'I can't tell you.'

'You will.'

'I can't.'

'Don't make me put the mouse back.'

'I can't tell you. I've sworn an oath to my buddies, my brothers in arms. There's no finer fellowship to be found on God's lousy earth, no bond of love more unbreakable than that. Compared to that, a man's love for a woman is nothing. It can grow cold with time, even with the best intentions it can, but the love forged in the crucible of battle never dies and never wanes. I would happily die rather than betray those beautiful comrades.'

I took the mouse out of its cage and popped it under the Pyrex dish. 'Beautiful speech, Caleb. I'm touched. It's not often a man gets to express such noble sentiments on his deathbed. For most of us in this mundane quotidian fallen world, the best we get to say is, "Please find a good home for the cat." But you! You, my friend, are different. You have transmogrified this bleak grey December afternoon with the beauty of your requiem. You have transfigured this filthy evil-smelling room you inhabit, and turned it into a palace. On this day, though you are about to die unpleasantly, you should scorn to change your state with kings.' I relit the firelighters.

This time Tiresias went straight to work on the tunnel project. Caleb began to scream.

'I'm leaving now,' I said. 'Is there anything you want to say to me?'

'Go and jump in the lake!'

'You're a brave guy, Caleb, I'll say that much. I'll tell them at your funeral.'

I stood up and walked to the door. 'Bon appétit, little mouse.' I walked out and listened. He screamed a couple of times and then said, 'Wait! Come back.'

I went back in. 'Yes?' 'Over there by the window, there's a knapsack ... Oh my God, this hurts. Please!'

I took the mouse out of the glass bowl. 'What about the knapsack?'

'In the front pocket on the right, there are some ampoules of morphine. Can you fetch them?'

'Huh?'

'For the pain.'

'What are you talking about?'

'I don't think I can bear the pain.'

'That's the whole bloody point.'

'No it isn't.'

'Yes it is! It's supposed to hurt so much that you scream and yell and cry out for your ma and eventually, unable to bear it any longer, you tell me what I want to know. It's called torture.'

'But I'm not going to tell you, I would die before I told you. All I'm asking is for you to give me a dignified death.'

'You don't give someone morphine if they're being tortured. It wouldn't be torture if you did.'

'No one will know. I won't tell. I'll be dead.'

'What is wrong with you? I don't care about that! I'm torturing you. You can't have morphine. Jesus!'

'All right. Keep your hair on. I only asked.'

'The whole point is you tell me because you can't bear the pain. That's what torture is.'

'Look, I understand that you're upset. But I can see you are a merciful man.'

'No, I'm not. I'm not!'

'You are. You are driven to do this by some desperate need that I do not ask about. I can see the gentleness in your soul. And because of that I ask for some relief from the pain.'

'The answer's no. No morphine under any circumstances.'

'In that case, you may as well proceed.'

'Caleb, please tell me about your secret shame. Don't make me do this.'

'I cannot.'

I reached for the mouse.

'One other thing,' he said.

'Yes?'

'You're doing it wrong.'

'Doing what wrong?'

'The torture. If you carry on like that the mouse will die of suffocation. You're supposed to use a cage – that's what they did. And you're wrong, it wasn't the Romans, it was the Spanish Inquisition. If you use a metal cage, the mouse can still tunnel through the flesh but he gets plenty of air.'

I looked at him and was unable to control my expression. It

was one of the purest astonishment. 'But why should I care if the mouse dies?'

'Because it's me you want to torment, isn't it? This has got nothing to do with Tiresias.'

'What if I spare the mouse? Will you talk?'

'Don't be stupid. I just thought—'

'Look, you fool, all I want is to hear the story. I don't care if I have to kill you to get it, so why should I give a damn about the mouse? OK, I tell you what I'll do. I'll put a little wedge under the edge of the dish so some air can get in. How does that sound?'

He thought about it and said. 'Yes, that should do it. And please, when I'm dead, don't let the cats get him.'

'Is there anything else you want? You strike me as a pretty damn fussy guy.'

'Despite everything I believe you are a fair man, a merciful man.'

'Don't bet on it.'

'A Christian.'

'Definitely not that.'

'Ah, yes, you deny it but I've presided at scenes like this too often in the past to be fooled. And because I can see the goodness in your heart I want to make one final request.'

'If it's cigarettes I'm fresh out.'

'No, I want a strop.'

'A strop?'

'You know, a piece of leather to bite on so my screams don't upset Tiresias. Loud noises spook him.'

'What about my shoe? You could bite on that.'

'I am in no position to bargain. The offer of your shoe is acceptable.'

I took it off, held it over his mouth and looked with horror as he raised his head towards it. He said, 'I'm sorry, it might scuff the polish a bit.'

'It's OK, there's a shoeshine kid at the Cliff Railway Station.'

'Make sure he doesn't overcharge you. Farewell, Tiresias, I forgive you.' He clenched his teeth on the shoe and closed his eyes.

I watched for a second or two, holding the struggling mouse by its tail. I put the mouse back into its cage and tore the shoe out of Caleb's mouth. I sat down onto the floor, defeated by either his magnificent spirit or a magnificent bluff.

Caleb opened his eyes and saw my dejection. 'Please don't take it to heart,' he said. 'It isn't easy to torture a man to death. Very few people are capable of it. I tried telling those people from Odessa, they were the same when they tortured me. I said to them, "Don't regard my refusal to tell you what you want as a criticism of your skills. You are excellent torturers, all of you."'

I smiled weakly and said, 'I bet they were glad to see the back of you.'

'They were.'

I began to wrench to nails from the floor. Once one arm was free Caleb used it to pull the other one off the nails.

'Would you like a drink?' he asked. 'It is Christmas.'

I nodded dully and he brought a bottle of sherry from out of the shadows and took a swig from the bottle. He handed it to me. 'Sorry I don't have glasses. I never get visitors.'

I drank from the bottle. We sat on the floor and said nothing for a while. Scenes like that are hard to follow. The torturer drinking a Christmas toast with his victim – there's no protocol to observe.

Eventually Caleb said, 'This Hoffmann guy, he sure has caused a lot of trouble.'

'If he exists.'

''Course he exists. He stole my bleeding coat, didn't he?'

'Then why don't you know who he is?'

'I do know.'

'You know?'

'Yes.'

'And you let me do the "mouse tunnelling through your stomach routine" and you wouldn't say?'

'You didn't ask me who Hoffmann is, you wanted to know about our secret shame. I will never tell you that.'

I looked at him once more in astonishment.

'Oh, Lord, yes! I can remember it as if it was yesterday – I was lying wounded in the field hospital and he came and took my coat and left me to freeze to death. I told my interrogators all about that bit. I didn't tell them that the item they were looking for was no longer in the coat, that I had taken it out.'

'Let me guess: you can't tell me what it was because it's connected to your secret shame.'

'That's right.'

I sighed. This was turning into a very exasperating Christmas.

'Are you OK?'

'I'm just a bit taken aback that you were prepared to die a few seconds ago and now you're telling me this.'

'But there's nothing to hide any more about Hoffmann. You can walk down to the Pier and see him.'

'Don't tell me he's the laughing policeman.'

'He's appearing at the carol concert tonight.'

'I thought that was just a wild rumour.'

'Oh, no. That Tadpole girl has been giving out leaflets. Come and be redeemed. Hoffmann will expiate the sins of all townspeople who turn up tonight. Tickets five pound. There's a leaflet here somewhere.'

'I guess they'll have sold out by now. Just my luck.'

'You're better off not going. There'll be a riot when they find out who it is.'

'So who is it?'

'Hoffmann's not his real name. That is just a . . . what do you call it? Acronym or something. It's from my torture dossier. That's quite a famous item in the world of the spooks. Those guys who tortured me wrote everything down in German. The name comes from the letters HFM which were scribbled as an abbreviation on my dossier. From "*Horizontalischer Falte Mensch*". Do you speak German?'

'No.'

'I told them, you see, about the coat. How I lay there coming round from the anaesthetic and everything was all misty and confused; I looked up and saw this blurry face. The only thing I could remember about him was the horizontal crease in his face that looked like a smile. So they called him "Horizontal Crease Man". In German that's "*Horizontalischer Falte Mensch*", which becomes HFM. Or Hoffmann.'

Chapter 22

In the bleak midwinter, frosty wind made moan

The Prom was a mixture of late-winter afternoon greys: mist and drizzle and drab, brooding cloud; a filmy luminescent quality to the light that gave the faintest whisper of snow. There was only one way to describe a light like that: plangent. Never before had I longed more deeply, or more simply, for the chaste and temporary purification that snow brings. I wandered along the Prom towards Sospan's kiosk. Up by the kids' paddling pool I could see the lone figure of Eeyore on his way to the Pier with a donkey for the crib at the carol concert. I could tell from the slight limp in the donkey's step that he had chosen Abishag this year. He saw me and waved. Outside the bandstand a group of men in dark coats held silver tubes of metal and blew into them. It sounded hopeful.

Earth stood hard as iron, water like a stone

Sospan poured out a mug of mulled wine and handed it to me. 'On the house,' he said, and we chinked mugs and wished each other a better year next year.

'I suppose you'll be going to the concert, then?' he asked.

'Maybe. What about you?'

He looked sheepish. 'Oh, I might pop my head round the door later.'

It meant that he wouldn't.

'Who do you reckon it is, then?' I said, changing the subject. 'This fat guy in the red and white coat. Is it Odin or the fourth-century Bishop Niklaus?'

'That's an easy one. It's Odin.'

'You sure he's the man?'

'Has to be. How would a fourth-century Christian bishop be able to deliver all the presents and put them in your pillowcase?'

I chuckled politely. 'But he doesn't really put the presents in the pillowcase, does he?'

'Who doesn't?'

'Father Christmas.'

Sospan look puzzled. 'Who does, then?'

Llunos pulled up in a prowl car. 'I can't stop,' he said. 'I have to go back to the hospital.'

'How is she?'

'She's holding on. Maybe she can make it.'

'The Lord will provide,' said Sospan in clear defiance of the available evidence.

Llunos looked annoyed and pulled me over to the railings. The sea was going out, and down below the wet shingles gleamed in the streetlight. The sea returned and gently sucked. You could watch it for hours.

Snow had fallen, snow on snow

'There's a man crying in your office,' he said. 'A Jewish guy.'

'I'm going there now.'

'Thought you'd also like to know, we found Erw Watcyns dead an hour ago. He was stabbed, down near the harbour.'

Snow on snow

'He won't be mourned.'

'We don't think it was anyone local.'

'How can you tell?'

'Too merciful. Whoever did it wept for the victim. We found this next to the body.' He handed me a small phial of artificial tears.

In the bleak midwinter, long ago.

* * *

I went to Smith's to buy some wrapping paper for the Pinkerton manual and returned to the office. Elijah was sitting in my chair. There was a suitcase next to his feet. He looked up, old eyes glistening with tears.

'Ah! Mr Knight, my poor old heart is broken. Never will it be whole again.'

'Really? How sad.'

'Yes, truly.'

'They sure teach you how to cry well at Mossad spook school.'

'My tears are real. You can taste them if you wish.'

I slumped into the client's chair and began to wrap the book. 'No, thanks.'

'My brothers, my two lovely brothers, Mr Knight. Lost. Both of them lost. One dead, one worse than dead. Lost in Aberystwyth. *Oy vey*!'

'I'll mention it to the mayor. What do you want?'

'I have come to apologise once more for that ignoble scene involving the gun and your daughter.'

'How about the ignoble scene where the same gun gets planted, covered in my prints, in the room of a dead Pieman? You going to apologise for that?'

He wiped his eyes and looked at me in puzzlement, genuine or feigned, who could tell? He'd probably lost track himself. 'But I wiped the gun. You think I would frame you for the murder of the Pieman? What would it benefit me?'

'You admit you killed him, then?'

'Yes, I killed him. You left me with little choice after the danger you put me in with your ingenious counter-surveillance technique.'

'What was that?'

'You said you would put my name on your incident board. Yes, I killed him; who shall cry over that? He was a man who had killed many people in his life, and I at least killed him with more compunction than he would have killed you or me. And now I must say goodbye.'

'Aren't you going to hang around for the concert tonight? Apparently Hoffmann's on the bill.'

'I care nothing for that *Schlemiel* Hoffmann.'

I raised my eyebrows.

'You look surprised.'

'I thought the fact that you cared about Hoffmann was the one piece of solid ground in this quicksand of a case.'

'I despise Hoffmann, whoever he is. He is a *Momzer*, a *chiam Yankel*, a . . . a . . . a *Putznasher*. I throw pepper in his nose! I spurn the quest; it has cost too much blood. Whoever he is, he cannot be worth a single drop of Ham's blood. The only solid ground amid this metaphysical quicksand is the promise I made to my dying mother that I would find the sons she lost to the fiend Hoffmann.'

'So it was Absalom who cared about Hoffmann?'

'Absalom cared about Ham, my sweetest, youngest brother.'

'Now I'm lost.'

'It all started, you see, many years ago, when I became captivated by the gaudy chimera that is Hoffmann. And to my ever-lasting regret I infected my dear brother Ham with my obsession. We lost him at Checkpoint Charlie in January 1968, the year of the Prague Spring. Ham made contact with a Russian émigré who had information about the original dossier relating to the interrogation of Caleb Penpegws. This Russian introduced him to a Czechoslovakian dancer who had been the mistress of the Soviet military attaché in Ljubljana who had connections to a KGB agent by the name of Alekhin who once served in North Africa and drank Ricard at a bar in Algiers with a Foreign Legionnaire who had been incarcerated in a military prison in Marseilles with a man who flew covert missions for the CIA in Laos; his co-pilot was a man who once forged papers for a fugitive Nazi who told him about the perplexing reference in the

Hoffmann dossier to the horizontal crease in his face that denoted a smile. What did it mean? They assumed it must have been some sort of code. The same CIA pilot introduced Ham to a secret procedure being developed by his organisation, called forensic physiognomy. Ham became obsessed by this new technique and his obsession took him to all four corners of the earth on the trail of the perplexing smile motif. We never saw him again; we just received postcards in which he described, in handwriting shaking with excitement, the various leads and discoveries that, he felt, were taking him ever closer to his goal. He claimed to have found glimpses and subtle allusions to the mystery in the tales our grandmothers used to tell us of the bogeyman of Jewish folk tradition, the Golem; and in the various troll traditions of northern European myth – the so-called 'eat me when I'm fatter' tales embodied in the story of the Three Billy Goats Gruff. As the years passed he receded more and more; became ever more remote from us; the postcards ever rarer, the writing on the cards ever more shaky, the language and idiom ever more crazy as he followed a trail of hints glittering like lost pennies in the dark forest of the world's folk literature. Our beloved young brother turned slowly insane and relayed the symptoms of his sickness to us through the medium of the international postal service.'

He paused and blinked back tears. 'When the cards stopped coming, my brother Absalom and I went our separate ways across the face of this earth in search of him. We did not meet again for many years. Then earlier this month Absalom sent me a letter from Cannes where he had seen a trailer for the movie *Bark of the Covenant*. Quite by chance, in the audience he met a Welshman who kindly invited my brother to his home; he put before him a dish comprising lamb and cheese. He called it *cawl*. My brother was astonished. This was the very same dish that Eichmann had spoken of in his interrogation, the dish he claimed the spy in the library had used in the honey-trap. The Welshman told him it was very popular in his homeland. Truly Absalom was amazed.

All these years we assumed that Eichmann had invented this aspect of the case. It seemed not possible that people could make a stew of lamb and cheese; and yet here was a Welshman claiming it was true. It meant that the entire supposition about Etta Place had been wrong. We all thought she had gone back to Kansas, and that was where we conducted our searches. But it appeared she must have travelled to Wales, that her daughter and grand-daughter would have been Welsh. The revelation was shocking. My brother set forth for Aberystwyth at once, because he knew that here finally he might find the bones of dear Ham.'

'The lamb and cheese helped you find your Ham?'

'I'm sorry?'

'Nothing.'

'And so here he came. And here he died, leaving that message in his blood, knowing I would follow. But why he would hide a picture of Butch Cassidy in the alley I do not know. The Butch and Sundance angle has been understood since the movie came out in 1969. That is a puzzling aspect of the story.'

I took out the photos Mrs Dinorwic-Jones had given to me and slid them across the desk.

'He hid these, too. This is a simpleton who lives in a house belonging to a girl called Tadpole. I don't know its significance. This headstone is from the grave of Sundance's daughter, Laura. She married a man called Llantrisant. It means that the grand-daughter will bear the surname Llantrisant. It is a very rare sur-name and only one person has it round here: Gertrude Llantrisant, a woman who used to swab my step. She was the woman in the reading room of Buenos Aires library, the one who stole the coat.'

Elijah picked up the pictures and examined them. He put down the picture of the grave and held the other one, the picture of the simpleton at Tadpole's house. He stared sadly at the image and said, more to himself than to me, 'I have met this Tadpole yesterday. She tried to sell me a ticket to see Hoffmann at the Pier.'

'I wonder how Tadpole knew about Hoffmann?'

Elijah tapped the photo with his finger. 'This man, the simpleton who chops wood and hauls coal, a man who dresses like a little boy because he does not have the wits of a man any more, ... he told her long ago who Hoffmann was. He knew because this man is my brother Ham. Or at least he used to be. What is he now, I do not know. A man who wears the outward appearance of Ham, but from whom everything inside, all the sweetness and grace, has been sucked out, leaving ... leaving behind just an oaf. A man who mined the ore of the horizontal-crease motif in the caverns of folk mythology, who sought a troll but acquired only the wits of one. And so the quest devours itself. This I now see is the revenge of Hoffmann. This is the bell-jingling cap of motely that Fate places on the heads of those who pursue him. What could have robbed my brother of his wits like this? It is my belief that it was fear, the nameless terror that gripped his heart one day when he looked into the mirror and beheld that familiar mocking smile upon his own face.

Chapter 23

TINKER, TAILOR, teacher, preacher, doily salesman, war veteran, misery-guts, rocking-chair maker . . . and the people from my client's chair. They had all come to the Pier to see Hoffmann. Two fat middle-aged men with short necks stood at the entrance and marshalled them, wearing evening dress and looking like tough penguins. People say it's a profession now, nightclub bouncer, with a fancy new name like Door Supervisor or Ingress Manager; just as the guy on the train who checks your ticket is now a Train Manager. They study psychology and adopt police techniques of diplomacy and violence de-escalation. It's not like it used to be. They don't break heads any more. That's the theory. But the reforms haven't reached Aberystwyth. 'De-escalation' isn't a word the police bandy around much, either, even at Christmas.

Tinker, gaoler, soldier for Jesus, librarian, whelk catcher . . .

To my surprise, Tadpole had put me on the guest list and after a cursory frisking I was admitted. Traditionally the main hall is used for dancing, or fighting; but tonight the people filing in were a noticeably different crowd, older and slightly unsure of themselves, as if it was many years since they had been to such a place. The dance floor had been taken over, with tables set for a banquet. Waiters and waitresses stood at the side, awaiting the beginning of proceedings. On stage, framed by red velvet curtains, there was a live tableau of the biblical stable: school children dressed as Mary and Joseph; a bright pink doll in a manger of real straw. Abishag stood placidly in attendance, because that is the great art of being a donkey and probably why she got invited to the first Christmas. Eeyore stood behind her, running a soothing hand on her mane; he was dressed as a shepherd, in that mixture of dressing gown and towel on the head which traditionally represents the Biblical shepherd.

Tinker, tailor, mason, Rotarian, hotelier, hotdog seller, shepherd from Palestine . . .

The tables filled quickly, and soon the hall was throbbing with an intense air of anticipation that even I was not impervious to. I pushed through the crowds, who were searching for their seats, and went towards the back. People began to stamp their feet and shout, 'Hoffmann!' This venue had, in its time, borne witness to all the manifold manifestations of the human condition: fights, and the unrestrained outpourings of lust; deaths; even children had been born in the middle of a ring of handbags. So many acts that cried to the stars for the redemptive balm of a saviour; but it had never seen a town gathered on the strength of such a promise as tonight. 'Hoffmann! Hoffmann!' they cried.

Tadpole took the stage. She was wearing a party frock, made of checked cotton with what looked like a doily at the neck. It reminded me the things people wear to go square dancing. She raised her hand to silence the rabble. Her cheeks shone like a well-polished saddle and her hair was plastered down and gleamed like a fish in the light thrown by the twirling disco balls, the tinsel and the single star behind her, above the stable.

'I guess you are all impatient to be redeemed,' she began. 'God knows you need it!'

There were hoots and jeers.

'You've been swimming in the swill of iniquity for long enough.'

More jeers and shouts of 'You can talk!'

'Yes. It's about time someone did.'

'Get 'em off!'

'I've seen you: coupling and rutting like dogs on heat; drinking liquor at all hours of the day—'

The crowd shouted 'Woooh!' in mock horror. It began to dawn on me. They weren't here to be redeemed at all. They were here for the entertainment.

'Sharing the bed with your own kith and kin!'

'Look who's talking!'

'Or with farmyard animals!'

Laughter.

'Oh, yes, if anyone needs to be saved, it's you lot, you bunch of slimy moral toads! But the funny thing is, you don't know the worst bit yet.' There were more catcalls and jeers, whistles and hoots. They were drunk and happy.

'Well, tonight you're going to find out the truth. You're going to find out about the terrible sin on the conscience of this town. The reason why the good Lord saw fit to blight us; why He sent a big flood five years ago. The reason why everything in this town is wrong; why the ewe miscarries, why the bread is stale and the hearts are cold. Tonight I'm going to tell you.'

'Get on with it!'

'All right, I will, but you've all got to shut up first.' She paused. The laughter subsided amid snorts of suppressed mirth.

'It's because we are party to a terrible deed, a secret shame that those horrible soldiers did in Patagonia.'

There were gasps of mock horror.

'We all know about the terrible war in Patagonia. How the Lord saw fit, even though we did not deserve it, to send us one of His angels on the eve of battle. We've all seen the pictures of brave Clip and the beautiful angel who came to see us. You'd think those soldiers would be grateful, wouldn't you? You'd think after seeing something as nice as that they would go and fight like men. But no! it wasn't enough that they made us lose the great colony of Patagonia.'

The words 'great colony' produced ironic laughter.

'When the angel went back to see them again, you know what they did? They were rude to her.'

There was an uproar of laughter and a barrage of bread rolls rained down on the stage.

Someone grabbed me by the sleeve; it was Calamity. She pulled me away and towards the door at the back marked 'Private'. We walked through into the kitchen.

'I have to tell you something.'

'Can't it wait? We're going to miss the unveiling of Hoffmann.'

There were more roars from the main hall and Tadpole's words floated over.

'. . . put your hands together . . .'

'I know who it is,' said Calamity. 'I know who Hoffmann is.'

'. . . come all the way to be with us here tonight . . .'

'I know who it is, too. It's Herod Jenkins.'

'. . . to expiate the grievous sins . . .'

'How did you know?'

'Caleb Penpegws told me.'

'Pretty measly sort of redeemer, huh?'

'The crowd won't like it. How did you find out?'

'Absalom said he saw him in the cinema queue, right? We all thought he must have met him, but there's a poster of Herod and the circus there, too. Maybe that's what he saw. I just sort of thought—'

'That's very good. Don't you want to go in and see the big moment?'

Calamity looked wistful.

'What's wrong?'

'Everything's turned out wrong, hasn't it?'

'Has it?'

'I've been a dope. And now Myfanwy—'

I flinched slightly.

Calamity saw something in my eyes and retreated.

'It's OK,' I said. 'I know she's going; she's leaving after the concert. What's wrong?'

'But . . .'

'What?'

'She isn't coming. She's left already ... on the bus to Shrewsbury.'

'Oh.'

'I thought you knew.'

'She's supposed to be singing.'

'She can't sing.'

'She got her voice back.'

'No, she didn't, she was lying. She told me to tell you not to stop her.'

'She said that?'

'She insisted I tell you before seven thirty this evening. That's when the bus leaves. She said, "You must promise to tell him not to come after me, and make sure you tell him before seven thirty."' She looked at her watch. It was seven forty-five. 'As I said, I've been a dope.'

'No, you haven't.'

'Yes, I have, a prize dope. None of that Pinkerton manual stuff worked out; the new office is a dumb idea. The Pinkertons never answered my fax. The only reason I didn't come back was I am too ashamed. And I was scared you wouldn't want me.'

'You don't know how wrong you are.'

'Everything I did was a failure.'

'What about that phoney leg routine? That was a piece of detective genius. It cracked the case wide open. Because of that we found out about the Butch Cassidy angle, and about Elijah and the people from Mossad. And now we've found the key to the whole thing because of your ballistics thing with the knitting needle. Remember Jack Ruby?'

'It didn't work.' She blinked in surprise. 'Did it?'

'Llunos had a complaint from Dinorwic-Jones about your torch beam. We went round to see her and she sang like a canary.'

Calamity's eyes sparkled. 'Wow! I thought I was a hopeless bungler.'

'You've still got plenty to learn.'

She smiled. 'What was it you wanted to see me about?'

From inside came the climax of Tadpole's introduction. 'Your redeemer and mine. Please give a big hand . . .'

The band struck up, the crowd roared.

'The saviour of saviours, the most sacred, most blessed truly holiest of holies. Hoffmann!'

More roars. And then, from the hall came the sound of five hundred drunken revellers booing. We walked to the door. Herod Jenkins, wearing his circus strongman's leotard, was on stage, glowering at the mob. Someone threw a bread roll and it hit Herod on the chest. 'Who threw that?' he thundered. He cast an accusing eye at the front row; they cowered. 'Was it you?' he pointed indiscriminately. 'If I catch anyone throwing anything again you won't get redeemed.'

'What a shame!' someone cried.

'Who said that?' The years had evaporated, he was back haranguing the school assembly. 'Come on, own up, or I'll keep you all behind after this concert.'

'Get off!'

'Any more of this cheek and no one gets baptised in the river tonight.'

'In this weather?'

'What's wrong with it?'

'Too bloody cold.'

'You namby-pambys!'

'Woooh!'

'Right, that's it.' He pointed at a man in the second row. 'I'm not redeeming you for a start.'

'I don't want you to.'

'What the are you here for, then?'

An old woman in the third row stood up and pointed at Herod. 'You can't be Hoffmann, Herod Jenkins. You're a troll.'

That went down well with the audience.

'No, I'm not.'

'Your father came out of the mountain at Devil's Bridge and your mother coupled with him. I was there. We threw her out of the village.'

'It's a lie!' shouted Herod.

Someone else cried out, 'All right, then, how come you're so strong and hairy?'

The crowd roared and demanded to be answered.

'If you must know,' said Herod, 'I owe my tremendous upper body strength to an accident when I was little.' He stared defiantly at the crowd and waited for quiet. 'I fell into a vat of special strength-development liquid, like Obelisk in the Asterisk cartoons.'

This time the laughter was cut short by the entrance of a new player. It was the Army chaplain, the man I had seen preaching on an orange box at the shelter, the man who they say lost his wits in Patagonia after seeing something terrible at the Mission House siege. He walked onto the stage and took the microphone off Herod. Quiet suddenly descended as the mob sensed something even better than the Obelisk story.

Tinker, tailor, teacher, preacher, doily salesman, war veteran, misery-guts, rocking-chair maker . . .

'You're all completely mad!' shouted the priest. 'And this girl . . .' – he pointed at Tadpole – 'would made the maddest of you look sane. You want to know the truth?'

The crowd cheered.

'There was no angel. It was a hoax made up by General Llanbadarn because it was the only way he could get the troops to go on his suicide mission.'

'It's not true!' shouted Tadpole. 'Of course there was an angel! Don't listen to him.'

The priest ignored her. 'Oh yes! The angel was just a silly girl in fancy dress, riding through a crowd of fools. God isn't punishing us for that. He doesn't give a damn. He probably thinks it was funny. I do.'

'We don't believe you!' cried Tadpole.

'And I'll tell you another thing,' he shouted with glee. 'This thing about the secret passage that only Clip knew about, *el pasadizo secreto*. There was no secret passage; that was code for something else. You want to know what it was? I'll give you a clue. They also called it *la entrada trasera*. That's Spanish for 'the back entrance.' It was code for sending a despatch by secure channels. You know where they put the secret despatch? Up Clip's anus.'

There was a riot. The people abandoned the tables and tried to storm the stage. A column of bouncers filed out of side doors. The priest continued, undismayed. 'Clip was a turncoat, you see. They used to tie messages to his collar, but the enemy put sausages out for him and he let them read the secret messages. He was a turncoat. A hand-licker. The Lord Haw-Haw of dogs. That's why they had to use the secure channel.'

The bouncers fought furiously with the mob. I grabbed Calamity and dragged her towards the rear fire exit. The townspeople were almost out of control and very angry. The disappointment at finding their redeemer was Herod Jenkins the school games teacher was bad enough. But this slander to the sacred memory of Clip was too much for any human heart.

Tadpole turned on Herod Jenkins and shouted, 'Say it isn't true! Say you never did that!' Herod looked round in bewilderment. Tadpole picked up a mop handle and advanced on him, the fury in her eyes flashing like bolts of lightning. 'Say it isn't true,' she demanded. 'Say you never did that to Clip.'

The auditorium erupted; men and women picked up their chairs and used them as weapons in the manner of the saloon-bar brawl familiar from old cowboy films. I watched, temporarily immobilised by astonishment. The priest slipped out through the upstage curtains; and a shepherd, whom I took to be the Pinkerton, helped Eeyore and the donkey out by the same route. The mayhem spread through the crowd like fire in a fireworks factory. I grabbed

Calamity by the hand and we ran for the exit as the fighting crowd surged towards the stage. The thin black line of bouncers fought heroically until, on the point of being overwhelmed, they bowed graciously to the inevitable and joined in. We slammed the fire door behind us and wedged it shut with a wooden chair. The last image I saw within was that of Tadpole raising the mop handle high over the head of the cowering games teacher and demanding to be satisfied. 'Say it isn't true!' she cried. 'Say you never did that to Clip.' Herod looked up at her in terror and then appealed to the howling brawling mob for understanding. 'But we all did it,' he wailed. 'We had to! Don't you see? We had to . . .' And then came the time-honoured plea for exculpation, the last refuge of all moral pygmies: 'I was only following orders.'

Chapter 24

THE SNOW WAS falling thickly now, and softly; slowly transfiguring the sea front. It gathered silently on ledges; formed a little conical hat on the fibreglass boy soliciting for charity; and melted wetly on the black muzzle of Abishag. Her eyes shone, her flanks trembled with fear. No one had told her it would be like this. There was no riot at the stable the first time round in Bethlehem. Eeyore ran a comforting hand down her neck. Joe Winckelmann, wearing a dressing gown and a fedora hat, held the halter. Two police vans pulled up and officers piled out with truncheons gleaming and raised like kendo swords.

Calamity and I stood and watched the cops pile in. The snow formed leopard spots on the dark fabric of her parka.

'So what did you need to see me about?' she asked.

'Oh, I was going to ask you to help me find a new assistant.'

Calamity's face dropped. 'An assistant?'

'Yes, I thought you could ask around. You know, see if any of your friends want the job.'

'Oh,' said Calamity. 'Sure.' The stricken look on her face pierced my heart. 'I'd be glad to help. Yes, of course. Sure.'

'I'm going to need an extra pair of hands in the new year.

'Yes.'

'Especially with all the new responsibilities.'

'Yes, you will— What new responsibilities?'

'Oh, you know, being an associate partner of the Pinkertons and stuff. There's bound to be more work, at least that's what Joe Winckelmann says.'

Calamity looked at me in astonishment. 'What are you talking about?'

'Joe Winckelmann, the guy from the Pinkertons. I would have asked you to help out, but it wouldn't be fair. I know you're probably snowed under—'

'Louie?'

'What?'

'Louie!'

'What?'

'Is this a joke?'

'Of course not.'

'He's here? In Aberystwyth?'

'Yes. Don't pretend you didn't know.'

'It's a joke, isn't it?'

'He's over there, holding Abishag.' I pointed and Joe Winckelmann waved.

Calamity stared, eyes wide with wonder and disbelief; she looked at him and looked at me.

'I guess you were probably trying to keep it a surprise but—' The rest of my words were lost as she lunged into me and threw her arms round me.

'Oh, Louie.' She squeezed the air out of me. 'You pig. You absolutely horrible wonderful pig.'

I put my arms round her and let her squeeze and we rocked back and forth on the balls of my feet, oblivious of the world; it could wait. When she finally let go I took her over to meet Joe Winckelmann. He reached out and shook her hand.

Calamity opened her mouth to speak, but only a puff of air and a tiny hiss came out. She tried again twice more, but each time could manage only a laryngitic squeak.

'She's very pleased to meet you,' I said.

'We're going back to the stable for a Christmas drink,' said Eeyore. 'Are you coming?'

'Maybe later. There's something I need to do first.' I turned to leave, but Calamity touched my arm and walked over to the sea railings with me.

'I've got something for you. Llunos gave it to me, I forgot about it.' She reached into her coat pocket and took out a manila envelope. 'It's the trace on the phone call, remember? For the Queen of Denmark.'

Our eyes met in an unspoken understanding.

'You haven't opened it.'

No, I thought I'd let you do that.'

'Sure, I can do that.' I held the envelope gingerly, as if it was radioactive.

'You know,' said Calamity, 'I quite liked having the Queen of Denmark around.'

'Me too. She was a fine lady.'

'It sort of brightened the day up a bit.'

'It certainly did.'

'It was like she was our friend.'

'That's exactly what I thought.'

'And, you know, if she's our friend it feels a bit wrong to trace the call; it's like prying.'

'Yes, I know what you mean.'

'It's silly, anyway, because it had to be her, really, didn't it?'

'Of course. As you said, no one would make such a thing up. And who else would have that kind of money?'

We both stared at the unopened envelope. I remembered the sign I had been considering for the office: Pandora Inc. And I recalled the look of baffled wonder on the face of a little boy in pyjamas, imprisoned in the reflex of a Christmas bauble. A child with the wisdom to accept the gifts that life offers and not enquire too closely; wisdom that the people in my client's chair have lost.

'You're right: we shouldn't pry.' I said. 'What's the point? We know it was her, right?'

'Absolutely.'

I put the envelope in my pocket. 'No need to open it, then.'

The town hall clock struck eight. Calamity looked over in the vague direction of the sound. 'Myfanwy will have reached Bow Street by now,' she said.

'I know.'

I walked back to the office and stopped to speak to a man by the bandstand. The man wore a distinctive black leather coat. It was Caleb. He turned to face me and gave a slight nod.

'That's a nice coat,' I said.

'Yes. I got it in the war. It's German. Real leather.' He rubbed the lapel appreciatively between finger and thumb.

I said, 'I think I understand it all now: about a man, a woman and a stolen coat. I understand how long ago a group of men played cards and conceived a terrible crime; one so shocking it made the priest go mad. I understand why all their names were on a list left in the pocket of a coat. And I understand why a man met a woman in the reading room of the library and went across the street with her to a cheap hotel. And in the morning this woman stole the man's coat and with it the list of names. She sold it to a soldier and that man was you. And when a while later some spooks turned up asking about the coat, this woman, who it turns out was Mrs Llantrisant, sent her lover to get the coat back and he stole it from you as you lay wounded in hospital. That thief became the celebrated Hoffmann.

'Over the years, many men have searched for the list. Some have sought the woman who stole the coat; and they have taken the path of genealogy; because she was, it seems, the grand-daughter of the Sundance Kid. Others have sought the man called Hoffmann, and their quest led through the dark, sequestered vales of physiognomy. Because he was, it seems, defined by that tantalising, insubstantial horizontal crease in his face which generations of school children have been informed was a smile. All the people – be they wayfarers on the high road of genealogy, or pilgrims on the low road of physiognomy – have reached journey's end in the chimerical town called Aberystwyth. And there they have all come to a sticky end at the hands of two men who were guardians of the secret; men called Erw and the Pieman. Oh yes, I understand it all now, except two things. What was the crime? And if Hoffmann stole your coat, how come you're still wearing it?'

Caleb nodded like a schoolteacher pleased with my progress. He looked down at Tiresias, who appeared to be listening intently; as if I had put my finger on the two aspects of the case that had always puzzled him.

'You see,' he said, 'there were two names on the list that shouldn't have been there, two men who had no business being in that weekly card game. One was General Llanbadarn; and the other was Sánchez, the bandit leader.'

'Llanbadarn was playing cards on the eve of battle with the enemy?'

'Yes. Llanbadarn had four of a kind; Sánchez had a straight flush. Sánchez would raise and Llanbadarn would see him and that old pot just got bigger and bigger. Sánchez put his boots on the table, and Llanbadarn his shirt. Then came Sánchez's hat and Llanbadarn's Sam Browne. After that they bet the dog, the mistress and the locket containing a picture of dear old Mama. Llanbadarn bet the farm; and Sánchez raised him with a gold mine. Eventually they had nothing left in the world to bid with, and that's when Llanbadarn played the big one, the ultimate stake; perhaps the greatest since the gods on Mount Olympus played dice with human destiny.'

'What was it?'

'He bet the 32nd Airborne.'

I gasped, and stumbled against the railings. 'He bet his own troops?'

'Yes. Agreed to send them into an ambush.'

'And you were one of them?'

'Yes. I was there.'

I paused to reflect. 'I can understand why the military would want to keep it secret, but why should you?'

'Because of what we did when we found out.'

'How did you find out?'

'General Sánchez was kind enough to tell us. After the battle the son-of-a-bitch sent us a message via the secret passage.' He shook his head as he relived the horror of it. 'The crazy bastard told us about the card game! You can imagine how we felt. We weren't bad men; we were just like everyone else out there. Good boys, mostly; lost in something we didn't understand. That day we had been twisted beyond the limits of endurance. We saw our comrades slaughtered by an enemy blessed by an uncanny fore-knowledge of our battle-plan, who seemed to anticipate our every move. It was as if they knew we were coming, we said. And of course they did.' He reflected for a moment and grasped his head in anguish. 'If only that damned stupid angel hadn't turned up again.'

'So your terrible sin has something to do with the angel, but you will never say what because of your vow.'

Caleb took a folded newspaper from inside his coat. It was the late edition, carrying a report of Erw Watcyns's death. 'It doesn't matter any more. He was the last one. They are all dead now; only me left . . . me and Tiresias.' He hesitated and looked down at Tiresias, who seemed to nod in encouragement. Caleb said, 'We nailed her to the church door.'

I groaned. 'But it wasn't a real angel, just a girl in fancy dress.'

'Yes, we could see that the second time round.'

'Did she die?'

'No, but she was never the same again. It was Miss Evangeline, the old woman up at the nursing home. She was General Llanbadarn's niece.'

'And the priest went mad.'

'Yes. He knew her, you see, from back home. A lovely girl, she was; sixteen years old, sweet as candy, always a bright smile for everyone. She'd won the Borth Carnival Queen and then someone had got her up the duff. The social services took away the kid and her uncle shipped her off to Patagonia out of harm's way. The priest was supposed to keep an eye on her. When we grabbed her, he tried to intervene. We tied him down and made him watch.'

'Why didn't she tell you who she was?'

'She did. She screamed, "No, no, please don't, please don't! There's been a mistake, I'm not an angel. I'm Evangeline, General Llanbadarn's niece. Please don't, please don't! I'm not an angel, I'm the General's niece." And the priest looked on in horror and heard what we said next and lost his wits.'

'What did you say?'

'We said, "Yes, we know."'

He spoke no more for a while, just stood there still holding my arm, as if only the touch of another mortal could save him from the abyss.

I said, 'Who killed Clip?'

He hunched himself deeper into his old leather coat as the snow fell more thickly, and said, 'The peasants. They watched it happen, you see. And then the little goat girl said her angel had stopped appearing to her. It reeked of opportunism to me, but you could hardly tell the peasants that. Word got round that the Welsh gringos had killed the little girl's angel. It was a hearts-and-minds disaster. Someone poisoned his sausages.' He shook his head in sad disbelief, as if that was the real tragedy. Perhaps it was.

'You know, sometimes when I wander this Prom late at night, when the drunks have all gone home and the only sound is the rasp of the sea on the shingle and Tiresias's breathing, sometimes I think I can hear the sound of that dog barking.'

'I met a girl whose father killed himself because of that dog's smile. The taxidermist.'

Caleb nodded wistfully. 'Yes, that is something else that will for ever lie heavy on my conscience. It was me who killed him.'

'I thought he hanged himself from Trefechan Bridge.'

'He did. But why? What made him do it? I made him do it. I met him in the cinema queue, you see. He told me all about himself. How his heart and indeed his whole life had been broken by that extraordinary expression on the dog's muzzle. "How on earth was it achieved?" he asked me. And in one of those stupid moments one regrets for the rest of one's life I told him.'

'About . . . about the . . . secret passage?'

'*El pasadizo secreto*. You should have seen his face. I will never forget it.'

He laughed without mirth and began to move away, then stopped and turned. 'As for this coat you see me wearing, it's simple. Hoffmann took the wrong one. I wasn't wearing it that day. I keep it for best, you see.'

We locked gazes, perhaps simultaneously amazed at how a simple mishap like that could have affected the destiny of so many people.

'You seem . . . wistful,' said Caleb.

'No, I'm just a bit surprised. It seems to me that, despite having become the greatest spy enigma of the Cold War, Hoffmann's role in all this was rather minor.'

'That's right. Very minor.'

'He wasn't present at the Mission House siege?'

'No.'

'And he wasn't connected to you at all?'

'No, he was just the man Mrs Llantrisant sent to get the coat back. Could have been anyone. Tiresias and I often comment on the irony of it.'

'Just a gofer.'

'Or maybe the errand boy of destiny.' At the sound of the word his gaze clouded. 'I hear you were with Miss Evangeline when she died.'

I nodded.

'Did . . . Did she say anything about . . . you know . . . it?'

'Yes. Her last words were, "Tell Caleb Penpegws I forgive him."'

He didn't take his gaze from me, but I could tell as the words sank in that he was no longer thinking of me. His features slowly lit up and then he grinned and looked down at the mouse.

'Hear that, Tiresias? Did you hear that? She forgave us!' He reached out and shook my hand. 'You're a good man, Mr Knight, a truly good man. A Merry Christmas to you.'

He walked off down the Prom humming 'The First Noel'; and it seemed to me that Tiresias bobbed his head in time to the beat. As I turned my steps to follow, a Black Maria drove past and for the briefest of seconds I fancied I glimpsed Tadpole's face pressed against the grille of the back window, looking at me; her fist digging into her eye, her mouth a twisted figure of eight on its side. Tadpole permanently on the road to Calvary.

I drove slowly through the streets of a deserted town; up a hill peopled only by ghosts. I didn't need to speed; I knew sooner or later I would overtake the bus. It could be at Taliesin or Machynlleth, it made no difference. I listened to carols from London on the radio; and turned the wipers to a higher setting as the snow grew heavier and heavier the further I drove inland. There's something so soothing about the hum of wipers in the night. And the songs of choirboys in a distant cathedral, wrapped in golden light, filled with wonder . . . smocks of scarlet and white. The cold stone nave filled with the sweetness that Antonini Stradivarius found a way to capture in a box of wood. His secret, his genius, to use timber that grew with immemorial slowness and thereby distilled the silence of a dark alpine forest: falling feathers of snow; drooping, thick, heavy doorsteps of snow; the hoot of an owl; the thin bleat of a posthorn as a vehicle with big wooden wheels struggled through the growing drifts; because no mission is more urgent than the one to get the messages of human warmth across the silent, frozen world. Just after Rhydypennau the eyes of a fox glittered at the roadside, greener than a brook.

I intercepted the bus just before Tre'r-ddol, and flagged it down.

'This had better be good,' said the driver.

Myfanwy was sitting on the front seat near the driver. She had one small suitcase. Her face was puffed and swollen as if she had been crying. Sitting next to her was an old woman. Something in the complicity of their attitude suggested the woman had been interrupted in the act of comforting Myfanwy.

'I told you not to try and stop me,' she said.

'I know you did, but I'm here anyway. I've come to fetch you.'

'It's too late.'

'No it isn't. It's never too late.'

'You said if you love someone, let them go.'

'That's right, I did. But I've been doing some thinking about that, and it seems to me there are two schools of thought. One you find in gift shops, written on trinkets adorned with pink hearts, on little notebooks and diaries and teddies and stuff; it says, "If you love them, let them go." And then there's the other school of thought, the Louie Knight school, which says, "If you love someone, don't let them go." The first one is fine if you live in a gift shop or if your supply of happiness on this earth is as plentiful and uninterrupted as the gas that comes through the mains. But if you're like me and you find that most of the time the gas is cut off, you can't afford to be so prodigal.' I picked up her case. 'You're coming with me.'

'Why should I?'

'What do you mean, "why"?'

'Why? Why?'

'Why? God, I don't know, dammit Myfanwy. Because . . . because . . . my life is nothing without you, and if you go now I will die like a dog in a marketplace in an unknown town and strangers will spit on my corpse and throw rocks on my grave. That's why.'

Myfanwy stared at me in wonder.

'And also because you are a silly goose.'

The old lady nudged Myfanwy and said, 'Well, go on then, you silly girl. What more do you want? Jam on it?'

The caravan looked like an iced bun. Thick snow was piled up on the roof, on the step, even on the crappy vinyl washing line that strung the caravan to a crooked pole. A faint breeze stirred the falling flakes and made them dance, made the sky tingle. The Lyons Maid sign outside the shop swung silently; the only sound was the crunch of our footsteps. Everything shone or glistened; all the grey and drabness had been erased; the sharp edges, the junk and bric-a-brac, milk bottles and gas canisters, TV aerials and dustbins, had all been softened and cushioned; the contours of the world rounded and worn away as the falling snow veiled the earth and revealed the deeper contours of the heart. All gone, invisibly mended; even the defiling plod of Tadpole's hoofprints across the roof of my home. The caravan park had been glazed with crystal.

Myfanwy climbed out of the car and raised her face to the dark sky, the edge of her cheek gilded by the strange milky efflorescence that filled the world. I opened up the caravan and conducted her inside. I lit the soft yellow lamps; rummaged around and found rum, mince pies and Ludo; and set them on the table. I walked back outside to the bins and threw away the envelope containing the wire trace on the Queen of Denmark.

I'll find out soon enough. One fine day, when I take that slow boat to Ultima Thule; in springtime, when the golden light returns, and the thaw begins. I can see it so clearly. The sea is darker than a bluebottle's eye; the timbers creak and groan; the sails tug and the rigging sings in the breeze. Off the starboard bow we see land, empty except for the crocuses and lichen and wild seabirds. A single polar bear emerges from the long winter hibernation with that puzzled look on his face, the one that says, 'My, oh, my! That must have been some night I had last autumn.' I turn and offer some smoked seal to the Inuit pilot and say, 'Tell me, fellah, what's the name of this beautiful place?'

And he says, 'My people call this place Louie Knight Sound.'

A NOTE ON THE AUTHOR

Malcolm Pryce was born in the UK and has lived and worked abroad since the early nineties. He has held down a variety of jobs including BMW assembly-line worker, hotel washer-up, aluminium salesman, deck hand on a yacht travelling through Polynesia, and advertising copywriter. He currently lives in Bangkok. His previous three books, *Aberystwyth Mon Amour*, *Last Tango in Aberystwyth* and *The Unbearable Lightness of Being in Aberystwyth*, are also published by Bloomsbury.

A NOTE ON THE TYPE

The text of this book is set in Fournier. Fournier is derived from the *romain du roi*, which was created towards the end of the seventeenth century for exclusive use of the Imprimerie Royale from designs made by a committee of the Académie of Sciences. The original Fournier types were cut by the famous Paris founder Pierre Simon Fournier in about 1742. These types were some of the most influential designs of the eighteenth century, and are counted among the earliest examples of the 'transitional' style of typeface. This Monotype version dates from 1924. Fournier is a light, clear face whose distinctive features are capital letters that are quite tall and bold in relation to the lower-case letters, and *decorative italics, which show the influence of the calligraphy of Fournier's time.*